PRAISE FOR ALEXANDRA SOKOLOFF

Huntress Moon
A Thriller Award Nominee for Best E-Book Original Novel
A Suspense Magazine Pick for Best Thriller of 2012
An Amazon Top Ten Bestseller

"This interstate manhunt has plenty of thrills . . . keeps the drama taut and the pages flying."

—*Kirkus Reviews*

"The intensity of her main characters is equally matched by the strength of the multilayered plot . . . The next installment cannot release soon enough for me."

—*Suspense Magazine*

The Price
"Some of the most original and freshly unnerving work in the genre."

—*The New York Times Book Review*

"A heartbreakingly eerie page-turner."

—*Library Journal*

"*The Price* is a gripping read full of questions about good, evil, and human nature. . . . The devastating conclusion leaves the reader with an uncomfortable question to consider: 'If everyone has a price, what's yours?'"

—*Rue Morgue magazine*

D1147222

The Unseen

"A creepy haunted house, reports of a forty-year-old poltergeist investigation, and a young researcher trying to rebuild her life take the "publish or perish" initiative for college professors to a terrifying new level in this spine-tingling story that has every indication of becoming a horror classic. Based on the famous Rhine ESP experiments at the Duke University parapsychology department that collapsed in the 1960s, this is a chillingly dark look into the unknown."

—*Romantic Times Book Reviews*

"Sokoloff keeps her story enticingly ambiguous, never clarifying until the climax whether the unfolding weirdness might be the result of the investigators' psychic sensitivities or the mischievous handiwork of a human villain."

—*Publishers Weekly*

"Alexandra Sokoloff takes the horror genre to new heights."

—*Charlotte Examiner*

"Alexandra Sokoloff's talent brings readers into the dark and encompassing world of the unknown so completely that readers will find it difficult to go to bed until the last page has been turned. Her novels bring human frailty and the desperate desire to survive together in poignant stories of personal struggle and human triumph. But the truly fascinating element of Sokoloff's writing is her deep dig into the human psyche and the horrors that lie just beneath the surface of our carefully constructed facades."

—*Fiction Examiner*

Book of Shadows

"Compelling, frightening, and exceptionally well-written, *Book of Shadows* is destined to become another hit for acclaimed horror and suspense novelist Sokoloff. The incredibly tense plot and mysterious characters will keep readers up late at night, jumping at every sound, and turning the pages until they've devoured the book."

—*Romantic Times Book Reviews*

"Sokoloff successfully melds a classic murder-mystery whodunit with supernatural occult overtones."

—*Library Journal*

The Harrowing
Bram Stoker and Anthony Award Nominee for Best First Novel

"Absolutely gripping. . . . It is easy to imagine this as a film. Once started, you won't want to stop reading."

—*The London Times*

"Sokoloff's debut novel is an eerie ghost story that captivates readers from page one. The author creates an element of suspense that builds until the chillingly believable conclusion."

—*Romantic Times Book Reviews*

Poltergeist meets *The Breakfast Club* as five college students tangle with an ancient evil presence. Plenty of sexual tension, quick pace and engaging plot."

—*Kirkus Reviews*

The Space Between

"Filled with vivid images, mystery, and a strong sense of danger . . . Sokoloff interlaces psychological elements, quantum physics, and the idea of multiple dimensions and parallel universes into her story; this definitely adds something different and original from other teen novels on the market today."

"Alexandra Sokoloff has created an intricate tapestry, a dark Young Adult novel with threads of horror and science fiction that make it a true original. Loaded with graphic, vivid images that place the reader in the midst of the mystery and danger, *The Space Between* takes psychological elements, quantum physics and multiple dimensions with parallel universes and creates a storyline that has no equal. A must-read."

hunger moon

Also by Alexandra Sokoloff

The Huntress/FBI Thrillers

Huntress Moon: Book I
Blood Moon: Book II
Cold Moon: Book III
Bitter Moon: Book IV

The Haunted Thrillers

The Harrowing
The Price
The Unseen
Book of Shadows
The Space Between

Paranormal

D-Girl on Doomsday (from *Apocalypse: Year Zero*)
The Shifters (from The Keepers trilogy)
Keeper of the Shadows (from The Keepers: L.A.)

Nonfiction

Stealing Hollywood
Screenwriting Tricks for Authors
Writing Love: Screenwriting Tricks for Authors II

hunger moon

Book V of the Huntress/FBI Thrillers

alexandra sokoloff

THOMAS & MERCER

Published by Thomas & Mercer, Seattle

www.apub.com

Amazon, the Amazon logo, and Thomas & Mercer are trademarks of Amazon.com, Inc., or its affiliates.

ISBN-13: 9781503942721
ISBN-10: 1503942724

Cover design by Ray Lundgren

Printed in the United States of America

This book is dedicated to the young women of End Rape on Campus (EROC) who are fighting campus sexual violence through direct support for survivors and their communities; prevention through education; and policy reform at the campus, local, state, and federal levels.
Now more than ever, their fight must be our fight.

Chapter One

The sandstone spires reach like alien fingers from the depths of the canyon.

The gorge cuts through the Arizona tablelands, a vast, prehistoric gash. Inside lies a 230-million-year-old natural wonder: a cathedral of wind-carved sandstone walls in every possible hue of red, gold, and white, adorned with the gleaming black curtain-like sweeps known as canyon varnish. Ancient ruins of cliff villages nestle in natural caves at impossible heights. Sedimentary deposits lie in distinctive round piles, like stacked pancakes.

And the famous double sandstone spires rise 750 feet from the canyon floor, at the exact junction of de Chelly and Monument Canyons.

Navajo legend says the taller spire is the home of Spider Grandmother, the goddess who created the world. She stole the sun and brought fire to the Anasazi. At the beginning of time, monsters roamed the land, and she gave her children, Monster Slayer and Child-Born-of-Water, power to kill the monsters and protect the First People.

Her stories are only told in the winter months.

And only to those who will listen.

A bleak sky, streaked with white, stretches over the desolate South Rim of the canyon. There will be snow tonight.

The grinding of a pickup truck grates through the silence.

A four-door Tundra. Tonneau cover over the bed. Two men dressed in camouflage inside. Fast-food and jerky wrappers litter the wells at their feet. In the back seat, a cooler packed full of beer.

And three rifles, three-inch twelve-gauge magnums, strapped to the padded back-seat gun rest.

Hunters, driving the rim.

The front-seat passenger sets his sights on something moving ahead of them, leans forward greedily. "There we go, there we go."

The driver follows his gaze, fixes on what he is tracking. Not a deer, but a young girl, shining black hair underneath the hood of her parka. Schoolgirl's backpack on her shoulder.

On the men's faces, something crude and capering.

"That's some tasty-looking pussy."

"Oh, yeah, that'll do."

"Let's go."

"Get her."

The driver swerves the truck over to the side of the road, squealing brakes.

The girl hears the sound, stiffens, is starting to run before she even completes the glance back.

The truck skids to a stop in the snow. The doors fly open; the men are out of the car, grabbing for their rifles.

The girl runs for the rocks, but her pursuers are bigger, faster. Two of them, grown men, against a teenage girl.

They move forward into the strong wind, a military-style formation, heavy boots crunching in the sandy snow.

They pause at the rock outcropping, looking out over the boulders. The girl seems to have disappeared. Then a scrabble on the rocks betrays her. Hearing it, the men grin at each other.

The driver rounds the rock first, his mouth watering. He is already hard in anticipation . . .

The tire iron bashes him across the face, breaking his jaw. He staggers back, howling inarticulate pain.

The girl kicks him viciously in the knee, crumpling him, then swivels as the second hunter rounds the edge of the rock. She slams the tire iron against the side of his head.

Now both men are collapsed on the ground, moaning and cursing.

She steps forward, no longer feigning that youthful, hesitant gait.

She lifts her arm and uses the tire iron on their skulls. Two, three, four blows, and there is no more moaning. Thick crimson drops spatter the snow. Her breath is harsh. Her face is ice.

There is only the wind, swallowing the sound of her breathing.

Cara stands at the edge of the canyon, looking out at the spires of Spider Rock, the vast open gorge.

Below her is an icy crevasse. The canyon has any number of them, deep splits in the rock wall where whole sheets of the cliff have broken away. Behind her is the hunters' pickup truck.

Their bodies lie at her feet.

She drags one, then the other, to shove them over the cliff's edge, stepping back to watch each body hurtle down into the crevasse, tumbling into oblivion.

The snowfall tonight will cover all trace of them. Later, birds and animals will pick the bones clean.

Another offering to the canyon, and the gods and ghosts that haunt it.

She disposes of the truck at one of the settlements along the rim, parks it with keys left under the seat, per her arrangement. It will disappear overnight, will be quickly and efficiently stripped for parts. Spirited away into motor vehicle oblivion.

Then she descends into the canyon on foot. The height of the sheer cliff face is breathtaking, stomach turning, but her feet are deliberate and sure as she walks the ancient Anasazi trails, past the pale, eerie alien handprints of the prehistoric canyon dwellers pressed into the rock.

At the bottom of the canyon, a sandstone arch leads into a more secluded part of the valley.

The creeks on the canyon floor are icy, the fruit orchards and cornfields now buried in snow. The Diné who make their home in the canyon have left the small wood houses and ceremonial hogans for the winter. The canyon is deserted, except for her. And perhaps the goddess who is said to inhabit it.

In a circle of cottonwood trees, there is a crude cabin of three rooms, and its eight-sided hogan.

Her home now, for as long as she is allowed here.

Canyon de Chelly had not been on her mind on the night she fled the derelict farmhouse in Napa Valley and the events of the Cold Moon. Seven weeks ago, she cut the throat of the predator Darrell Sawyer, with FBI agent Matthew Roarke standing across from her, watching Sawyer bleed out.

She had known, in that moment, looking into Roarke's eyes and feeling the monster's blood gush warm over her hands, that she would have to leave California. For a long time, if not for good.

Even now, the thought is a pang. The state is as close to a home as she has ever had. No one part of it—more like the whole of it: the roads and mountains and beaches and forests and deserts. But she cannot be sentimental. Attachment is fatal. There is more danger to her now than ever before, not just because she has jumped bail. She is on the radar for the first time in her life. More than on the radar: she has become notorious. Her image has been widely circulated.

The media has been stupefied by what she has been doing, by her simplest of solutions to the devastation *It* wreaks on the world. Men like those she has just dumped in the canyon—their intent is clear. Their brutality is soul crushing. They have no place on the planet. She has long ago given up on the world understanding.

But her work is no longer under the radar.

It is no longer just Roarke and his team hunting her. In fact Roarke may have ceased his hunt entirely. But now the entire country knows her name.

Leaving had been the only option. Leaving Roarke with the corpse of the predator in the icy farmhouse and driving, under the steady guiding light of the moon.

She had driven ten straight hours to get out of California.

South first, on I-5, because in the dead of winter the Sierra Nevada mountains are snow traps, an effective natural roadblock to any state to the east. A stop in Bakersfield to pick up the set of automobile master keys she had mailed to one of her many postal drop boxes for safe-keeping. Then crossing over on the 58 to I-40, old Route 66, into the desert, through Tehachapi, Barstow, and finally across the border into Arizona. No small highways or back roads, either: she wants major interstates with anonymous traffic.

The next state over is New Mexico, possibly the most beautiful of all the states. The Southwest has been a frequent site of her restless driving; the long miles of unpopulated areas and natural beauty are her safe haven. The next state after is Texas, always unsettling, always the biggest danger to her, but she can stay on the road, drive through it quickly, a day and a half max. And next is Louisiana. She has not been to New Orleans in two years. Too long. Tourists will be flocking in for the long buildup to Mardi Gras, costumed and perpetually drunk, and she can hide in plain sight . . .

This is her first torrent of panicked thoughts. But the road slows her down, calms her body and mind. It is guidance she needs. The guidance that has always been there for her.

She must be still and let it come.

So she drives, and listens only to as much news as necessary to be sure that the hunt has not focused itself.

Halfway across the state she stops for gas at an isolated station. There is a cluster of roadside stands in the back lot, beside a row of windblown cottonwood trees, where Native vendors display an array of produce and crafts. After filling the tank, she walks over to the stands to stretch her legs. She is drawn to a table where a tiny Navajo woman sells necklaces of silver spiderwebs, symbol of the creation goddess, Spider Grandmother.

The little woman does not look at her. But as Cara browses, the older woman silently touches a filigree web set with star-dots of obsidian. And pushes it toward her.

She buys the necklace and returns to the road. And when she sees the turnoff toward Indian Route 15, into Navajo territory, she takes it.

The land base of the Navajo Nation covers 27,000 square miles of the Southwest, expanses of unparalleled beauty and largely unpopulated wilderness spread through the states of Utah, Arizona, and New Mexico. As she drives, wind-sculpted buttes and mesas loom up out of grasslands like ancient idols.

The landscape stirs memories of her fourteen-year-old self, the year she had been released from *The Cage*, the youth prison in Camarillo.

And a plan begins to form.

She spent much of her teenage life in proximity to Indian reservations. So she knows something about them. Indian land is sovereign territory, with its own laws and justice system. Right here, in Navajo territory, no US lawman can arrest her—the laws of the United States do not extend to tribal land. On this long stretch of highway, she is free.

She looks at the necklace, the spiderweb hanging from the rearview mirror. It catches the clouded sunlight in a silver gleam. And suddenly she knows where she is going.

At the town of Chinle, the flat planes open into a stunning red gash in the earth. Canyon de Chelly, the second-largest canyon in the US, only eclipsed by the Grand Canyon itself. Located between the four sacred Navajo mountains: white Blanca Peak, turquoise Mount Taylor, yellow San Francisco, and black Hesperus Mountain. A place of power and healing. And the site of the massacre that began one of the most horrific travesties of US history: the atrocity known as the Long Walk.

It is not her first visit here. She has camped beside the canyon's staggering beauty, has hiked its depths, has felt the peace and the heartbreak of it. She knows its rhythms and its rules.

In this small town at the mouth of the canyon there are only a few hotels: two chains and the Navajo-owned Thunderbird Lodge, located in the original 1896 trading post, right at the canyon entrance. The gift store still sells blankets and sand paintings, jewelry and kachina dolls. In the cafeteria chefs cook traditional meals: blue corn fry bread and green chili stew and red chili pork posole.

Off-season, it is not as deserted as one might think. It is winter, and the rates are half off.

The clerk at the desk is Diné, as are all the hotel workers, the clerks at the gas stations and convenience stores—which means here, her coloring conceals her. She is just another *Bilagáana*, not worth their attention. And when she speaks to the clerk, it is only a few halting words, in a German accent. She knows German tourists abound in the Southwest, and lone German female travelers are not unusual.

She impulsively asks for a room for three nights.

The room is clean and cozy, with thick walls and Navajo-themed decor. She sinks into the bed and sleeps two nights and a day.

When she is rested, she drives out to the canyon rim and hikes the trails allowed to her. By law, most of the canyon interior is accessible only with a Diné guide.

She sits and looks over the canyon for hours.

She walks and she waits and she watches, eating in the cafeteria by herself, observing the comings and goings: the cleaners and the clerks, the tour company owners in their Western boots and black hats with bands of silver conchos and flashy SUVs, and the guides with their geriatric Jeeps and wary and haunted eyes.

And that is how she hears talk of the Hunting.

It has become a sport, discussed in private forums on the Internet with titles like "How to rape and get away with it." Predators taking advantage of a loophole in US law that in practicality means a white or non-Native man can assault a Native girl or woman on tribal lands and the tribal authorities have no jurisdiction over him. No ability whatsoever to prosecute.

In the past not even six months, three teenage girls have been attacked while walking the rim route.

And now she has a purpose to her hiking.

Now she knows why she has come to the canyon.

She kills the first hunter a week later, under the growing Bitter Moon, and she drops the body into the gorge, in full view of the spires of Spider Rock.

And that night she walks the rim, in the cold, under the frozen stars, feeling the deep sense of peace that comes after a successful battle with *It*. The diamond canopy above her puts her in mind of Spider Grandmother, who began the world by taking a web she had spun, lacing it with dew, and throwing it into the sky.

She stops, touching the silver necklace she has worn every day since she bought it, and looks out over the canyon to find the double sandstone spire, where the goddess is rumored to live, surrounded by the bleached bones of the wicked she has killed.

When she turns away toward the path, three figures stand in silhouette on the trail before her. Three black shadows, appearing without sound.

Her pulse skyrockets, adrenaline shooting through her entire body . . .

And then she recognizes that they are women.

And they are there for her.

This is how she has come to have the use of one of the small wooden houses at the very bottom of the canyon. It had been a straight exchange. The Diné of the canyon have a problem, a white problem. She has agreed to take care of the problem. The small house, and the refuge of the canyon, is her payment. She has lived in the cabin in the canyon throughout the Bitter Moon of January. Patrolling the rim . . . eliminating the predators.

The dwelling is small, crude, low to the ground. The wind outside the plank walls is a constant, a live thing, pushing against the timbers of the cabin and the hogan outside. It slides along the windows, slips icy fingers into cracks of the sills. But the woodstove heats the rooms, and the fire talks to her in crackles, hissing and popping.

She gathers wood every day, venturing out along the creek beds and collecting from the fallen cottonwood trunks.

She chops the wood and cooks simple meals: canned soup, beans, fry bread. She hikes the trails snaking up the sheer walls, learning the curves and splits of the rock. She visits the ruins, ancient stone houses in the same colors of the sandstone, and listens to the murmur of dead voices in the rocks.

The starkness of the land is healing. By day, vast bleak white spaces and bare crags jutting through the ice. At sunset, the sky blood red above the cliffs. And at night, a galaxy of diamond stars.

She luxuriates in stillness, in the absolute peace that is the absence of people—the emptiness of desert and the infinity of sky. Gradually it draws away all that is still toxic in her from the jail and her period of confinement.

On her walks there are hawks and squirrels, rabbits and antelope. She feels the presence of the ancients, but in a month she has seen only four people, all Diné. The predators stay up on the rim roads, as if afraid of the canyon ghosts.

She feels these, too, raging and wailing in the caves where so many were slaughtered. A constant reminder of her own possible fate.

But for now, she is alive.

Alive.

Not only alive, but free. It is so unlikely after everything she has been through, after the events of the last few months. She has no idea what to make of it.

Something has always protected her.

But she knows that this time, her survival, her freedom, is in large part due to Roarke. She had held his own gun on him in that frozen, derelict farmhouse—but she suspects if he had wanted her caught, she would be dying in a jail by now.

She is not sure how long she has stayed in the canyon, not in days. Time is different when there are no hotels or checkouts. It has been through the waxing of the moon. Bitter Moon. Wolf Moon. The moon of her teenage awakening.

She has had her rest. But it is coming to an end.

A vast darkness has spread across the land. Even in her canyon hideout, she feels it.

She has heard some news of what has gone on since the election and inauguration, on the radio while driving, on televisions hung from the ceilings of convenience stores. But mostly she dreams, and she watches the signs in the canyon. The clouds that throw shadows against the sunset like some massive dark bird.

The dreams are worse every night: Dreams of white men raping the land. Dreams of burning buildings and soldiers in the streets. Dreams of Apocalypse.

It is loose in the country. Everywhere, now. In the very highest corridors of power. There will be a showdown. But she is only one person.

Only one, against this vast army of darkness.

It is coming.

She waits.

And she tries to sleep.

Chapter Two

Roarke couldn't sleep.

He never could before a big meeting. And tomorrow morning he was headed into what was possibly the most important meeting of his FBI career. Scratch that—it was the most important meeting of his life.

No pressure there. No, not at all.

He lay in his bed for another minute and a half, and then threw off the covers. The tossing and turning was just tying his stomach in knots.

Need to burn off this nervous energy.

He was not one of those people who could do well on no sleep, and he knew he might regret it in the morning, but he got up and pulled on sweats. Maybe not a run, but a walk, at least.

He jogged down the stairs of his Victorian apartment and stepped out into the San Francisco night.

As soon as he'd closed his front door behind him, he knew getting out was the right thing to do. The night air enfolded him in a soft mist, and he felt calmer just being free of the confines of his house.

He walked. Dark buildings loomed around him, and fog wreathed the streetlamps, drifted in the alleyways.

His city. So familiar, and so loved.

He'd been away for just a month.

But it had been mere days since his return from the—*Case? Sojourn? Odyssey? Dream?*—in the Southern California desert and he still felt scraped raw, overwhelmed by the pace of the city and the necessity of dealing with people. His neighborhood was the gentrified Noe Valley, with its upscale boutiques, yoga studios, and natural-food stores. After that month living in the stark simplicity of the desert and the Mission *asistencia*, it all felt alien. Too big. Too crowded. Too distracting.

But just blocks away was the Mission, which, despite the Silicon Valley hipster invasion of the city, remained its colorful, criminal, rough-and-tumble self.

And it was that way that he found himself headed.

It was not a walk that many people would want to take at night. Gang graffiti adorned the alleys, and criminal elements skulked in dark doorways, though they faded back as they saw Roarke coming. Criminals had a sense for cops in the same way cops had a sense for criminals.

The darkened stores he passed were heavy on the taquerias, bodegas, and botanicas, the Mexican occult shops with their candles and herbs and charms. As he continued down the street, deeper into the heart of the Mission, he found himself drawn almost inevitably toward a side street.

The facade of a building ahead blazed with a mural, the wildly colorful Mexican artwork so typical of the district. The painting adorned a tiny shop squeezed between a liquor store and a bar. Its front window glowed softly. He moved toward the shop and stopped on the sidewalk.

A life-sized skeleton figure stared down on him from behind the glass. She was dressed in a white gown, globe in one hand, scythe in the other. An owl nestled in the folds of her robe, and electric candles of all colors glowed at her feet along with offerings: candies, tequila, cigarettes, roses.

Santa Muerte, the unconsecrated Mexican saint known as Lady Death.

Roarke stared up into the idol's bony face.

It gave him the eerie feeling of stepping right back into the case he'd abandoned two months ago, at the end of the year: the December Cold Moon.

And that was just one indicator of his transformed life view—that he now thought of the months in terms of their moon names. December Cold Moon. January Bitter Moon—which it had been, in every possible way. And this month, February. Hunger Moon. The very name gave him a queasy feeling.

Too on the nose, there.

The month of the Cold Moon had started with the arrest of the suspect he had been pursuing for what felt like a lifetime: mass murderess Cara Lindstrom. She'd killed a pimp named Danny Ramirez, a lowlife predator who ran teenage girls on the streets of the Tenderloin. It was the only murder Roarke's team had ever been able to pin on her, though Roarke was sure Cara was responsible for hundreds of other killings over the last sixteen years. But this time they had a witness: a precocious, volatile sixteen-year-old runaway who called herself Jade Lauren. Ramirez was Jade's pimp, and the girl had been right there to see Cara cut his throat in a tunnel in Golden Gate Park.

But before they could get Jade to testify, she'd disappeared.

And then another pimp turned up dead, his throat slashed in Cara's signature M.O. Except that Cara had been in lockup at the time.

It was enough to get her released on bail, and she'd jumped it.

And the bodies kept dropping. Pimps. Johns. In the Tenderloin and across the Bay on Oakland's notorious International Boulevard. All with their throats slashed.

The crime scenes were linked by the shrines and offerings to Santa Muerte.

For a time every woman Roarke knew seemed equally capable of the killings. Cara. Cara's cousin Erin McNally. Rachel Elliott, the social worker Roarke had been briefly, painfully involved with. The girl Jade. He'd even at one point suspected his own Agent Singh.

And of course, any one of the followers of a radical anonymous cyber organization that called itself Bitch, who had taken a keen interest in Cara and her crimes.

The month had ended with Roarke in a dangerously compromised state of mind. Obsessed with Lindstrom. Traumatized by what felt like the futility of combatting atrocities that society refused to look at: the sexual abuse and trafficking of children.

He'd tracked down Cara, and Jade—and tragically, Rachel—at a derelict farmhouse in Napa, then stood helplessly by as Cara had cut the throat of Jade's stepfather, Darrell Sawyer, a piece of filth who had sold Jade to his poker buddies for turns when the girl was just twelve.

Roarke hadn't intervened, partly because Cara was holding his own gun on him. But he doubted he would have stopped her even if he could have.

When he let Cara, Jade, and Rachel flee from that farmhouse, he'd committed a laundry list of criminal acts: destruction of evidence, destruction of property, aiding and abetting a fugitive. Two fugitives.

And at that point, he simply didn't care.

He'd gone out into the Southern California desert looking to escape all responsibility. He'd never intended to return to the Bureau again.

But it was as if someone, something, karma—some force he couldn't explain—wanted him to continue as an agent.

That next month, the month of the Bitter Moon, had been a strange time warp into an old, unsolved case of atrocity. He'd started off following fourteen-year-old Cara's footsteps deep into her past. And ended up solving a sixteen-year-old cold case and capturing a vicious serial rapist.

He had walked the same streets that young Cara had: her group home, her high school, a Mission *asistencia*, a derelict shack where she'd killed a monstrous predator—and Roarke had nearly killed another. He'd almost *lived* her fourteen-year-old life.

He knew now that for Cara, Santa Muerte was real. She had been a girl Cara's age, Ivy Barnes. A schoolgirl abducted, raped, burned alive. And Cara had known her, had taken her vengeance.

But Roarke suspected Ivy had never left her, that she traveled with Cara now, and possibly pointed her bony finger at men she saw into with her hollow and sightless eyes.

Images like that haunted him. He struggled to make sense of them.

But his experience in the desert had returned his purpose, focused it. He'd been given a second chance at life and his career, with the help of an unconventional nun and the ghostly memories of three fourteen-year-old girls who had suffered more than a lifetime of hell in their brief time on earth.

His feelings toward Cara had changed.

Now he knew her better than he ever had. Knowing more had loosened the grip of what he fully acknowledged had become a dangerous obsession. His physical hunger for her had turned into something more tender. Protectiveness. He could see her as a child now, feel her suffering. She looked like an adult, but she remained as his mentor had described her—fixed in the trauma of her childhood.

And he'd found a reason to return, out there in the wilderness, under the Bitter Moon. On his terms.

He had a vision now. A task force focused entirely on combatting the sexual abuse and trafficking of children.

There was a pressing urgency to make the task force a reality. So many federal programs were in chaos under the new and unprecedentedly destructive regime. Combatting the sexual abuse and exploitation of women and children was far from the priority of the new administration. In fact there was every reason to believe that a generation of progress on the issue would be undone.

And he might never again have as much pull as he did at this moment.

He stared up into the face of the skeleton.

And suddenly he realized the walk, and his visit to the saint, had focused his thoughts, had outlined his pitch. He felt entirely ready for the morning meeting with SAC Reynolds.

He nodded a silent thanks to the statue.

And then as he turned, out of the corner of his eye, he saw the skull face open her jaws in a bony smile.

He whipped back around, unnerved.

Of course she hadn't moved.

Of course not.

But there was suddenly a knot of dread in his stomach. An overpowering feeling that she was out there, too, tonight, walking the streets as restlessly as he was.

Doing what, he had no idea.

But if she was out there, he was about to find out.

DAY ONE

Chapter Three

The Basement was deep under the house, a huge three-story clinging to the cliff edge in a row of oceanfront houses along Del Playa. Outside the wall of windows and a sliding glass door, the long, well-used wooden deck overlooked the Pacific Ocean, and the sound of the surf was a constant rhythmic rumble.

The room inside was lit only by strings of Christmas lights. The chairs and sofas were occupied by the shadowy figures of nine or ten young men in the prime of their lives. They were uniformly handsome: chiseled chins, silky tanned skin over taut six-pack abs, strong thighs. Any one of them could make decent money modeling for an ad depicting the Southern California experience.

At the moment, though, in the shadows, faces lit by the flashing lights of the digital sound system and the screens of their smartphones, they were so wasted that they looked more like thugs. They were seated around the table, sprawled on the sofas, sloppy drunk, with various bottles and red plastic beverage cups littering the end tables, the floor.

And on the low table in front of them, a mirror smudged from lines of snorted substances.

Above them, one wall of the room was completely papered in photos: a collage of naked female body parts. Shots of breasts and thighs branded with Greek letters drawn in marker on the skin. Beaver shots, anal shots. Some full-length, candid photos of naked and half-naked girls, passed out, one or two in their own vomit. In some pictures boys were having sex with the girls—in these, the boys' faces were never shown.

One of the young men addressed the wall. "Gettin' tired of looking at the same ol' tits and ass. Need some fresh wallpaper."

Another one chimed in. "Hell yeah. Pledges are getting derelict. Gotta make 'em up their game."

The first young man spoke again. "This time next week I want to see all new booty up there."

There was a groundswell of approval. "Fuckin' A right. New pussy."

A chant started. "New pussy. New pussy. New pussy."

"We need a challenge."

"A fucken challenge, *yeah*."

Their leader stood, unsteadily. "It's coming to me . . ." He took a dramatic pause. "Valentine's Day."

A chorus of groans, boos. "Fuck that!"

"Hold on. Think it through. That shit is bait for the hos. We throw a big blowout, hearts and flowers and thongs . . ."

Now hearty laughs.

"The bitches will love it, and we get our pick of the gash. A Valentine's party for them—and a Hunting Party for us."

The room took up the cry. "Hunting Party! Hunting Party!"

"All pledges need to bring in twenty-five points. Five for titty shots."

"Extra points for best heart-shaped ass!" a brother contributed from his seat on the floor.

"Extra points for asses with K-Tau letters written on 'em. Brand the bitches."

"Ten for full frontal. Twenty for penetration. And—"

"Twenty-five for anal!" a big guy finished.

"Hey!" someone else protested. "Why should pledges get all the action?"

"Anyone can participate," the alpha said magnanimously. "Cum one, cum all." He raised his glass in a toast.

The boys all pounded their shots, then the room exploded in drunken chatter.

"We be fucking tomorrow. Totally fucking."

"Get some bad bitches over here."

"Cooper be flicken mo' bean than an epileptic Mexican chef in a kitchen fulla strobe lights."

"I'm goin' hunting *now*. Got to crank out a few so I can last longer later."

The leader turned and looked over the table, the smudged mirror. "Oh hell. Look at that. Someone's hoovered up all the refreshments. Cutler, Vogel, you're up. Bring back fortifications."

The two frat brothers staggered out of the house into the fog. At the end of the block, Del Playa ran into a trailhead, turned into twisting sand paths through a labyrinth of beach scrub on the bluffs.

Cutler and Vogel veered onto the trail, slogging in the sand. They panted with exertion, squinting through double vision, stumbling in the dark. The dorm complexes of Manzanita Village and San Rafael were distant, blurry lights in the fog. The Kappa Alpha Tau house's main dealer lived in San Rafe and would be meeting them in the usual spot on the bluffs.

An occasional gleam of moonlight flashed on the rumbling dark expanse of the Pacific below. Otherwise, darkness. Silence.

Vogel kept turning, glancing into the dense woodland gloom beside the path.

"Dude, what is your problem?" Cutler complained.

"Someone in there," Vogel slurred. "Inna scrub. Following us."

"Yer trippin', dude . . ."

"Huh-uh. Listen—"

Both boys jumped as the carillon bells suddenly tolled from Storke Tower in the center of campus. Cutler burst into manic laughter.

"Yeah, I'm hearing it now. Totally."

He stumbled on ahead, leaving Vogel muttering behind him. "There was. There was someone—"

He staggered on in the dark—and nearly ran into Cutler, who had stopped in his tracks and was staring out over the thick scrub truculently. "Somebody out there? Who the fuck is following us? C'mon outta there, asshole."

The shadows moved. Cutler tensed, his fists balling at his sides. The ocean thundered below them.

A figure loomed up, dark, hooded.

"Holy shiiiit!" Vogel yelped.

The figure advanced through the fog, pushing back its cowl to reveal a gleaming white face, hollow eye sockets. A skull.

The frat brothers stumbled backward, screaming, and the skeleton figure barreled toward them, implacable in the fog.

Chapter Four

F og drifts through the silent, towering redwoods of north campus in the cold, gray dawn.

A lone girl huddles into her coat as she scuttles on a meandering path through the grove, en route to an early TA meeting. Her breath is puffs of white in the fog. Squirrels scatter in front of her, frantic red zips of motion.

The path opens up in front of a looming curved stone wall, like the outside of an ancient Roman coliseum. Rough gray brick with black iron gates.

The girl halts in front of the gates, staring upward. She jolts backward . . . and begins to scream.

Two male figures hang from the arches of the stadium, by ropes around their necks.

Roarke stood in front of the gates with Special Agent Damien Epps and San Francisco Police Homicide Inspector Clifton Mills, looking

up at the figures hanging from the famous arches of the historical wall. They were male, dressed in football uniforms and fraternity hoodies.

Below their dangling feet, a plaque set in the looming gray wall read Simpson Center for Student-Athlete High Performance.

Spray-painted across the wall in red were the words **DEATH TO RAPISTS**.

Mills turned from the sight to look at the agents. "Not too vague, is it? I'd say that's not too vague."

"It's also not homicide when the victims are mannequins," Epps said. "So what exactly are we doing here?"

Roarke was silent. He'd been wondering the same thing.

After his midnight pilgrimage to commune with the store-window saint, he'd returned home and dozed off . . . only to be awakened almost the next minute by a phone call from Mills, asking him to drive across the Bay in blinding fog on some urgent call related to a case they'd recently worked together.

They'd come because it was Mills, of course. The eccentric detective was a piece of work, but they owed him, and they trusted him.

But Roarke had *one* mission to focus on and it wasn't this—whatever this was.

"Lemme spell it out for you two sleeping beauties," Mills drawled. "Two of the athletes in this here program are under investigation for sexual assault. The university is under federal investigation for Title IX violations. I assume I do not have to familiarize you with Title IX and violations thereof."

The agents were perfectly aware of Title IX and violations thereof. Title IX was a federal law mandating that colleges and universities have a responsibility to protect students from discrimination and sexual assault. In the last two years a grassroots movement led by young rape survivors had spread to campuses throughout the country. Because of their actions, over two hundred colleges and universities were currently

under federal investigation for their responses, or nonresponses, to rape complaints against students, athletic teams, fraternities, and faculty.

Mills stabbed an index finger upward toward the hanged effigies. "So you tell me that isn't related to your never-ending mindfuck of a case."

Roarke felt a surge of anxiety, denial . . . and a hollow hunger. Everything he always felt when Cara was mentioned. Everything he hoped he'd left behind in the desert.

He composed himself, shook his head. "Cara Lindstrom didn't do this." He glanced to Epps.

"Not her style in any way," Epps agreed.

Cara didn't hang effigies. She killed. Brutally, mercilessly, and prolifically.

Epps added, "Besides which, it's Berkeley. If there's something to protest, they're going to protest it here."

The notoriously liberal campus had been host to who knew how many thousands of protests over the years: from the 1960s sit-ins and takeovers of campus buildings in opposition to the Vietnam War, to the 1985 tent city staged calling for UC divestment in apartheid South Africa, to the Million Student March demanding tuition-free higher education and the cancellation of student debt . . . and just weeks ago, a controversial, fiery riot over the scheduled lecture of a right-wing Twitter troll.

And Berkeley students spared no theater when it came to political protest. Roarke had seen "die-ins" with thousands of students sprawled prone in Sproul Plaza, activists chaining themselves to the gates of the Livermore Lab. A dozen environmentally protective young people had lived up in the branches of redwood trees, some for a staggering 649 days, to protest the construction of this very sports facility.

"Yeah, it's Berzerkely. My alma mater." Mills thumped a satirical fist on his chest. "And the protests have been nonstop since the

Cheeto-in-chief took office. There's a Hashtag-Not-My-President tent city on Sproul—have you seen it? Kids are losing their shit."

"Who isn't?" Epps asked.

Nobody had to answer.

Roarke had returned from the desert to a whole new world order. The election upset had caused a nationwide wave of protest, unprecedented in the modern US political landscape.

Mills continued. "What you're not getting is that this was not just Berkeley, comrades-of-mine. Whilst you boys were catching up on that aforementioned beauty sleep, *this* was going on all over the country." He stabbed a finger upward at the hanged dummies, the spray-painted threat. "They hit close to a hundred campuses that we know of so far."

Now Roarke and Epps looked at each other, stunned.

"And reports keep coming in." Mills passed over his iPad. The agents looked down at the top image. It was a photo of a mansion with a columned portico. Large Greek letters, prominently displayed, identified it as a frat house. Underneath the letters someone had spray-painted **YOU'RE NEXT, RAPIST**. And beside that warning was a painted pictogram of a skull with a crown of flowers.

"Santa Muerte," Epps said.

Santa Muerte. The skull with the crown was a clear reference to her.

Roarke thought of his midnight walk, his moment of communion with the botanica idol. This had been going on, even while he stood there in front of the saint's altar. It was an eerie feeling.

He swiped to the next photo. Another frat house, mannequins hanging by their necks, the same spray-painted threat, and the same skull pictogram.

The next photo: a college football stadium. Spray paint and skull.

Roarke looked up to see Mills watching him. "Yep. All over the US. Overnight. We have no idea of the final count. Colleges and universities in Northern and Southern California, North and South Carolina,

Florida, Kentucky, Michigan, Massachusetts. Zero warning. Some of them have the skull, some don't. Same message, give or take a death threat or two.

"The skull thingy is a stencil, suggesting it was made available for download on the Internet. According to your Agent Singh—who apparently gets up earlier than you two do—most, but not all, the universities that were hit are under federal investigation for Title IX violations."

"Bitch," Epps said, tightly.

Mills pointed at Epps. "Bitch. Exactly. Amiright? How else could anyone organize that?"

Roarke nodded, lost in thought. It was true—he had no doubt that Bitch had the online infrastructure in place to instigate a coordinated action.

Like the Internet hactivist group Anonymous, the feminist organization Bitch was a philosophy more than an actual structure. "Affiliation" was probably a better word for it. It was an underground, off-the-grid operation that claimed to have no headquarters, no corporate location. There was no telling if there were forty members, or four hundred, or four thousand. Anyone who wanted to could use the name Bitch to claim credit for a certain kind of action. In Bitch's case, that action was exposing sex criminals.

Last month, when the pairs of pimps and johns started turning up dead on infamous prostitute strolls in the city, no one had used Bitch's name to claim credit for those murders. But the crime scenes were linked by the shrines and offerings to Santa Muerte, and Bitch had adopted the symbols of the saint when they were staging protests against the incarceration of Cara Lindstrom. Roarke highly suspected Santa Muerte was Bitch's new mascot.

He turned to Mills. "Was anyone hurt in this . . ." He had to stop to figure out a word for it. "Vandalism? Anyone murdered?"

"Not that I know of," the detective admitted.

"So these campuses contacted you—why?"

"To request help finding and arresting the perpetrators."

Roarke held up the iPad. "Seems to me the perpetrators have been identified."

Epps shot him a look, but said nothing.

Mills shrugged. "You could take that view, and I prolly wouldn't argue with you. In other quarters, though, including your own backyard, they're calling it domestic terrorism."

Roarke didn't even have time to laugh at the absurdity of it. It was Epps who exploded. "Are you shitting me?" The agent walked a circle on the path in complete disbelief. "In the last month there's been a seven percent surge of reports of hate crimes against Muslims, African Americans, gays, women. That barely rates a blip in the media—and a protest against *rapists* is suddenly terrorism?"

Roarke couldn't agree more. "Sorry, Mills—you're on your own with this one." He glanced up at the hanging dummies. "This is street theater. Performance art. It's vandalism, yeah, but it's not terrorism and it's certainly not murder."

And yet he had an uneasy feeling. The new administration had been calling more and more stridently for FBI crackdowns on any protests that opposed its agenda.

This could get ugly. Fast.

Mills gave the agents a hard look. "If you'll remember, I'm investigating a serial murder. I'd say this is loosely related, or tightly. So hey—you can blow me off, or just blow me. This is a zero-casualty action right now. But it's not the last of it, we all know it. Later or sooner, shit's gonna get real." He jerked his head toward the words spray-painted in red. **DEATH TO RAPISTS**.

And Roarke knew he was right. People were going to die.

"And FY-fucking-I, it wasn't my idea to get you boys over here. That was your boss."

Roarke and Epps stopped on the path and looked at each other.

"So ask *him* what he has in mind. I gave you the tour, as requested. Go with God. Or with that skull thing. Your choice."

Roarke and Epps walked a meandering path down through north campus, under towering redwoods, past neo-Gothic buildings and brutalist cement structures, over wooden bridges spanning a low creek. The path wound through a eucalyptus grove, the air spiced with the fragrance. The cold early morning was heavy with mist.

"It sure looks like Bitch," Epps said, finally.

If so, there was no doubt it was worrisome.

Bitch had continued to take action in the weeks since the December protests over Cara Lindstrom's arrest and the mysterious, still-unsolved Santa Muerte killings. The organization, or someone in it, had released online lists of names and private, identifying information about pimps and "mongers" and other sexual offenders in several doxxing campaigns. But doxxing was a fairly standard armchair operation.

There had been nothing remotely on this scale of planning, coordination, and execution.

Roarke wrested himself out of those thoughts. Bitch was not his case. He was out of that business. He had a plan. He had a task force to organize, once he sold it to his SAC.

"Not our problem," he told Epps. "Not anymore." He glanced at his phone for the time. "I've got to get back."

"The meeting with Reynolds?" Epps asked.

"Ten a.m."

"Get it done, boss—"

Epps fell silent, staring ahead of him. The look on his face was so odd, Roarke turned instantly to look. And he felt his pulse leap.

Pale figures were materializing in the mist between the trees. A whole group of young women, in what looked like bloody shrouds. As they came closer, Roarke saw that they were college girls, draped in white sheets splashed with red, like blood. Dozens of them, walking ghostlike through the eucalyptus trees.

The agents stood and watched them pass, unnerved.

"Berkeley," Epps said uncertainly.

Roarke was silent, watching the girls disappear again into the fog.

Only it's not just Berkeley anymore, is it?

A hundred campuses hit overnight.

There's something happening here. No doubt about it.

Chapter Five

Roarke strode into the concrete monolith of the San Francisco Federal Building, in the heart of downtown. Flashed his Bureau ID to the guard in the giant bulletproof glass cube in the blue-veined marble lobby. Rode the elevator up and stepped out into the gleaming corridor, lined with framed newspapers and photos depicting the history of the Bureau. Walked past the windows with their views of the Bay—always breathtakingly beautiful—and the seedy squalor of the Tenderloin.

He paused for a breath in the outer office of his Special Agent in Charge. And he forced himself to relax, to remember his circumstances. The publicity from the case he had cracked open last month—almost in spite of himself—had gone viral. He was returning a hero. He was walking into his SAC's office holding all the cards.

He opened the door with confidence.

It all began so well. Reynolds behind his wide desk, intently listening as Roarke paced the office, laying out the proposal for his task force.

The first step was a complete overhaul of ViCAP, the Bureau's Violent Criminal Apprehension Program. The database was supposed to have revolutionized law enforcement, especially in regard to sexual assault cases. Unlike Canada's successful version of the same program, it still hadn't happened. Out of 18,000 police agencies in the US, only about 1,400 currently participated in the ViCAP system. Far less than one percent of violent crimes were ever reported to the database.

So Roarke's first priority was to get ViCAP up to speed.

The second, but simultaneous, action would be to tackle the national rape kit backlog. Hundreds of thousands of rape kits, with crucial DNA evidence that could convict tens of thousands of serial offenders, currently sat unprocessed in police labs across the country. The case he'd just solved, the horrific attack on fourteen-year-old Ivy Barnes, abducted, raped, and burned alive, might very well never have happened if the rape kits of two previous victims had been tested and entered into the ViCAP system. Roarke wanted a national clearinghouse for rape kit processing. He knew his teammate, Antara Singh, could really sink her teeth into that one.

He spelled these first two pillars out for Reynolds, and concluded with the third aim.

"On our own turf, I want to shift the focus of the team. Use RICO laws to pursue and prosecute traffickers. If there's anything we learned from the killings in Oakland and the Tenderloin, it's that there's nowhere near enough law enforcement focus on trafficking. At present the only nationwide task force dealing with domestic sex trafficking is Operation Cross Country, a once-a-year sweep."

Last year's OCC action had resulted in the recovery of 82 children being victimized by prostitution, and the arrest of 239 pimps. Less than a drop in a bucket of filth.

No, it's not enough. Nothing could be enough.

"There needs to be a year-round task force. A dedicated unit here in the Bay Area will mean more resources, higher penalties, more kids rescued, more pimps put away for so long that the gangs, cartels, and independents will start thinking long and hard about going into the racket."

He took a breath. "And, most importantly, we can be a pilot program for other field offices. And branch out to work with other organizations like Thorn, Polaris, MISSSEY, and Children of the Night, who are using innovative strategies to combat trafficking online and in the streets."

And there was so much more to do. Taking Social Services and the juvenile justice system to task, aggressively prosecuting abusers of all kinds, from parents to pimps to law enforcement officials.

But it was all possible.

His team was the best he could hope for. Special Agent Damien Epps, the most moral man he'd met in his life. Street cred. Uncanny instincts. True outrage about the evil that men do.

Special Agent Antara Singh. A brilliant tech expert, researcher, and analyst. India-born, Cambridge-educated, with a keen perception of the international issues of trafficking.

Crime scene techs Lam and Stotlemyre, supervising the forensic aspects of the task force's investigations. Coordinating the overhaul of ViCAP.

Roarke hoped as well to recruit his old mentor, retired Special Agent Chuck Snyder, as the task force's go-to profiler.

When Roarke had finished speaking, Reynolds nodded for a long time. "I'm extremely impressed, Matt. You've put a lot of thought into this. You're addressing systemic failures and it's all sound. More than sound."

Already Roarke was tensing up. He could feel the "but" coming.

"Sir, I appreciate that—" he began.

"But before we get into more specifics, I'd like to know what you saw over there in Berkeley this morning. Is this Bitch?"

Roarke tried to keep his voice even. "All due respect—that's not what I'm here to discuss. You know my conditions for coming back."

"I do," his boss assured him. "But I'm getting pressure to investigate these campus attacks." He opened a manila file, and Roarke looked down at a stack of faxed photographs. A spray-painted stencil of Santa Muerte stared up at him. "They were nationwide, but they were particularly concentrated in California, so—"

Roarke couldn't wait for him to finish. "Bottom line—it's vandalism. I don't know why we're even—"

Now Reynolds spoke over him. "The Bureau is extremely concerned with cyberterrorism right now, and this was a coordinated attack, organized online, through social media and encrypted accounts. It's clearly the opening gambit in a protracted action, if we don't move to shut it down."

Roarke had to force himself not to answer in anger.

If the Bureau is so concerned with cyberterrorism, where was it during the election, when democracy was being hacked by a totalitarian power?

He thought it, but didn't say it. It was one of the ongoing questions of the new world order.

He was silent for a moment, forcing himself calm. And then he spoke again.

"There's only one reason I'm coming back on, and that's the task force."

"And you'll get your task force. This vandalism . . . this action," Reynolds was struggling to name it, "this is *now*. This is top priority. You know the potential players. You have the contacts. There's no one else in the country more prepared to handle it. And we need to handle it, before . . ."

"Before what?"

His boss paused. "I don't know. I've never seen anything like it before."

No one has seen anything like it before. But the protests are only a reaction to a government that no one in the US has ever seen before.

"What do these campuses expect us to do?" Roarke asked, keeping his voice neutral.

Reynolds started, "They know we're familiar with the organization Bitch—"

"My team ceased investigating the organization in December, when Cara Lindstrom was arrested. It was never a full investigation to begin with, just an avenue of inquiry. But that's beside the point." Roarke pointed to the file of photographs on the SAC's desk. "Since when is tagging a federal crime?"

"The campus boards say it's creating a climate of fear."

Roarke laughed. He couldn't help it. At the same time, he felt the familiar sick churning in his gut, the sense that they were living in a system turned on its head.

He gathered himself and spoke as evenly as he could. "So for decades these campuses have been covering up rapes, protecting rapists, intimidating the victims into silence—or in some cases, suicide—and never *once* have those campuses asked for federal help to deal with their rape problem. But there's a rash of graffiti—and suddenly they want federal intervention?"

"The administrators claim other students also feel threatened."

"Only if they're rapists." Roarke didn't even try to keep the edge out of his voice. "The message is pretty clear: don't rape. The answer is pretty clear, too. These campuses could get rid of the problem by expelling the rapists." He stared at his supervisory agent. "You're not seriously suggesting we get involved with this."

Reynolds lifted his hands, placating. "All I'm asking is that you go down to Santa Barbara for a day or two."

Despite himself, Roarke was curious. "Why Santa Barbara?" *If the protests had been all over the country . . .*

"The situation there is—elevated. It's the only campus where a couple of students were actually attacked."

"Attacked how?"

"That's one of the details I hope you'll be able to clear up."

Roarke had the sense the SAC had just evaded the question, but the older man continued. "It's a simple job. Go down there, find out what happened, see if there's anything to it." He spread his hands, appealing. "You know how this works, Matt. You give a little to get a lot."

The implication was clear: do this and I'll support your task force. *So that's it. The offer I can't refuse.* Roarke had to hold down the surge of resentment. *Go along to get along.*

He was blindingly angry when he left the SAC's office.

He slammed into his office and indulged himself in a way he rarely did, by kicking the side of his desk. It felt so painfully good he turned and punched the wall.

Then he caught sight of Singh, standing outside the window of his office. Her shimmering dark hair, luminous, her watching dark eyes. Still as only Singh could be.

He had no doubt that she'd seen his outburst.

She met his gaze. Then she quietly opened the door and closed it behind her. "Not good news, then."

He shook his head. His breath felt like an animal trapped in his chest, clawing to get out. He turned away from her and gripped the windowsill, staring out. "Of all the fucking jerk-off assignments. Now. *Now*, when . . ."

His memories closed in on him: fresh, raw, agonizing.

Ivy Barnes. Laura Huell. Jade Lauren. Marlena Sanchez.

The young rape victims he had come to know over the last two months. Girls who had been abused beyond his comprehension, and betrayed by the very systems charged to protect them.

He'd sworn to himself, sworn to *them*, that he was not going to leave these kids to fight *It* on their own.

The sense of urgency was back, more oppressive than ever. *Running out of time. Your days are numbered.*

He was on the verge of walking straight out again and never coming back. Instead, he summoned himself.

I owe them this.

"Get Epps," he told Singh. "Tell him we're taking an early lunch. Meet me in the plaza."

The agents met up in the Civic Center Plaza—a Beaux-Arts square surrounded by the classical architecture of the City Hall, the state building, the library—and walked its octagonal paths past pigeons and wandering homeless.

Singh and Epps strode side by side, professionally formal, not touching, yet moving in tandem. They had been a couple for months, at first staying completely under the radar. Now they had submitted a domestic partner declaration to the Bureau, with Roarke's complete approval. But their conduct on the job was impeccable.

The agents bought coffee and street tacos from a food truck and sat on a bench along the alley of pollarded sycamore trees. By unspoken agreement they fell silent any time a pedestrian passed nearby.

Roarke could pretend to himself that this outdoor meeting was to clear his head.

The truth was he no longer felt safe to speak in his own office.

It was a sign of the new *Not Normal*—an extraordinary sense of paranoia that Roarke's team could feel even a continent away in California.

There was a cloud permeating the whole Bureau. FBI officials in Washington were being overtly pressured by the administration to back "alternative" versions of events, to deny the White House's ties to Russia and the Russian influence on the election itself. The administration had the whole intelligence community in its sights. No one knew who might be collaborating.

How quickly democracy fails.

At least Roarke had his team. It was just him, Singh, and Epps, now. They'd recently lost their newest member. Special Agent Ryan Jones was young, hungry. When Roarke had taken his indefinite leave of absence, Jones had requested a transfer. Roarke understood perfectly, wished him well. Roarke himself hadn't intended to be back, ever, so why wouldn't Jones move on to a more conventional arrangement?

It was for the best. He hadn't had the chance to fully know Jones. An ambitious agent was susceptible to the attention and promises of his superiors.

Whereas Epps and Singh, he would trust with his life.

And even that. That's the way I'm thinking now.

What have we come to?

Is this the end of America? Is it?

He put his chaotic thoughts aside and gave his agents a terse version of the meeting. Even outdoors, this far away from the Federal Building, he was speaking in a hushed voice, wary of passersby.

Before he'd finished he could feel Epps seething.

"So that's the deal," Roarke ended. "Not in those words, but—no task force, not even a discussion of it, until we handle this investigation of whatever the hell it was that went down last night."

The men both glanced automatically to Singh, knowing she would have the latest.

She nodded, always centered, always serene. "I have been monitoring the reports that have been coming in all morning. There have been over three hundred campuses hit. All in the same night."

"Holy mother . . ." Epps murmured in disbelief—and admiration.

Roarke had to admit he was stunned by the scope of the—*Action? Protest? Demonstration?* He was having as much trouble naming it as Reynolds had been.

"It is astonishing," Singh agreed. "Less than two months ago, we saw Bitch turn out over a thousand women to protest Cara Lindstrom's arrest. That number is not especially unusual for San Francisco. But that was before the inauguration, and the Women's March."

The protests in January, the ones Roarke had missed, the Women's March demonstrations, had changed everything. The day after the inauguration, an unprecedented number of women, men, and children had poured into the streets. In city after city across the country, there had been such a mass of humanity there was no way to police it. It had been the largest political protest in America, ever. Three to four million people, all told.

Astoundingly, there had been no violence, no arrests. But it was still early days. The marches had shown the size of the opposition.

How many ways could that energy be harnessed?

The administration had cracked down immediately. In eighteen states, more every day, laws were being proposed and expedited that would severely curtail peaceful protest. The legislation had been started in Southern states in response to the Black Lives Matter protests of the fall, but now more states were jumping on that bandwagon, ramming harsh legislation through—even one law that would decriminalize killing a protester with a vehicle, if that protester was blocking traffic. A law like that was nothing less than an open invitation for a certain element to commit vehicular manslaughter.

And now Bitch had responded with an escalation of its own.

Singh concluded, "I believe it is clear what higher-ups are really afraid of. The sheer scope of Bitch's action is worrisome. A nationwide, coordinated blitz attack that is not simple protest, but something more actively threatening."

Given the current political landscape, Roarke could hardly blame the protesters. But Singh was right. What was alarming about this campus-centered vandalism was the consistent symbolism of it. The skull, the hanging dummies, the focus on rapists. It was on point, it was an overt threat of violence, and it continued to coalesce, even anthropomorphize, around the mythic force of Santa Muerte.

Now that Roarke was recovering from the sting of the setback, he had to admit that there might be some merit in assigning him and the team to investigate.

He asked, "Why do you think Bitch targeted campuses? Why that focus, particularly?"

Epps was the first to answer. "Because it worked. They sure as fuck got their message out there. But I'm not the one to explain it."

Both men looked to Singh.

She took her time, answering slowly. "I would say that there was already a large network of activists to tap into. Before the election there had been a surge of grassroots activism. A coalition of young women who have survived sexual assault only to be victimized again through the legal and university systems. Young women willing to make a stand, to fight their rapists and their college administrations for justice. Hundreds of these young women. On hundreds of campuses. With a tech and social media savvy unprecedented in the history of protest."

Roarke nodded, intent.

"And now there is the added, profound distress of the election, the normalization of sexual assault by the most powerful of our leaders, in the very highest offices of the land. And those lawsuits these young women have worked so hard for, against such odds, are in peril because of the new regime. The new secretary of education has so far refused to commit to taking these lawsuits forward. So, Bitch knew that there was anger and youth to be tapped into. There was—there is—a willing and able army."

She looked at the men with her dark and luminous eyes. "It seems a perfectly obvious move, does it not?"

Roarke stared at her, unnerved. "That sounds like war."

"Yes," she answered softly. "I believe it is a declaration of war."

Chapter Six

It is not even dusk when she sees her, so it cannot be blamed on the shadows, or a trick of the light.

She stands on a rise, looking down on Cara. The skeleton girl.

Forever fourteen. Flesh burned away, down to her bones.

The specter of Ivy Barnes. A girl from her past. Abducted by a monster, a vicious predator, one of the worst incarnations of *It* she has ever encountered. Raped, burned alive, miraculously surviving, her flesh eaten by fire.

She will not come near, but she watches Cara as she gathers kindling for the stove.

The girl Ivy is long dead. Sixteen years ago Cara avenged her, killing her torturer, and had helped her die. But her ghost, the skeleton girl, is back, and has been an almost constant companion for the last month.

At night Cara curls by the fire and dreams, and the skeleton girl crawls into her bed and lies against her, just as she had that night, all those many years ago.

And now, she is here in the daytime as well.

For what?

Cara straightens with her armful of kindling, and stands still, willing her to speak, to step forward, to give her some sign.

But Ivy stands without moving, and when the molten sun drops behind the rim of the canyon, she is gone.

Chapter Seven

Roarke stood looking out the tall windows of his living room at the lights going on all over his city.

He and Epps would head down to Santa Barbara in the morning. Roarke hated having to waste precious time, but he was resigned to it. If this was the hurdle he had to jump over to get the task force, it was better to get to it.

He turned from the windows, sat down in front of his computer at the dining table he never used for dining.

He avoided looking at the news updates. It was nothing but bad. The constant state of unreality was exhausting.

But as he had done every night for the last two weeks, he logged on to the online "men's rights" forums.

Of course tonight the forums were buzzing with talk about the Santa Muerte campus attacks. The meninists were having as much trouble as the media trying to find words to describe the action. But instead of phrases that the media used, like "coordinated protest" and "nationwide anonymous demonstration," in these forums the word that came up over and over was "terrorism." And the ever-popular "feminazi terrorism."

If the feminazis want a war, they're gonna get a war.

A rape war. Hell fucken yeah.

Rape the bitches.

And on, and on, and on.

A large number of the protesters thought that Cara was behind the protests.

This is Lindstrom and those bitches.

Rape the Lindstrom bitches.

Roarke felt helpless anger rising.

Tens of thousands, hundreds of thousands of these monsters out there. Threatening real crimes.

And we're supposed to clamp down on protests about unprosecuted criminals? What kind of world is this?

What are we heading into?

He ordered himself not to read any more. Instead he skimmed through the forums for the names he knew to be handles used by Detective Gilbert Ortiz.

Ortiz. A demon from Cara's past who had followed her into the present. A supposed lawman who'd been peripherally involved in the manhunt for the vicious pair of serial rapists who had attacked Ivy

Barnes at Cara's high school, and raped dozens of other high school girls, in dozens of different states, over dozens of years.

Instead of pursuing this unholy pair of predators, Ortiz had abused his power to stalk fourteen-year-old Cara. And even now, sixteen years later, he was creating whole forums like these. Forums with titles like "Rape Cara Lindstrom" and "Kill That Lindstrom Bitch."

Roarke's long experience, as a profiler and as a man, was that no one talks about doing sexual violence to a woman without being a sexually violent person.

He had seen Ortiz's anger up close. Ortiz's old partner had called him a wife batterer. And Roarke thought there was even more to it than that.

Ortiz knew that Cara recognized what he was. She'd seen what she called *It* in him. She had seen evil.

Face-to-face with Roarke, not only had Ortiz not denied it—he'd almost admitted it.

So Roarke clenched his jaw and scrolled through the cesspool of posts.

He made himself do it because Ortiz had put a bounty on Cara's head. He was offering to pay for "any verified Lindstrom sightings." There was an email address attached to these posts, which Roarke was constantly tempted to ask Singh to hack.

But he hadn't. The fact that Ortiz kept posting variations of that same message, periodically, meant that he probably, *probably* hadn't gotten any useful tips.

Yet.

Cara had been off the radar for nearly two months now. Roarke hoped to God she had the sense to stay off the radar.

He had his own guess where she might be.

It had come to him during his month out in the desert, as he drove the state roads crossing in and out of Indian reservations.

He didn't know exactly where, not even exactly which state. But he was pretty sure how one would start looking for her, if one were inclined to find her.

But he wasn't.

Cara was not his case anymore. She'd jumped bail, which made her the jurisdiction and responsibility of the US Marshals Service, Northern District of California.

Roarke hadn't been following the marshals' activity—not entirely. But he knew the division hadn't made any progress in locating her.

And what he'd learned about her childhood made him the last possible person to want to catch her.

But he combed the men's forums every night, to make sure that Ortiz wasn't on his way to kill her.

DAY TWO

Chapter Eight

She rode through the fog, up over the mountains, galloping under the canopy of ancient oaks, splashing across streams. Feeling the horse's gleaming flanks heaving with muscle underneath her, the heavy hooves trampling everything in her path. Melded to the horse, she was huge, powerful, invincible. No one could touch her when she was riding.

On the ridge, she dismounted, feeling her thighs shaking. But her stance was strong, her legs like roots, tree trunks, an extension of the earth.

Jade stood, panting, and leaned against Christobel, and looked out over the valley, through the sunlight just piercing the mist. It was stunningly beautiful, so quiet and deserted, with sleepy ranches tucked away in the folds of the hills. Coyotes roamed by day and night, and deer, in pairs and trios and whole herds. There were hawks and owls, rabbits and raccoons and squirrels, lizards and hummingbirds.

And almost never any people. They were just an hour and a half north of Los Angeles, half an hour inland from the beaches of Santa Barbara, and there were towns within riding distance nearby, touristy wine towns like Los Olivos and Santa Ynez, with their quaint main streets of Old West storefronts, craft breweries, outdoor wine-tasting patios.

But here, in the valley, so many of the ranches were uninhabited. Vacation homes for their wealthy owners, occasionally rented out through Airbnb or VRBO. So much luxury, untouched, unused.

This, the Santa Ynez Valley, had become Jade's whole world. The valley, the hills surrounding it, and the ranch.

They'd been keeping her there at the ranch for almost two months now. Elle—Rachel Elliott, the social worker from the Belvedere House. And the women who called themselves Bitch.

They weren't holding her hostage, exactly. It was their version of inpatient hospitalization. Well, and there was the little matter of the murders.

Last month Jade had killed three people, if you could call a scuzz-ball pimp and two douchebag johns "human." Possibly four—it had gotten a little crazy for a while there, what with the meth and the blood, and the blond one, Cara Lindstrom. And the skeleton. Jade had been so fucked up it was hard to tell the memories from the nightmares.

She knew she'd done DeShawn the pimp and that fat fuck monger Goldwyn, or Goldman, or whatever. And Cranston, in Santa Cruz, may he *not* rest in peace. She sincerely hoped there was an afterlife and that Clyde was down there eternally roasting on a spit. There were a couple of others she wasn't so sure of. But yeah, enough dead pimps and johns that if she didn't keep her head down, she'd be thrown into some concrete hole for the rest of her life.

When Elliott had first brought her to the ranch, they'd kept her locked up in a single room. Oh, she'd been fucked up, no doubt. They—mostly Elliott, but others, too—nursed her through meth withdrawal. Round-the-clock supervision so she'd had no choice but to kick it.

She'd been pretty crazed through that. She didn't remember a whole lot, but she knew there had been screaming and breaking things, trying to fight people. Maybe hurting them. She wasn't entirely sure, but she thought she remembered restraints.

Of course that could have been from *Before*. When she'd first been dragged down into the hell known as "the life." When there had been the systematic torture pimps called the "seasoning" of a new girl—

She pinched herself hard. *Before* wasn't something she needed to think about. *Just shut that shit down now.*

After those first two weeks of detox . . . the IV hydration, the shakes . . . when she was actually able to walk again . . . she was allowed out of the room into other parts of the ranch house. With supervision, of course. Always with someone watching her.

But this time *It*, the meth, that ravaging hungry thing, didn't seem to have its claws so deep inside her. After a month and a half she was clean, cleaner than she'd been in a year, two—she couldn't even remember, really.

Now when she looked in the mirror, she had to stare hard to find herself in the reflection. Her wild and heavy hair had been cut to a bob and dyed a dark brown, along with her carefully reshaped eyebrows. She never stepped outside without a long-sleeved, flesh-toned bodysuit under anything else she wore, to conceal the art that covered pretty much her entire body. The Bitches weren't taking any chances. Jade wasn't on the Most Wanted list or anything, but she was pretty sure a couple of San Francisco cops wanted a word or two with her.

Of course the Bitches had a lot to lose from being discovered, themselves. Jade got that, right enough. Illegal shit was going down here for sure, beyond hiding a murderer. Or "harboring a victim of the patriarchy." However they wanted to say it.

She was shocked that they let her out at all.

But it wasn't prison. She could have run, by now. She could run anytime.

The real reason she didn't was the horses.

They'd started her on the horses after those first gnarly weeks—the raging and shaking and vomiting, the out-of-her-fucking-mind withdrawal.

She knew how the positive reinforcement shit worked—it was to get her in line. But. But. When they started letting her ride the horses as a reward, it kept her mind off the crystal.

And then she'd fallen in love. Gotten completely hooked on the wild beauty of them and the speed—they were so *fast*—and the awesome power. Christobel—any one of those massive animals—could crush her to death without a thought. Crush her, or anyone.

They belonged to the wild. They let themselves be enclosed in the barn, where they were groomed and fed and sheltered. Who wouldn't want someone catering to your needs like that? But behind all of their huge, liquid eyes was the knowledge that on any ride, they could throw their rider, trample them, and take off, never to be found.

From the beginning, Elle had made her groom and feed and water them, too. No riding without brushing down the horses, and mucking out the stalls. Saying "thank you" by keeping their stalls clean.

But that was as good as the riding, somehow. Lifting one of those legs and having that huge beast trust you to clean her hooves.

Even pitching out horseshit felt like . . . somehow felt like . . . like pitching shit out of her own soul. Emptying herself of every drop of spunk from those pathetic losers. Every foul touch, every swallow. Getting cleaner with every mucking out.

It was as good as counseling, although there was plenty of that, too. Elliott had started that and the detox even before the ranch, when Jade had been in the Belvedere House in San Francisco for those few days after the blond one, Lindstrom, offed Danny right in front of her—

Danny.

For one shuddering second she was back in the dark, stinking tunnel . . .

The pimp's body at her feet in a pool of his own blood.

She pinched herself hard again, banished the image.

Beside her, Christobel nickered in her ear, and Jade turned automatically to pet her.

"There now. There," she crooned, nuzzling the horse's nose with her own.

Lindstrom had killed Danny and freed her. But Jade had turned around and freed Lindstrom right back, hadn't she? Planting the razor Lindstrom had used to kill Danny at the scene of DeShawn's murder. That had been a stroke of genius, no doubt. Exculpatory evidence, they called it, and it made them give Lindstrom bail. Get out of jail free.

Lindstrom was back on the street, probably killing the shit out of more scumbags.

That's how come sometimes Jade wasn't even entirely sure she'd done it, the other pimps and the mongers. 'Cause for sure Lindstrom was out there doing her thing.

And then . . . well, yeah. There was the skeleton that she saw sometimes. She didn't know if that was the meth, or her brain, or what. Sometimes it was just hard to tell reality from the drug fugues and the detox hallucinations and the crazy freaking flashbacks.

The skeleton had been there, too, when Danny died. And that fat fuck monger.

So maybe the skeleton did it.

Or maybe I did.

But the main thing was, they were dead. And that felt *good*.

"How do you like me now?" she whispered.

Chapter Nine

She could groom Christobel in a half hour, but she often took twice that long, just 'cause. It wasn't a chore at all. And she was in no hurry to get back to the house. It was always so freaking tense. Every day some new drama.

The Bitches at the ranch came and went, staying a night or two, or a week. There were some of what they called "survivors." Jade knew the black wariness in their eyes. Some were counselors like Elliott. Rape crisis, social workers, lawyers. Dykes, trans people, and even some good old-fashioned cis women.

They had secret meetings, and Jade wasn't allowed in to those. So she knew stuff was up, stuff that she could entirely fuck up if she had a mind to.

The Bitches weren't out there killing. Not yet, anyway. It was all cyber attacks, so far. There was constant, furious blogging going on. Petitions. Twitter campaigns.

And the cyber storm had stepped up to hurricane level since the election, the hostile takeover of the pussy grabber. Like that was any surprise to anyone? They were fucked, of course, the entire country was entirely fucked—but they always had been.

She took apples from the barrel and fed Christobel, then the other three horses, stroking their long noses, looking into their ancient eyes.

Then she headed for the ranch house.

It was huge. She'd gone around and counted one day: ten bedrooms of different sizes, although a lot of them were always locked. Whoever owned the place had the bucks, obvs, but if that person was ever there, Jade hadn't sussed her yet.

But it was more homey than fancy. The furniture was old and lived in. It seemed kind of like something out of an old black-and-white movie you'd see on cable at Christmas. Jade had her own room, with a four-poster bed and doilies and shit, like she was a real person.

She came in the front door and dumped her riding boots in the mudroom.

Just walking into the main hall, she knew something was up. First of all, no one was in the great room or the kitchen.

That left the library. But to get there, she had to walk by *Her*.

There was an alcove in the hall that had been set up as an altar to Santa Muerte, the skeleton woman. Lady Death.

Jade approached, as always, with trepidation and stopped in front of her, staring up at the five-foot-tall idol: A skeleton dressed in purple velvet robes, with a lace shawl over her skull. A cigarette stuck jauntily in her bony jaw.

The altar was covered by a glittering cloth. Fat candles burned on top of it and offerings were piled in front of the saint: coins, flowers, candy, a bottle of tequila.

Her hollow eyes glared out at Jade, and Jade shivered. But she couldn't look away.

The rest of them, the Bitches, they didn't really believe in her. They were using her as a prop, some kind of mascot for their cause. But *they* hadn't been out there on the filthy streets of the Tenderloin and International Boulevard. They hadn't seen the skeleton hovering in the shadows, watching the mongers cruising teenage girls and younger. They hadn't felt the rage heating the ancient bones as she watched the forced blowjobs in alleys. Hadn't felt her lust to kill.

The Bitches didn't believe. But Jade knew that you didn't have to believe in something for it to be real.

Every gift they put in front of her, every chocolate, every dollar, every cigarette, all of it—was making her more alive.

Alive enough that Jade could see her almost all the time now.

She stared into the hollow eyes and whispered, "What do you want? *Just say it.*"

The black buzzing thoughts rose, like a swarm of wasps inside her . . .

Voices.

But this time the voices weren't in her head. They were coming from the library.

She stepped quickly back from the altar and moved down the hall.

The library was the best: a two-story room with shelves of books all around the walls of the first floor and also on the top balcony. The Bitches used it as a conference room. Now the door was closed and she could hear the raised voices behind it. A lot of voices, talking fast over each other. A fight.

She made her steps soft and moved across the floor silently, then hovered outside the door, listening.

"*. . . front page news . . .*"

"*. . . hit before. We're out ahead of the curve—*"

"*Barely. It's going to come any minute.*"

"*Let it come. Let him announce. We're ready, now.*"

Judging from voices, the layered quality of sound, there were more than two dozen women in the library. Three, maybe. Something big was up.

Jade knew the layout of the room; she could picture it in her head. They were having their meeting around the old oak table on the lower floor. And she knew that she could get onto the balcony through a second-floor door. If she was careful, no one on the ground floor would see her come in.

She turned for the stairs, crept up silently in her stockinged feet. On the second-floor landing, she stopped at the door and twisted the knob carefully, cracking the door open. The voices were louder now.

She pushed the door just enough to slip through. Inside the room, she pressed her back against the wall.

The voices came clearly from below.

"We've got the media coverage now."

"Which is exactly why we have to push it."

Jade suddenly heard Elliott's voice, raised, and sounding distressed. *"It's too far. We can't . . ."* and there was something Jade couldn't hear. *"Not their way."*

There was a bunch of shouting, then.

Jade still didn't know what they were talking about. But she knew how to find out.

She eased back out of the library door. Elliott was down there in the library, so she had a few minutes at least.

She hurried to Elle's bedroom, quietly opened and closed the door, and sat down at the computer.

She wasn't allowed to get online without supervision. But if they didn't want her online, they shouldn't be teaching her hacking. Which one of the Bitches, Miranda, had been doing for some time now. And Jade had figured out the passwords long ago.

Someone had said something about "front page" so she googled the *LA Times*. It took her all of ten seconds to find out what all the shouting was about.

She looked down at the screen at the photos of hanged male dummies, the painted Santa Muerte skulls. And she felt her heart start to race. It was so much more interesting than she'd thought.

Someone was out for blood. Someone was ready to *do* something.

It was the sign she'd been waiting for.

It was like—like war.

She was so engrossed in reading she forgot to watch the time. And suddenly the door slammed open behind her.

She jumped up from the chair, her heart pounding.

Elle was in the room already before she even noticed Jade. She shut the door behind her and leaned into it.

Jade stared at Elliott's back. She was shaking.

What? What the hell?

Elle turned around . . . and jumped back a foot, seeing Jade. "Jade! What are you—"

And then instead of yelling, she burst into tears.

Now Jade was really freaked out. She'd never seen her do that before. Everything Elliott had done, everything she'd seen, and she'd never cried. Not for anything. It was truly weirding Jade out.

"I'm sorry," Elle said, through sobs, as if she'd done something wrong. "I'm sorry." She sat abruptly on the bed, as if she couldn't actually stand.

Shit.

Jade swallowed. "Can I . . . Do you need anything? Can I get you anything?"

Elliott didn't answer. She just cried.

This was definitely *not okay*. Elle was the strongest person she'd ever known.

She knew Elle thought she'd killed those pimp daddies, and the mongers. For real—Elle totes knew Jade was a murderer. But Elliott didn't try to pretend nothing had happened. She didn't tell her to put it all behind her and focus on other things. She didn't get mad when Jade was mad; she said she had every right to every bit of the anger.

And she said . . . she *said* . . . that none of it was her fault and that she'd believe that one day.

She was everything a teacher was supposed to be. Yeah, and everything a mother was supposed to be. And now she was losing it. It seemed . . . it actually seemed like she was breaking apart.

Things must be really bad. Worse than bad.

And suddenly Jade wasn't scared. She was furious.

Chapter Ten

The agents flew into Santa Barbara on a day so beautiful it almost hurt to look at it. The gently rolling Santa Ynez mountain range encircled the coastal city, with its opulent State Street lined with Spanish architecture. The Mediterranean-style enclave was in many ways the epitome of California mythology: sun, surf, wineries, wealth.

The plane descended toward the vast gleam of ocean. Looking out the window, Roarke could see black dots in the waves along the shoreline.

In the seat beside him, Epps looked out in disbelief. "Those fools are actually out surfing? In February?"

"Best time of year for it."

"And you know this from experience."

"Little bit."

In fact Roarke had done some surfing right down there, the year he'd dated a UCSB sorority girl and regularly drove the hour and a half down from his own college in San Luis Obispo.

Epps shook his head. "You have hidden shallows."

Roarke wasn't about to argue. *Those were the days,* he thought dryly. A time so simple it seemed like seven centuries ago.

The airport was a bit north of the city proper, and a mere half mile from the university.

The two students who had been attacked the night of the Santa Muerte action were fraternity brothers from the Kappa Alpha Tau fraternity. Apparently they'd been accosted by a skull-masked, caped figure on the way home to their chapter house.

Roarke knew UCSB's fraternities and sororities were all clustered in the student village of Isla Vista, north of campus. But the agents' first contact was Kirk Sandler, the attorney for the university's Interfraternity Council. Sandler had offered a car to pick them up, but the agents had declined in favor of renting a vehicle up front.

Their meeting place was only a few miles from the airport: the Bacara Resort and Spa. Roarke had a vague recollection of a golf resort north of campus. But the agents were in no way expecting the luxury of the Bacara.

It was a five-star hotel on Highway 1, meaning right on the ocean. Gleaming Mercedes and BMWs and limos lined the long drive in front of the main building: California mission-style mixed with Mediterranean-style architecture in blinding white.

The agents left the rental car at valet parking and walked through the grand entrance into a lobby with thick columns, arched nooks, patterned marble floors with Persian rugs, several huge fireplaces, iron chandeliers. Well-heeled guests milled at a wine and cheese tasting going on in one of the alcoves.

Epps muttered beside Roarke, "Think this Sandler has something to prove?"

Roarke gave him a grim smile. It was startling, but not surprising. Santa Barbara was the whitest of all the UCs and the average parental income for incoming freshman was the highest in the state. Conspicuous consumption was par for the course. Affluenza, it was called.

Sandler was waiting for the agents in a conference room overlooking the ocean. Five-thousand-dollar suit and manicured nails, Republican haircut, Botoxed forehead. He stepped forward, stuck out a hand.

"Kirk Sandler. Appreciate you coming down."

So polite. But it was just a formality, a surface sheen over the man's arrogance.

At Sandler's cue, the agents took seats at the conference table. Roarke fought with himself not to be distracted by the stunning, shining ocean view, and focused on the man in front of them.

"Mr. Sandler, why don't you tell us why we're here?"

Sandler glanced from one agent to the other, annoyed. "I'd have thought your SAC had told you that."

"We'd like to hear it from you."

Sandler gestured impatiently. "There were a couple of young men attacked the night before last."

"And by 'attacked,' you mean . . . ?"

"Assaulted on campus. In the dead of night. At the same time as that—grotesque attack on Storke Tower."

The vandalism had been similar to what they'd seen at Berkeley: a male mannequin hung by the neck from the campus's central bell tower, the same spray-painted skull stencil, and the words **NO RAPISTS** spray-painted on the tower in red.

"Has this been reported to the police?" Roarke asked politely enough.

"Of course," Sandler said, offended. "But the National Council has been in discussion with the Bureau since these nationwide . . ." he paused to find the word, settled on "assaults."

Roarke had no doubt. There were plenty of fraternity alums in the Bureau. And he was sure plenty of calls had been made, plenty of strings were being pulled. The fraternity lobbyists would be out for blood.

Sandler continued. "The Bureau reached out to me immediately, given that our young Tau brothers were witnesses to this attack."

Roarke was confused. Surely there were other witnesses, nationwide. And then he had the sinking sensation that he and Epps were not the only agents dispatched to investigate in this case. Was this a nationwide Bureau action?

He leaned forward, cut to the chase. "Mr. Sandler, has either of these boys been accused of rape?"

Sandler reacted as if he'd been zapped by a cattle prod. "What kind of question is that?"

"The obvious one," Epps answered mildly. "Given the nature of the graffiti."

Sandler turned to Roarke, outraged. "You put up with that?"

Now it was Epps who stiffened. "Excuse me?"

Sandler didn't even give him a glance. "I'm not talking to you."

Epps' voice was quiet. "You are now."

Sandler looked to Roarke, obviously expecting backup. Roarke lifted his hands. *You're on your own, asshole.*

Epps spoke evenly. "In every instance across the country, these demonstrations have a specific focus: rapists. If these two young men were attacked, it's the logical question."

Sandler gave both agents a hard look, drew himself up in his chair. "I'm retained as a risk-management consultant and counsel for the Interfraternity Council, here. Do you want to know what, in my experience, is the biggest risk to our young brothers?"

The agents waited.

"Drunk female students," Sandler said, with a hint of triumph. "All it takes is one insane story by some hysterical coed to bring a whole fraternity system down."

"So there *has* been a rape charge," Roarke suggested, straight faced.

Sandler was startled, then angry. "No. Not at all. Why would you—not at all."

Roarke feigned confusion. "Maybe I wasn't following. I thought that's what you were trying to say." He could feel Epps beside him, struggling not to burst out laughing.

Sandler turned an alarming shade of red, clearly on the verge of another explosion. "These boys were attacked completely without provocation. Your superiors are taking it seriously—"

"*We* are taking it seriously," Roarke said sharply. "Which is why we're asking for any information you have that will help us do our job here."

Sandler's face went cold. "There've been no rape accusations. Not against these boys. Not against anyone in the house."

By this point Roarke was sure they'd get no useful information from him. And he wasn't in any mood to debate the definition of rape or consent with this man, given what they'd already heard. He stood, and Epps rose with him. "I'm glad to hear it. We'd like to talk to the boys, now."

Sandler stood as well, passed over a file folder. "Here's the chapter house address, chapter officer contact information, and the names of the two young men. I've arranged rooms for you here at the hotel—you can check in at the front desk."

The agents exchanged a glance. "Does SAC Reynolds know about this 'arrangement'?" Roarke asked.

Sandler's glance was pure condescension. "Of course. I'll be hearing back from you today, then."

It took everything Roarke had to answer neutrally. "Thanks for your information." The agents walked out without giving him more.

The Bacara's grounds were so big the agents had to be driven to their villa in a golf cart. Epps sat, tight lipped, as the cart motored past round white mission-style buildings with red-tiled roofs, double swimming pools with a Jacuzzi in the middle, stone walkways under palm trees between villas, mosaicked fountains, mysterious stairwells. There were endless ocean views, a sandy jogging trail along the cliff, a pier just down the beach.

Their driver pulled the cart up to one of the villas. Roarke tipped him, and both agents declined to have their overnight bags carried in before they went to their separate doors.

Roarke unlocked his door . . . and stepped into a deluxe king room with an arched doorway leading out to a private patio. On a table was a gift basket with a bottle of wine, nuts, fruit, chocolates.

He slid open the glass doors and went onto the patio. Through the banana palms discreetly surrounding the secluded space, he caught glimpses of a huge alfresco dining area overlooking the ocean, a yoga class taking place on a wide lawn.

Epps came out through the sliding door of the next room and looked over the hedge at Roarke. "I just looked online. Rooms start at $750 a night."

The price was a jolt.

"But there's free Wi-Fi," Epps pointed out, straight faced.

"Thank God for small favors. The tips alone are going to kill us."

"Get the feeling we're bein' bought?" Epps said dryly. "What do we think he's paying for?"

"I guess we'll find out. Let's go check out this innocent frat that's being so vilely targeted."

Chapter Eleven

Jade turned in a circle, looking around at the open, sprawling Santa Barbara campus: the big clock tower and the palm trees and the wide green lawns.

She'd left the ranch with just a backpack, some money, and an iPad.

Well, those—and a car.

Every day since she'd been allowed out, much of her time had been spent exploring the buildings of the valley: barns, garages, homes—many without complicated security systems, which made them a cakewalk to break into. And there were all these cars just sitting in garages at neighboring ranch houses, left as spares for weekend retreats.

The rich people would never miss one.

She followed the flow of students walking past the University Center, "The Hub," with its student store, study hall, eating venues. The building overlooked a lagoon and she could see out to the ocean. Students ran on a track curving beside the water. Rowers skimmed over the rippling surface.

A million years ago in tenth grade, before she'd followed Danny the scuzzball out of school to the San Francisco streets, her math teacher had said she was a shoo-in for college if she kept her grades up. Apparently math was the Golden Ticket these days, and she'd always been good at math.

She was aware of waves of emotion inside her, rumbling like the sound of the sea.

This is what Elliott kept pushing at her. The promise of college, of doors opening, of walking through those doors and into a future where she was not an abused victim, but a privileged member of a power class.

Elle said *she* could have all that, too.

Jade felt a seductive pull . . .

But she shut that down real fast.

Elle's breakdown, that crying jag—whatever you wanted to call it—had hardened her. If things were this fucking fucked up, then someone had to step up. Elle didn't know what to do? Well, Jade knew what to do. And this time she wasn't alone.

Santa Muerte had struck all over the country, all at once. Close to three hundred colleges in one night. *That* was freaking awesome. Somebody out there meant business.

Well, that somebody had her attention.

As Jade walked by a group of guys, one of them elbowed another and they turned to look her over. She gave the leader such a malevolent look that the leer died on his face.

That's right, asshole. Your days are numbered.

She walked faster to put distance between herself and them, kept moving down the main road past the bikers and the skateboarders until she found Storke Plaza, a big cement space under the sixteen-story clock tower, landscaped with palm trees and olive trees, a fountain and reflecting pool with lily pads and actual ducks.

This tower was where the rapist mannequin had been hung.

Jade stood beneath the tower and squinted up, picturing it.

They'd already painted over the words on the concrete, and the skull face, but you could see where she'd been, that pale splotch of not-quite-matching paint.

Dudes must've lost their shit. Must still be losing their shit.

Good. They should be scared. But it's not enough. The real key is follow-up.

When Jade put her head down, she was sun dazzled, so the figure in front of her was just a shadow, with hand outstretched.

For a second, her pulse spiked. Because what she saw was the skeleton. Hooded, robed, implacable. *La Santisima. Lady Death.*

But then her eyes focused and saw a girl in a hoodie. In her outstretched hand was a pink flyer. The girl kept the flyer extended, patiently. Jade took it, looked down at it.

HAD ENOUGH? COME TO OUR MEETING.
END RAPE CULTURE NOW.
IX

Jade and the girl looked at each other for a moment, and then the girl moved on.

And it was as easy as that.

A sign.

Chapter Twelve

Frat row was adjacent to campus in Isla Vista, a square mile of typical college town, casual, scruffy. The KAT house was instantly recognizable, with huge Greek letters mounted on the front of the house. It was one of a cluster of sprawling two-story stucco buildings with red-tiled roofs, built in a foursquare, taking up an entire block. Their parking lots had been turned into courtyards, enclosed by cheap wooden plank fences for privacy and with a few palm trees for landscaping. And just as Roarke remembered from the bad old days, a blizzard of red plastic drinking cups littered the lawns, the tables, the sidewalk. Party central.

As the agents walked up to the house, Roarke glanced in through one open gate and saw volleyball nets, tall wooden rectangular structures arranged like bar tables, Coke and candy machines, Dumpster-sized recycling bins overflowing with bottles and cans.

Packs of frat brothers lounged out in the courtyards, sprawled on the filthy sofas, partying at barely four in the afternoon. The official uniform seemed to be cargo shorts or bathing trunks slung low on hips, and no shirt, the better to show off six-pack abs. There was an indolent and vaguely predatory sensuality about the groupings.

"Future captains of industry," Epps muttered.

"God help us," Roarke agreed.

They were met at the door by a tall, buff, square-jawed young man, fully dressed, with a practiced smile—and gray eyes as cold as steel.

"Agent Roarke?" The young man stuck his hand out toward Roarke without having to be told which agent was which, then turned to Epps with suspiciously exaggerated courtesy.

"And Agent Epps. I'm Topher Stephens, chapter president. Our IFC liaison said you were coming by."

As he ushered them into the front hall, there was thumping on the staircase beside them. A group of guys trampled down, looking the agents over as they passed, en route to the front door.

Stephens nodded to the group before he turned back to the agents. "Kirk called ahead," he said. "He said you'd want to talk to Cutler and Vogel. I've got them in here." Stephens led the agents through double doors into a smaller, more private, library-ish room. "Where you can talk in peace."

Roarke glanced around at glassed-in bookcases, an impressive bar. Two young men were seated in the room, both white and tanned, blandly good looking. One was taller, one was heavier, but they were otherwise indistinguishable from each other.

"Rick Cutler, Neal Vogel," Stephens said, gesturing to the taller one first, then the heavier.

"Thanks. We'll take it from here," Roarke said to Stephens, and looked at the double doors.

Stephens frowned, but he left the room, closing the doors behind him.

The agents turned to the boys, and Roarke got straight to the point. "Why don't you take us through what happened the night before last?"

The one called Vogel answered first. "We were studying at the house and needed some munchies to keep going?" The question mark at the end was typical Southern California—not a question, just a verbal tic.

Epps gave Roarke a neutral look that said exactly what Roarke was thinking. "Studying at the house" was code for "partying." Going for "munchies" was code for "beer run." They were maybe even meeting a dealer.

Cutler took over the narrative. "We were just going a few blocks to the 7-Eleven, decided to walk along the bluffs."

Roarke tracked this in his mind. The campus was a five- or ten-minute walk from the frat house. Cordoba Road ran right into the campus at Ocean Road, which ended at the bluffs. Everything was close in Isla Vista.

"This was about what time?"

"After midnight. Prolly close to one."

"Kind of late for a stroll, isn't that?" Epps suggested. "Any particular reason you headed for the bluffs?"

The bulkier one, Vogel, was instantly belligerent. "Why shouldn't we be out on the bluffs?"

"Not saying you shouldn't be," Roarke said.

Cutler shot the big one a look. "We were just walking."

"Not really much in that area, though, is there?"

Cutler stared at him. "The ocean. The lagoon."

"Out for the scenery, then," Roarke suggested. "In the dark."

The boys were silent.

Epps spread a campus map out on the table. "Show us."

Cutler traced a path with his finger—Cordoba Road to Ocean Road, then onto a trail that wound past two dorm complexes.

"So you were on the bluffs and . . ."

"We didn't see her coming," Cutler said. "All of a sudden she was just there. This—hooded thing. Cape and hood. And the face was a skull. I mean, yeah, right, it was a mask. But for a second . . ." He shuddered.

"So this figure was wearing a mask and cape."

"A cape, or a poncho, maybe. Something flowy."

Roarke nodded. "If this person's face was covered, and their body was covered, how do you know it was a female?"

Vogel frowned. "Well—a dude wouldn't do that to a dummy, right?"

"The dummy hung from the tower?" Roarke asked. "Which you didn't know about until the morning after, right?"

Vogel looked confused. "But . . . we know now."

Cutler gave Vogel another warning glance. "We figure it was a girl by the way she moved. Definitely not a guy."

Roarke raised his eyebrows. "The way she moved? Slinky? Girly?"

"No, she was fast. Really fast. But it wasn't the way a guy would move."

Roarke looked over the map Epps had spread on the coffee table.

The dummy had been hung from Storke Tower, which was just a minute or two away from the lagoon. Roarke figured there had been more than one—*Tagger? Vandal? Bitch?* He was at a loss for words to describe the perpetrators here.

But the Lagoon Trail looped around to the bluffs. So conceivably the hooded figure had been one of a few who had hung the dummy, then made a beeline toward the Lagoon Trail and ran straight into the boys.

"Did this person confront you?" he asked. "Attack you? Did she touch you?"

The boys shifted, without speaking.

"Did she try to injure you? Did she threaten you at all?" The brothers were silent.

Roarke walked in a circle, exasperated. "Look, guys. You reported that she attacked you—"

Vogel blurted out, "We didn't say 'attacked.'"

Roarke frowned. "That's what Kirk Sandler told us."

"Well, we didn't say 'attacked.'"

Roarke backtracked in his own mind. So it was Sandler who had exaggerated the incident.

But why?

"All right, so you didn't report an attack. But you did report an incident."

Cutler spoke up. "Hey, we didn't know what we were dealing with. If this chick was armed, or what . . ."

"Did you think she was after you in particular?"

The boys exchanged a glance. Again it was Cutler who answered. "Well . . . she came right at us. No joke, she was barreling down."

"How tall was she?"

Cutler stood and indicated a spot at about his collarbone. *Five-six, five-seven.*

Epps nodded. "Not too big, then. And there were two of you. Big guys."

They squirmed a bit, embarrassed.

Epps continued. "But you were stoned, weren't you? That's what freaked you out."

"It wasn't just that," Vogel said. Cutler shot him a look, and he amended, "It wasn't that. She was, like, hyped up. It wasn't normal."

Adrenaline, of course, Roarke thought. *If she'd just hung the dummy off the tower, she'd be flying with it.*

He shook his head. "Seriously, guys. You've walked those paths before, hundreds of times. I assume you've been high before. You've seen people in costume. So what I don't get is—why was this so freak-ish to you? Why did you feel a need to report it?"

"We didn't. Not at first," Cutler protested.

"It was when we saw what they did to that dummy. You saw that, right?" Vogel asked pointedly.

Roarke looked at him. "But the painting on the tower was very specific."

The boys looked blank.

"What it said was, 'You're next, rapist.' Any reason that should scare you?"

Cutler looked away. Vogel muttered, "Some crazy bitches are out there. How do I know what they're thinking?"

"But do you have a particular reason for thinking these protesters will come after you?"

Cutler understood the question. He looked up, glared at him. "No."

"Then is there anyone in the house who might be a more likely target than anyone else?"

The boys were silent.

"Because the targets here are really specific. You get that, right? If there's anyone here under suspicion of rape, for any reason, whether that's right or not, that guy is vulnerable."

Still no answer. Just a lot of seething.

Roarke and Epps looked at each other. Both stood at the same time, and Roarke spoke. "Guys, here's the thing. You're playing victim here—you seem to want us to protect you, but you're not telling us why. We can't help you if you're not going to be straight with us. You think a little harder about those questions, and when you're ready to answer, you let us know."

Chapter Thirteen

The IX meeting was on the fourth floor of a building on Storke Plaza, in a classroom with generic tables and chairs . . . and a wall of windows that overlooked the ocean.

The view actually stopped Jade in her tracks for a moment as she came through the door. Crazy that you could go to class and have the whole ocean right out there in front of you.

There were fifteen other girls scattered in the room, different sizes, different ages.

One girl stood at the front, beside a whiteboard with a huge scrawled *IX*. She was blond, white. She looked Jade over as she came in, and Jade stiffened, but the other girl's gaze was direct, friendly. "Hey, I'm Liz. This your first meeting?"

That was easy. "Yeah. I saw the flyer. I'm Tory," Jade lied without a second thought.

"Welcome, Tory."

Jade saw an empty seat and took it. No one even asked her if she was enrolled at the school. But really, people almost never asked that kind of thing. If you were there, they assumed you had a right to be there. She looked enough like the rest of them—but the truth was she was just sixteen. The street will do that to you. She knew she could pass for thirty, if she felt like it. So much of life was about playing into what people thought they were seeing.

By the time the meeting started, the room was packed, standing room only, students drawn by the vandalism at the tower.

The girl named Liz said, "I know we have a lot of new people here, so we want to talk about what Nine is all about. We call ourselves 'Nine' after Title IX: a federal law that prohibits discrimination on the basis of sex in an educational institution's programs and activities. Title IX requires institutions to take necessary steps to prevent sexual assault on their campuses and to respond promptly and effectively when such conduct is reported . . ."

Jade found herself fidgeting.

She knew the kind of cases Liz was talking about. Roofies in a drink, separate the girl from the pack—up to your room or down to the basement—invite your dudebros in for a turn. *Boys will be boys.*

Well, fuck that. Time to shake this shit up.

"So who did the hanging?" she asked abruptly.

Everyone turned to look at her. There were glances, some low key, some not.

"And seriously, how'd you get the dummy up there? 'Cause that was off the hook."

"That wasn't Nine," Liz said.

Jade widened her eyes. "FR? It must've been one of y'all." She looked around the room. "You musta had a plan about the campus cops and security cameras, right?"

There were exchanged glances all around her.

"I have no idea who did that," Liz said firmly.

Jade smiled. "Riiight. I get you. I just wanted to say, that was savage." She lowered her voice. "Is there another meeting for that?"

Liz looked uncomfortable. "We're working through the Title IX program. We collect data for lawsuits—"

Jade interrupted her, feigning innocence. "But Title IX is under the jurisdiction of the Department of Education, right?" She'd heard all about it at the ranch. "And who's running the Department of Education now? That Holy Roller flake? How are those Title IX cases going under her?"

Liz was completely flustered now. "That's why we have to keep the pressure on—"

Jade had had enough. "But what do you *want*?"

"In general?" Liz asked.

"In everything. What do you want?" Jade turned to others in the room, challenging.

After a beat, she heard murmurs from the girls: "No more rape culture." "End rape culture." "End rape."

"That's what I'm talking about." Jade looked deliberately around at all of them, a hard stare. "And you think that's gonna happen? With *laws*? Really? When sixty-seven percent of judges are men? When eighty-eight percent of cops are men? Eighty-one percent of Congress? Seventy-nine percent of senators? WTF, y'all?"

She'd been listening in those Bitch meetings, all right. She'd heard the numbers. She'd heard more than what she needed to hear to understand that shit wasn't changing without some serious revolution.

"You have actually *seen* what's running the country right now, haven't you? Well, good luck changing that in our lifetime."

She could feel the tension in the room, the girls shifting, the anxiety and fear. There were some whispers, but she ignored them. So what if it was harsh? It was *true*. "So what are we going to do about it?"

Someone raised a hand, asked tentatively, "What are *you* saying we should do?"

"I'm saying that you need to step this shit up." Her voice was hard and merciless. "You want to end rape, you need to start thinking about ending rapists."

Liz looked aghast. "That's not us. That's not what we do."

"Well, someone out there sounds ready." Jade stood, walked to the whiteboard, picked up the pen, and printed an anonymous email address on the board in bold strokes. "That's who *I* am. And that's the someone I want to talk to."

She turned around and walked out.

Coming out of the building, Jade was hyper. Her face was flushed, her skin felt too tight. She walked with a jerky stride back toward the plaza.

Inside she was roiling. She didn't know what to feel. Some of these girls—the single worst experience of their life was something she'd gone through on a nightly basis, sometimes four or five times a night. Sack of shit losers using her body as if she were some kind of trash dump.

You think one *night can ruin your life? Try living it for a year. Or two. Or four. That was how long ago it was that Darrell and his dumbfuck friends . . .*

Suddenly she couldn't breathe.

She is back in the farmhouse . . . men crowded around . . . hands holding her down on the bed . . .

She gasped aloud.

She was standing still on the path. A couple of girls looked at her warily as they approached.

She stared back at them until they moved on in a hurry.

Well, she wasn't about to say anything about all that to anyone. And have them look at her the way they would? Fuck that. She wasn't talking.

But someone—someone out there is ready to do some business. Maybe not anyone in that meeting. But someone.

She felt something, like eyes on her back, the feeling she used to get when she was being cruised on the street. Sometimes you could just tell somebody was watching.

She turned, glancing around her.

She saw a pale flash of face in the shadow of a building and froze. *The skeleton.*

Then that someone stepped into the late afternoon sunlight.

Another girl.

She moved toward Jade. Short black hair and a bowler hat. A black leotard under overalls. Older than Jade by a few years, but she looked older than that. Her face was strained and pale.

She jerked her head toward the building where the IX meeting had been.

"You said you wanted to know."

Chapter Fourteen

When the agents left the frat house, Topher Stephens was at the door to see them out. Roarke would have bet money he'd been within earshot during the whole interview.

The agents said their goodbyes and walked out to the street. Once they were a safe distance away, headed for the car, they looked at each other under the darkening sky.

Epps spoke first. "Bullshit, bullshit, and more bullshit. 'Attacked,' my ass."

"That was the one thing we did get out of them. It was Sandler who was calling it an attack."

Epps was silent, thinking on it.

"So why this intense reaction from Sandler?" Roarke asked, thinking aloud. "It's not just that those guys are spooked. *Sandler* is spooked."

"So he hauls out the FBI connections, calls in whatever chits he has with Reynolds or whoever to investigate this crap . . ."

Roarke shook his head. "That's not quite how he told it, though. Sounded like that frat council made a complaint, and someone inside the Bureau homed in on these guys here as potential witnesses."

The men had reached the car, but Roarke stopped beside it without getting in. He was sure Topher Stephens was watching them and Roarke figured it couldn't hurt to make these boys nervous. They weren't exactly rocket scientists—and he wanted them jumpy enough to slip up.

He stared off toward the ocean, a visible gleam four blocks away at the end of the street. Finally he said, "Someone's going to have to decide to talk to us. Until they do—" He ran his hand through his hair. "Go back to the hotel and call room service. Charge it to the room."

After all, Sandler was paying for it.

Epps stared at him, then laughed, catching on. "A steak would taste just fine . . ."

"Lobster. A nice bottle of wine . . ."

"All this hard work we're doing."

"Got to keep our strength up."

"Got that right."

"Fortify yourself," Roarke ordered. "Call your woman. I'll see you in the morning."

Epps looked at him questioningly. Roarke nodded toward the ocean, the sunset. "I'm going to take a walk. Clear my head. I'll Lyft back."

Chapter Fifteen

Bowler hat girl's name was Kris.

She was interesting. There was almost a trans vibe about her—or a femme who was experimenting with butch. But not really. "Genderfluid" was the word.

Which was cool. Gender was just another trap. But Jade got the feeling that whatever transition was going on was recent.

By silent agreement, the girls didn't speak as they walked down from the tower and along the lagoon path. The water was alive with waterfowl: ducks, pelicans, even a flock of white herons standing knee deep in the murky shallows, dipping for fish. The breeze smelled of the ocean. It was so peaceful, a whole sanctuary right here in the middle of campus.

The trail ended at a small beach cove, and other paths went up the bluffs on either side.

Instead of going up one of the paths, Kris continued straight toward the beach. Sandpipers scattered as the girls crossed the sand.

They sat on a soft dune between piles of boulders. Kris pulled out a joint and they smoked. The sun was going down and the weed turned the sky blazing and bloody. The waves rumbled and crashed, a rhythmic, lulling sound.

Jade watched the other girl without watching her. She was an expert at that. Tricking meant you watched everyone, all the time, doped up, sleeping, fucking—always.

When they were both good and relaxed, Jade spoke. "So you did the dummy."

"There were a bunch of us," Kris said vaguely. "You know, people've been following that group Bitch." She glanced at Jade.

Jade frowned, nodded, kept it vague herself. "Kinda like Anonymous, right? Are you in that—Bitch thing?" Kris wasn't anyone Jade had ever seen at the ranch, and she was dying to know how it had all come together.

Kris half shrugged. "I don't know what 'in' is. There are all these groups. On Tumblr, on Reddit, on the Gram. You get invited to a portal group and you can post there. I figure people in the inner circles are watching what you post, or maybe checking you out other ways. After you do enough of the right kind of posts they invite you into another group and then another, and it gets more and more hardcore."

Jade nodded. It made sense. She kept playing innocent. "So Bitch made this happen, all those colleges? There were dozens, right?"

Kris's eyes gleamed in the fading light. "Hundreds."

"How'd they do it?"

"They put out a call to action. You only would've seen it if you were already registered to some of these groups—had posted a bunch of times—I don't know, maybe even have donated? They were vetting people, for sure. And then you had to go through a bunch of levels and use passwords to get through to the instructions . . . and then they sent the actual details through Snapchat."

So whatever they sent would disappear. "And they used onion routers so no one could track them," Jade murmured.

"Yeah."

Onion routers wrapped messages with layers of encryption. Then successive computers unwrapped only one layer at a time, so the origin of the message couldn't be traced.

Miranda had taught her. She'd made Jade brush up on HTML and JavaScript, and taught her the programming languages SQL, Python, Perl, and C. She went on to all kinds of shit—a ton of practical techniques to get into a website. How to make cookie catchers to gain access to website users' accounts for websites with vulnerable logins. How to scramble her IP address to cover her tracks.

Miranda had shown her enough for her to know that Bitch had been working on establishing a network for a long time. Now Jade was starting to see why.

She spoke aloud, probing. "So that whole thing that night—"

"They posted across to the groups," Kris said. Now she seemed eager to talk about it. "They had this skull stencil that you could download. So it gave me the idea, and I just thought . . ." She stared out at the red ocean, and her voice hardened. "Yeah. *That.*"

Jade glanced back toward campus. "And what about them? In the meeting? Were they in on it?"

"Nine? They're cool. Liz is straight-up focused on changing the laws. Some of the others . . ." She shrugged. "I guess there are different levels of commitment."

Jade leaned forward. "So what's your level?"

Kris pulled her phone out of a pocket, tapped it, passed it over silently.

Jade looked down at a photo of a blond girl with fresh-faced model looks, more pretty than hot. They had passed by dozens of her in that short walk across campus.

"My sister," Kris said shakily.

Jade gave her a quick look. They didn't look even related. In fact, they couldn't have been more different.

Kris exhaled smoke. "I know, right? Miss All-American. Cheerleading in high school. Rushed here at SB. Caitlin was into all that shit. She never did know when she was just some stupid fuck toy."

Jade swiped through several more photos of Caitlin, then handed the phone back to Kris.

"She wanted so bad to belong. It was like a fuckin' target on her chest."

Jade nodded, and waited while Kris smoked for a while, got hold of herself.

"She went to this frat party on Halloween. She woke up in the morning on the lawn in a park down the street. And there were *Ks* stamped on her back, in different colors. And she was, like, torn up."

She stopped. But she didn't have to draw a map. Jade picked up a rock from the sand, flipped it into the surf. "Not her fault. World's full of assholes. Sooner or later you run into one of them."

"Four," Kris said, and her voice was colder. "There were four."

"She didn't go to the cops?"

"Not till it was way too late." She added, almost as an afterthought, "She didn't even tell me for weeks."

"How is she now?"

Kris looked away, and Jade knew exactly what she was going to say. "She's dead. Killed herself."

She didn't cry. She didn't shake. Her face was as blank as her voice.

Jade leaned over and took the pack of cigarettes from Kris's bib pocket, lit one, and passed it to her. Then did one for herself.

They sat and smoked together, watching the sun bleed out into the ocean.

And then Jade asked softly, "So why are these asswipes still breathing?"

Chapter Sixteen

Shadows from the setting sun poured across the trails as Roarke walked the bluffs.

He'd decided to check out the trail the Tau boys had been talking about.

When he turned off the street at the trailhead, he was instantly in wilderness. Sandy paths crisscrossed the cliff, weaving through a labyrinth of thick coastal sage scrub, waist high and higher, so that every curve of the path hid the next part from sight.

All street sound had disappeared; there was only the constant rumble of the ocean below and the twittering of birds in the saltbush. Wooden benches lined the trail at various lookout points over breathtaking views of the Pacific and the Channel Islands.

Two bikers pedaled by, dressed neck to ankle in black wetsuits, clutching their surfboards under their arms. They disappeared around a curve and Roarke was alone again.

He turned toward the campus. He could see the top of Storke Tower, and the two huge dormitory complexes that overlooked the lagoon and bluffs. Theoretically the masked attacker, or vandal, or whatever she was, could have been seen by hundreds of people from their windows or balconies. But there had been fog that night, the thick coastal stuff.

And there were no lights whatsoever along the trail. At night it would be dauntingly dark.

Spooky, he had to admit.

He stopped at a lookout and gazed over the waves of red emanating from the setting sun. He caught a whiff of the pungent green smell of pot drifting from the beach below.

And he felt some kind of peace for the first time all day. He craved this: The blank stretch of sand and the infinite perspective of the ocean. The roar of waves that muted human voices.

Would he ever hear the ocean again without thinking of Cara?

He had been so good about not thinking about her. Now, alone, he cautiously let his guard slip, let his thoughts go to her.

Where are you?

He was less and less sure that she would stay hidden. With everything, everything, going on in the country right now, she wouldn't be still. She couldn't be. She would surface. And it would be soon.

His gaze moved up to the sky. It was too early to see the moon, but he could feel it.

Hunger Moon.

It was superstition. It was supernatural. But in the eternity, the five months since Cara had come into his life, he'd learned one thing above all: the closer to a full moon, the bigger the danger.

Whatever it was, it would be soon.

Chapter Seventeen

Kris stared at Jade, seeming stunned by the question. "I don't . . . I don't know what you mean."

"Yeah you do," Jade answered.

Kris bit her lip, stared out at the ocean.

So she wasn't quite ready yet. But she was here. That said it all. Jade could wait.

After a while Kris spoke. "I went to an IX meeting after . . ." She swallowed. "After the funeral. I thought about filing a complaint. But what could they really do?"

"Nothing," Jade said flatly. "So then you see this call to action from Bitch . . ."

"Yeah. No. Really, it was before. It was that Cara Lindstrom thing."

Jade felt the name like a blow. *No. Not a blow. A razor cut.*

Kris was looking at her. "You know who I mean? Those murders in San Francisco?"

Jade nodded. Oh yeah. She knew. What *didn't* she know? Her heart was racing. She threaded her fingers through the cool sand and said nothing.

Kris stared off over the red-streaked water. "I read about what she was doing and I knew—I knew it could be different."

Jade felt a buzz that she couldn't define. This was all meant to be.

She took the joint from Kris, took a long toke, held, exhaled. "I was there."

The tunnel in Golden Gate Park is short, dark, and cold. It reeks of body fluids and that crack smell, like burning plastic, and any number of other things.

Danny has texted her to meet him there, one of his favorite rendezvous points. And when Danny texts, well—be there or else.

She can't see him in the dark, but she can feel him, and hear his breathing.

Then there is the flare of a lighter, held to a cloudy glass pipe, and she sees him ahead, illuminated in the arch of the tunnel.

And then her heart stops.

There is someone else there, too. A blond woman, slender and still, dressed in dark clothes. The one Jade now knows as Cara Lindstrom.

She can tell Danny hasn't seen the woman. Then he spots her and flinches, obviously startled. He hadn't known she was there.

For a moment he's amused. His smile is slow, dangerous.

"Want something, bitch?"

In one fast move, the blond woman strides forward and takes him by the hair, jerking his head back, exposing his throat.

Jade gasps.

There is a flash of gleaming metal and Danny's blood arcs in the tunnel.

The woman holds him hard, one fist twined in his hair, his body against hers as he struggles. He makes astonished, inarticulate noises as blood gushes hot and hard over the blond woman's hands. Watching, mesmerized, Jade can almost feel the wet heat on her own hands.

It takes mere seconds for him to bleed out.

Lindstrom releases her grip, lets Danny's body slip heavily to the floor of the tunnel. She stands in the darkness above the body, feet planted.

Jade's heart is pounding in her chest, echoing in her ears.

Lindstrom turns slowly in the dim blue light of the moon outside the tunnel, and looks right at her.

Jade can't move, can't breathe. All she can see is the blood . . . Danny's blood all over Lindstrom's face, her arms, her hands—

Jade jolted back to the present, looked out over the beach.

The skeleton was there, standing at the shoreline, silhouetted by the last rays of sun.

Jade turned to Kris. Her voice was merciless. "They raped your sister and she's dead. Don't tell me you haven't thought about it."

Now Kris was trembling. She answered cautiously, "I only know one for sure . . ."

"And?"

Kris's face hardened. "I want to know all the names."

Jade felt fierce triumph. *Game on.* "Okay, then. That's step one."

Now Kris's words came tumbling out. "It never fucking ends. They know they can do it to anyone they want because they'll never even get time."

Jade leaned forward, put her hand on Kris's ankle. "So what do *you* want?"

Kris's voice was so strained it was barely human. "I want to kill them. I want to kill them all."

They sat in silence, and for a minute there was only the sound of the ocean. Then Jade spoke. "So let's get these motherfuckers."

Kris looked at her, dazed. "But . . . why would you?"

"'Cause somebody has to."

Chapter Eighteen

Staring out at the last rays of light on the ocean, Roarke felt a jolt of unease.

The sound of the surf surrounded him. The smell of pot was gone. The sun had sunk below the waves.

It was getting dark. He should be getting back. For what, he was not so entirely sure.

But something.

He turned away from the sea and sky and headed down the winding path in the opposite direction, back toward the hotel.

Chapter Nineteen

Cara wakes in the frozen dark, to the touch of bitter wind on her skin and the frantic thump of her heart pounding in her chest.

She sits up, throwing off the thick blanket. The fire is out in the woodstove. The door stands open wide.

And the skeleton girl stands in the doorway, looking in on her with sightless eyes.

She nods to Cara and turns.

Cara rises from the bed and follows.

Out into the midnight black of the canyon. Into the moonlight spilling over the snow in a bright blue-white trail.

Ahead of her Ivy climbs sure-footedly up the cliff, following the Anasazi path up the towering sandstone wall.

Cara follows.

The wind pushes against her, keeping her upright. But walking is no effort, and Cara has no fear.

In no time they are passing the spectral hands imprinted in the sandstone, long, delicate fingers raised in greeting, in solidarity.

And at the top of the canyon, Ivy stops and points.

To a hunter's tent, a dark quadrangle against the rocks, its sides rippling in the bitter wind.

And Cara is paralyzed with fear.

Whatever Ivy has brought her for, whatever she wants to tell her, is in this tent.

And she would give her life not to know.

In the morning, in the time known as reality, she makes the long hike up to the rim. It is not so easy when she is awake, without her spectral guide. The path is icy. One slip and she will tumble hundreds of feet to a bone-shattering death. But her body remembers the nighttime journey, and her feet find the footholds in the rock.

The tent is exactly where it was last night, on the South Rim trail. It is thick, structured canvas, an Arctic tent. Camouflage pattern, of course.

She sits in the shelter of a rock outcropping and watches it, listening, for nearly an hour before she ventures toward it.

There is no sound except the rippling of the walls. No sense of human presence.

She carefully unzips the front flap . . . steps through it into the canvas room.

And looks into her own face.

The police mug shot of her is up on the tent wall, attached to some grotesque mockery of a female body—spread-eagled, vagina wetly gleaming.

She swallows back bile and contempt.

These men have not come here hunting girls.

They are hunting her.

DAY THREE

Chapter Twenty

The canvas walls of the tent shake in the wind.

Or perhaps she is the one who is trembling.

The dim cloth walls seem to close in on her. It is all she can do not to tear down the images, rend the tent.

There are more photos taped up on the canvas, all with the same theme: her photo and the police sketch printed out, attached to the bodies of *Hustler* models. Porn shots. Doggy position, with cheeks spread, anus exposed.

She forces herself to breathe, forces her body to move, to stoop and rifle through sleeping bags and backpacks. Most of it is camping gear, junk food—and of course the porn magazines the images have been torn from.

But there are also some papers in one backpack, and she just lifts the whole thing, slings it over her arm. She turns and peels back the top of the entrance flap of the tent to scan outside—the snowy rim, the sandstone rock formations on either side of it.

There is no movement that she can see.

She slips out of the tent and runs, swift footed and silent, back to her niche in the nearby boulder fall.

She finds a position out of the wind that conceals her, but gives her a view of the tent.

She settles in, her back against a massive rock, and keeps both ears trained for any sound as she opens the backpack, removes the papers, and starts to read.

Chapter Twenty-One

Roarke startled awake to the sound of his phone, vibrating and jumping on the table beside the king bed.

He reached for it, checked the screen, saw Singh's name.

"Singh. I meant to call you last night—"

"No need. I spoke with Agent Epps at length. He is on his way over."

Always that formality. Roarke had never even heard her refer to Epps by his first name.

Right on cue there was a knock at the door, Epps' familiar rhythmic rap. Distinctive enough to recognize, without being obvious code.

Roarke pulled on clothes and opened the door to let him in. He indicated the phone on the desk. "Singh's on."

He put the phone on speaker and her velvet voice filled the room. "I have been pondering the question of why our higher-ups are so keen to have you working in Santa Barbara, and I believe I have a lead for you to follow. You will remember Andrea Janovy."

The name was an odd frisson from the immediate past. When Cara had been imprisoned in the women's lockup in San Francisco, a mystery visitor had used a stolen driver's license as ID to get into the jail to visit her. The license belonged to an Andrea Janovy, a woman who had not been able to drive for two years—not since an accident that had taken the use of her legs.

In a phone interview Janovy had claimed no knowledge of the ID being used, much less who used it. But still, Roarke had wondered.

Singh continued. "You will also recall that we strongly suspected that the blogger who uses the name Bitch was the individual who used Janovy's ID to gain access to Lindstrom."

Roarke felt a prickling of significance. He knew that Singh was onto something, but it took him a moment to realize the connection.

"Janovy lives in Santa Barbara," he said.

"Just so. And it has occurred to me that Janovy could be the link to Bitch that you are being prodded to investigate. So I have been doing some research into Ms. Janovy. She is a Santa Barbara native who earned a BA at UCSB, then obtained her law degree at UC Berkeley. She is now a junior partner at the Goleta law firm Buchanan Thompson Kerr, specializing in insurance law. And Ms. Janovy's particular focus is bringing suit against fraternities."

"I'll be damned," Epps said softly.

Roarke knew the same thought had occurred to both of them.

If the secret purpose of this mission to Santa Barbara was to investigate Bitch, then maybe the key to the upper levels of Bitch had been right under their noses all along.

Janovy had agreed to an early appointment before work. The route to her house took them up into the hills, past Mission Santa Barbara, with its distinctive twin bell towers, red-tiled domes and crosses on the top. Roarke caught a glimpse of the skulls set into the garden wall, and images of Mother Doctor and Ivy skittered through his head. The Mission *asistencia* of Las Piedras, another stop on Roarke's weird foray into the past, seemed a hundred years ago now.

When he looked away, Epps was watching him. "What happened out there?" Epps asked, softly.

The team knew something of what had transpired in the desert. The barest minimum.

Roarke shook his head. It was a story that needed time, not just to tell, but to be able to tell. Epps nodded, and drove.

Janovy's house was a complete contrast to the Mission: upscale modern. "Thanks for seeing us," Roarke said as the agents followed Janovy up a ramp to a sleek, wide-open living space.

She had gone to considerable expense to make the house wheelchair accessible. There were ramps everywhere and an elevator up to the second floor. Of course the open floor plan was to give her as much room as possible to negotiate in the chair.

"I don't mind," she said over her shoulder. "But I did go through all of this with your Agent Singh back in December." Janovy wore fingerless athletic gloves and navigated her hand-powered wheelchair expertly, taut shoulder muscles straining under her NASTY WOMAN tank top. Her auburn hair was cropped close to her head, just a fuzz.

She spun the chair around to face a sofa, gestured with a hand for them to sit. "As I told her, I don't know who used my ID to get into a Bay Area prison. I haven't used my driver's license since my accident."

Roarke and Epps exchanged a glance. Janovy caught it.

"Is there a problem with that?"

Roarke was thinking, *Why no car?* Judging by her house and the way she manipulated that wheelchair, she was the poster child for mobility, and there were plenty of hand-controlled vehicles on the market. She obviously had the money for one.

Roarke began, "None of my business, but—"

She waited.

"Haven't you considered a hand-controlled automobile?"

She stared at him, stone faced. "Easy to say when you've never had a seventeen-ton truck parked on your legs."

Roarke felt the sting of the smackdown, and rightly so. "Point taken. Sorry."

"PTSD," she said shortly. "I'm working on it. But that doesn't mean I'm safe to drive. Now what can I do for you?"

After that inauspicious start, Roarke decided to ease his way into his questions. "This use of your driver's license seems so—random. Had you even heard of Cara Lindstrom? Before Singh contacted you?"

She raised an eyebrow. "Some of us remember real news."

An evasion. Roarke pressed it. "Had people in your circle been talking about her? The arrest, the trial . . ."

"In my circle," she repeated without inflection. Roarke was pretty sure she knew he was alluding to Bitch. But all she said was, "There was talk at work. Anyone who grew up in California . . ."

She didn't have to finish the sentence; Roarke knew exactly what she was going to say. Anyone who grew up in California knew about the Reaper, the family massacres, and Cara, the "Miracle Girl" who was the only survivor of that slaughter.

She shrugged. "Well. Of course I remember the Reaper. All that." She suddenly smiled, a not very humorous smile. "Let's cut to the chase, shall we? Do you actually think I know where Lindstrom is?"

It was an interesting take on why they were there.

Epps smiled back. "Do you?"

Janovy lifted her hands. "She's gone underground, hasn't she? I know *I* would. Leave the state, probably leave the country. But you'd know best about that . . ."

Roarke had the slight sense of being probed. It could just be curiosity, but he was more inclined to believe there was a game going on.

"You're probably right," he said, then took a moment, pretending to think. "You've heard of the cyber group Bitch?"

He watched her face as she replied, "After yesterday, who hasn't?"

Roarke and Epps looked at each other.

"What?" she asked.

"Ms. Janovy, to our knowledge, Bitch hasn't taken credit for the campus action."

"But it's pretty obvious, isn't it?" she retorted. "It's not my personal theory. Most of the media seems to think so."

"So do you or have you ever worked with them?"

She frowned. "Worked with them? As an attorney?"

"As anything."

"I'm sure I've 'liked' some posts on Facebook and Twitter." She looked from one man to the other. "Are you thinking someone from Bitch stole my identity? That's not good, is it?"

"How do you mean?"

"They're a powerful cyber group that a lot of people are calling terrorists. I'm sitting in my house talking to two FBI agents who want to know if I have ties to that organization. In this brave new world, that doesn't really add up to fun times. So you tell me—do I need a lawyer?"

Both Roarke and Epps shifted uncomfortably, and Roarke knew what he was feeling was shame. *It's come to this, already—every inquiry we make is going to feel like a paramilitary threat.*

He was on the verge of apologizing and leaving her alone. But the woman was ticking all kinds of boxes: a wealthy lawyer, an intersectional feminist—she was definitely someone who could be part of Bitch, even conceivably running it. So he tried a different tack.

"I didn't mean to give that impression. I'm sorry the subject made you uncomfortable. Let's put Bitch aside. What we're really interested in is your expertise."

"Expertise in regard to?"

"Fraternities."

Her gaze narrowed.

Epps had obviously picked up on Roarke's strategy. Now he expanded on the question. "In many of the instances of vandalism of the night before, fraternities were specifically targeted for threats. We'd like any insight you can give us about why that would be."

"In general, you mean."

"In general, of course."

She shrugged. "You asked for it." She leaned forward in her chair. "If your goal is to dismantle the patriarchy, fraternities are a good place to start. That's where all our best misogynists get trained. And of course, they're bastions of white male privilege as well." She looked straight at Epps as she said it. "Fraternities represent an almost cult-like white-cis-hetero-patriarchy—a closed chute that exists to isolate the sons of the privileged among their wealthy peers and keep them moving straight into the highest echelons of society. Fraternities are where the one percent systematically consolidate their wealth and learn how to keep the rest of society enslaved.

"Sororities are a chute into the upper echelons of society, too. The difference is sorority girls aren't being groomed as power brokers. The Greek system propagates and normalizes female inferiority. Sexual assault is a routine part of Greek life. Bluntly, the Greek system is a hunting ground. We are breeding entitled racist misogynists in a petri dish of rape culture. These thugs go on to make laws and enforce laws that perpetuate rape culture and racism."

She looked Roarke in the eye, and then Epps. "It's not accidental, lads. This is a finely honed system of oppression. It's taken thousands of years to build it. And it's not going away without *all* of us using our skill sets to bring it down."

Roarke took that in. "So your goal is to dismantle the patriarchy."

She smiled grimly. "You bet your ass my goal is to dismantle the patriarchy. But obviously," she gestured to her legs, "I'm not going around scaling university clock towers to do that. I wanted to pick the biggest offender I could go after with my skill set. And that's fraternities. I'm a fraternal plaintiff's attorney."

"Which means—you sue the frats? The universities?"

She grimaced. "That's an uphill road. College administrators are incredibly reluctant to discipline Greek houses or to publicize the crimes of individual members. They're much more likely to close ranks around them, block any outside investigation, because universities depend on rich Greek alumni. Also there are very powerful political lobbying groups aimed at protecting fraternities' interests." She paused. "So I go after the parents."

Nothing she had said so far had surprised Roarke. That last did.

"I've recovered millions and millions of dollars from homeowners policies. That's how many of the claims against boys who violate the strict policies are paid: from their parents' homeowners insurance."

Roarke and Epps stared at her, unnerved. "You don't feel the slightest bit guilty about penalizing the parents?" Roarke asked.

Janovy turned cynical eyes on him. "Did you happen to read the letter the Stanford Rapist's father wrote to the judge, pleading for leniency for his rapist son? Arguing that his precious boy shouldn't be penalized for 'twenty minutes of action'?"

Her loathing was palpable in the room.

"Yes, Agent Roarke. I go after the parents. It's proved pointless to ask them to instill basic decency in their sons. They won't lift a manicured finger to stop rapist attitudes, rape culture. So I go after them the only place it seems to hurt them. Their bank accounts. Enough high-profile lawsuits and they just might start getting the message."

Roarke had to admit it made sense. But he was after something more specific.

"Have you had, or heard about, any complaints about the Kappa Alpha Tau house in particular?"

She went still for only a fraction of a second, but Roarke caught it. Then she spoke. "Specifically K-Tau? Not that I know of. Why? Do you know of something?"

Roarke felt a warning stab at her interest. "Just asking."

She regarded him, unsmiling.

Roarke veered quickly to his last question. "Just one more question, if we may. I'm wondering about the timing of all this. This huge, coordinated action. Why now? It doesn't seem to be a reaction to anything in particular."

She tilted her head. "You don't see anything significant about the timing?"

Roarke glanced at Epps. "What significance is that?"

"We've been sitting here for fifteen minutes talking about fraternities. The demonstrations targeted fraternities specifically, if not exclusively. So the Taylor Morton rape trial? It's going to verdict any day now. Down in San Diego."

Taylor Morton? Roarke scrambled to identify the name. She gave him a cold smile. "Can't quite place it? Maybe because there are so many of these cases out there. Here's your brief. The accused is a star runner. White, upper-middle-class, frat boy. The judge is a white middle-aged man, Princeton law school graduate. Oh, and by the way—a Kappa Alpha Tau alum."

Roarke and Epps stared at each other. *Coincidence? Or something more?*

"Put all that together—and do we realistically think Morton is going to get jail time?" Her voice shook. "Brock Turner. Austin Wilkerson. These guys are *convicted* rapists and we can't get judges to sentence them. At a certain point, you have to start asking yourself how to actually solve the problem. Because a two percent conviction rate doesn't even begin to count. How long until we have an equal number of female judges? How long before we make even the slightest dent in rape cases? Given the political nightmare we're living in, what hope in hell do we have of that happening *now*?"

She paused for breath.

"So yeah. I'd kind of expect something to happen around that verdict and sentencing."

Roarke turned that over in his head for a moment. "So all of this vandalism was what—anticipatory outrage? Or are you saying that someone has gone to great lengths to set up some dominoes to make them easy to knock over when the verdict comes in?"

Janovy leaned forward. "You keep asking me what I think. What I think is that something's going to blow. There's just nothing left to lose anymore. The US government has declared open war on women. Officially, these fuckers are going to try to take away every right we've ever fought for. Women are angrier than you can possibly imagine. All we need is one last straw. It could happen any second. And then there's going to be rioting in the streets. There's going to be bloodshed."

She sat back. "And *that* trial? People are watching it. You know why? That misogynistic joke of a judge is on the predator-in-chief's short list for the Supreme Court."

The agents sat in the car on the street outside Janovy's house.

Epps was the first to speak. "She had a lot to say."

"She did." And all of it voluntary. That always alerted Roarke to an agenda. "But what if she's right? That the coordinated vandalism is a setup for when the Morton verdict comes down? Building a pyre in anticipation of the match?"

There was something about it that made sense, especially if the judge in the Morton trial was a contender for the open Supreme Court seat.

Epps was speaking, and Roarke had to focus on his words. "If she is with Bitch, why let us in on all that? She's flat out feeding this stuff to us."

He was right. And personally, Roarke thought Janovy was lying. About something, or about everything.

He leaned forward, hooked his phone to the dashboard port, and called Singh.

"We just got finished with Janovy. We need some information on a trial down in San Diego—"

"The Taylor Morton trial," Singh finished for him. "It is on a list I have compiled of potentially volatile situations."

Roarke shot a glance at Epps. Epps shrugged, but Roarke detected a ghost of a smile. No doubt—with Singh, Epps had won the lottery.

"Janovy basically just called the trial—the verdict—a ticking time bomb."

There was a brief silence as Singh considered it. "She may well be right. The presiding judge is Charles Blackwell. He has a history of handing down light sentences for sexual assault. His name has been floated as a possibility for the Supreme Court vacancy, though not as a top contender."

Epps spoke up. "Janovy says the verdict may be coming down any minute."

There was a brief silence before she replied. "'Any minute' would not be entirely correct. It is my understanding that the defense will conclude its presentation of its case in the next week or so. But in a criminal trial . . ."

She didn't have to finish the sentence. They all knew. Anything could happen, at any time.

Roarke started, "So either Janovy knows something that we don't . . ."

"Or she's trying to get us down there," Epps said. "Or just away from here."

"Maybe." Roarke frowned. "There is the Tau connection, though."

"So . . ."

The truth was, ever since he and Epps had arrived in Santa Barbara, Roarke had been on edge. Whether that feeling meant they were close to some kind of action, or too far away from it, he couldn't tell. But he had felt increasingly jumpy as the morning rolled on.

He weighed it, called it. "We split up. You stay here. Follow up with the county sheriffs and the Isla Vista Foot Patrol to see if there have been any reported rapes concerning the KAT house. Even rumors."

Epps looked surprised. "You're going down to San Diego?" For the slightest second he looked skeptical, suspicious. And why wouldn't he? Roarke had had no end of ulterior motives since this case began.

Epps mentioned none of that. He only asked, "What do you really think you can do there?"

Roarke had to pause. "Sit in at the trial. Be there in case something does go down. Yeah, it's hedging our bets. But if Janovy does have some kind of inside track, then I'm there on the spot."

There was another reason, of course there was.

But not one that Roarke was going to share.

Chapter Twenty-Two

After the call with Roarke and Epps, Singh sits in her cubicle and looks around the empty office. It is early, still some time before business hours; she is the only one in.

So she turns away from her Bureau computer and removes her personal laptop from a drawer. She boots up and logs in, to check up on a project of her own.

Using an alias, on an encrypted connection, she enters the Darknet and logs on to a forum titled "Rape Cara Lindstrom."

It is the hateful brainchild of Riverside County Sheriff's Detective Gilbert Ortiz.

Singh has been following Ortiz online for some weeks now. At first her surveillance was on a legal warrant for Ortiz's online activity, when he was a suspect for the rapes of more than a dozen teenage girls over the last sixteen years.

Ortiz was not part of that rapist team. Roarke had closed the case. But Singh has continued to track Ortiz, unofficially. And illegally.

Because of this forum.

It is a place where men who choose to do so can share their most despicable fantasies.

Singh has lived all her life with the knowledge that a random group of men can turn into a monstrous, ravening beast, with no thought, no morality, no consciousness. That any moment she herself could be seized, brutalized, left for dead or worse than dead.

So many relatives, friends, colleagues have been broken by *It*, the vile thing that slithers through the streets of her home country. The thing that terrorizes women, holds them in *Its* grasp. The thing she has always known is here in this country, too, but at least somewhat deeper in the shadows.

But *It* has free rein in these forums.

She is being careful to mask her movements. Using a laptop that cannot be traced to her. Scrambling her IP address to cover her tracks. But on another level, she simply does not care.

She knows Ortiz's aliases. She knows his habits. When he tends to access the secret forums. The order that he checks in on all of the forums he does haunt.

She has created her own identities and posted in the forums by copying the grotesque, almost invariably ungrammatical writing style of the forums' inhabitants. With her aliases, she has gained access to secret subforums on the Darknet.

There are extreme porn videos and forums with titles like "Top Ten Ways to Get Away with Rape."

Here also is where professional trolls recruit like-minded men to attack women who dare to post their opinions online. Scientists, actresses, journalists, politicians, game designers—anyone female is vulnerable to trolling. A target is posted in the forums and a harassment campaign is begun, in which the victim is deluged with insults, threats, images of sadistic porn.

Over the past several years, online trolling has been rising in an alarming wave. Singh has seen hundreds of female celebrities deluged with rape threats—not only against themselves, but against their children, their mothers, their sisters. A coordinated attempt to silence female voices.

These trolls have only been emboldened by the ascension of the ultimate troll, a sexual predator now determining national policy.

Singh left her own country in part to be free of the pervasive underlying belief that rape is normal, part of a woman's fate. In India the attitude is that the victim asks for it and the male is nowhere in sight of blame.

She does not see these forums or postings as innocent. From attitude comes action.

So she is collecting files on the posters. Trawling for crimes. She is hopeful that the task force that Roarke is spearheading will give her a platform to go after these monsters in some way.

In the meantime, she watches.

She searches all the forums she knows Ortiz frequents, checking for any recent activity. She only skims the threads. Reading closely is unbearable.

But Ortiz has not posted today. And as usual, it is not long before she has to sign off in revulsion.

She puts the computer away, sits back in her chair. She feels agitation prickling under her skin, and takes a moment to close her eyes.

She lets her workplace cubicle slip away and focuses on her breathing, identifying the sensations in her body.

They are too familiar.

Her body temperature is elevated, her face flaming. She is burning up, shaking from this toxic overflow of misogyny and racism and hatred.

Not just in the forums, but in the news, everywhere.

She feels often that she is losing her grip on anything rational. And as so often happens, in this moment she has literally stopped breathing.

She makes herself inhale deeply, exhale slowly.

Then she centers, visualizes the sun, the rays warming and surrounding her, and silently recites a prayer, the ritual of light.

Light before me.
Light behind me.
Light at my left.
Light at my right.
Light above me.
Light below me.
Light around me.
Light to all.
Light to the Universe.

She sits in the visualization, and feels her breath steadying. And it helps, of course it helps. But her prayers and rituals do less and less to calm her.

She spends her days in a haze of anxiety. By night her dreams are ominous: Of a dark force settling over the country. Paroxysms of malice. The constant sense of being hunted.

Nowhere to run. No place that is safe.

And a terrible, inescapable reality: there is no end in sight.

Chapter Twenty-Three

Cara huddles in her niche between massive rocks. The tent ripples in the wind, dancing with menacing presence.

She has been through most of the material in the backpack now, the printed-out emails and web pages. The directive is clear. There is a $25,000 bounty on her head.

"Alive and undamaged," is how the missive is worded. *"Bring her to me first, and you'll get your taste."*

She feels the presence of *It*, hovering, smiling at her through jagged teeth. She sits for some time, breathing through the horror.

The printouts are from an online forum. How many are hunting her, then? Hundreds? Thousands? There could be any number. These stunted beings congregate in the dark corners online, but all her life she has seen them walking in the daylight, every day. They are legion.

She forces down revulsion.

The others are the next problem. First, she will deal with these in front of her.

She tries to keep her mind focused, despite the overwhelming physical sensations telling her to flee.

Get out now. Drive. Put several states between you and these monsters.

The thing that is most stunning, and simultaneously not surprising, is that she *knows* the man who has sent the hunters on their grotesque mission.

His name is pinned to the wall of the tent, in the printout of the online message that amounts to a bounty offer. The message is anonymous, but the hunters had added their own notation, a name and address, in a town that she is quite familiar with.

An old enemy.

Ortiz.

This man from her childhood, who bore some intense, outrageous hatred of her.

He came for her as a teenager, barely fourteen years old, with *It* crawling behind his eyes and equal parts rage and lust in his heart. He suspected her of the killing of the group home counselor who had tried to attack her, and was bent on destroying her for it.

And now, it is clear that hatred has never died. Instead it has festered, metastasized.

She is so overcome by the malice of it that she can't focus. And that makes her vulnerable.

She coldly brings her mind back to the present, the problem at hand. The hunters.

There are two of them, she knows. Two sleeping bags. Two air mattresses.

Two is an easy number.

She must deal with just these two first.

Chapter Twenty-Four

W hen Jade woke, it was a moment before she knew where she was. Not the ranch, she knew that.

And there was someone in bed with her.

The realization was instant, blinding terror. Her whole body froze, and she was back in the endless hell of the street . . .

Shut up and take it, bitch. Swallow it, you little whore. Turn her over and let me at that sweet ass . . .

Jade gasped herself out of the memory, clutching the sheets below her, and bit the inside of her cheek to force herself into the present.

The sheets were soft, well worn, and there was a lavendery scent on the pillow. The breathing beside her in the bed was light, feminine.

The panicky sense of danger subsided.

She remembered now. They'd crashed at Kris's place, an anonymous utility apartment at the edge of the two square miles of Isla Vista.

Beside her, Kris woke with a jarring gasp. And Jade knew the thoughts going through her head. She knew her fear, she knew her rage.

They were the same.

One rape, a thousand rapes . . . or a lifetime living with the fear of it. It was all the same.

"Just me," she said softly. "It's cool." She looked into Kris's eyes until the other girl focused on her, recognized her.

They both lay there, remembering the talk of the night before.

And finally Jade spoke. "So let's go get a look at this prick."

They picked up grande coffees at a place called Equilibrium and walked under a cloudy sky over to the Kappa Alpha Tau house on Camino Embarcadero. It was one of four in a square block, backed up against each other.

A whole frat city, Jade thought, without amusement.

The dudebros were out in packs, in khaki shorts, shirtless, up on ladders, hanging lights on the front of the house, clipping paper hearts and angel wings on clotheslines strung over the back patio areas.

"Whaddaya know, it's party time," Jade said softly.

"Valentine's Day," Kris said.

Jade was startled by the thought. She'd completely lost track of time at the ranch.

How perfect is that? The possibilities danced in her head. *Costumes. Easy entry. We can do this tonight.*

"Where is he?" she muttered to Kris. "Do you see him?"

"He won't be doing grunt work. Probably kicking back at the satellite house."

Jade frowned. "Satellite house?"

"All the big frats have second houses on Del Playa. The main houses never get too crazy. They keep up a good front, so anyone official who drops in—the college, the frat boards, the cops—just sees what the frat wants them to see. The real . . ." She faltered. "The real action happens at the satellite houses."

"Show me."

Kris took her along the street, which curved into "the Loop," a strip of road around a small park, lined with restaurants, cafés, liquor stores, a party store, an Amazon fulfillment store. From there short straight blocks led down to the ocean.

Del Playa was the street that ran along the cliff. Big old houses alternated with condo complexes with surfboards lined up on balconies. Many of the front yards boasted long, tall rectangular tables and grimy sofas on the sidewalk, perpetually set up for the next party. A fair number of the smaller houses were painted with colorful murals of Hollywood icons: James Dean, Marilyn, Elvis. Red beverage cups were strewn everywhere, like oversized confetti.

When the two girls got to the end of the next block, Kris kept moving, but jerked her head toward the last house on the block. "That's it."

Jade followed Kris, glanced back casually.

The satellite house was a huge modern three-story clinging to the cliff in a line with the other oceanfront houses along Del Playa.

Kris murmured beside her, "There are decks around the back, on the cliff. You can't see the lowest level from the front. They call it the Basement. That's where . . ."

She broke off, shaky.

The two girls kept walking. Beside the house was a mini public park overlooking the ocean, with a swing set, an outdoor shower, stairs leading down to the shoreline.

Kris nodded toward the park. "We can watch from there."

The girls moved across the shabby grass and sat on the swings. The sound of the surf below them was a constant rhythmic rumble. Kris pointed out the patio overlooking the ocean, the triple level decks jutting out over the water. "The low deck is the Basement."

Jade studied the house, assessing the layout. "Gotcha."

Just then a group of guys spilled out the back door, onto the concrete side patio. Kris stared at the frat boys and froze. "That's him."

Jade got a glimpse of a tall, dark, and arrogant one. Kris stood from the swing. Jade followed as she darted away from the swing set, ducked under one of the twisty trees.

They watched from behind the branches.

Two of the guys carried a beer cooler between them. They set the cooler on the porch, on the house property, but an easy walk from the volleyball net.

A couple of them started to toss a ball between them, not a game yet, just fucking around. A lot of them carried red cups. Drinking already, or maybe they'd never stopped from the night before.

The girls hung back in the trees. "So this is the one," Jade said, not taking her eyes off him.

Kris's voice was hollow. "He hit on her first. All charm, so smooth. Of course he drugged her drink."

Jade squinted, lasering in on him. Square jaw. Six-pack abs. Shorts hanging off his hips to show the triangle of pelvic muscles. She knew the type. Alpha asshole. Daddy's little prince.

You're a cocky fucker, aren't you?

"Gimme your phone," she ordered. Kris passed it over and Jade zoomed to take a few photos, then switched to video mode. She wanted to memorize his face.

Through the phone lens, she could see their horseplay up close, how some of their touches lingered on ass cheeks, how fingers brushed across abs and thighs.

Homoerotic much? she thought, with contempt. *Why can't you all just fuck each other? Leave the rest of us out of it.*

Finally she lowered the phone. "Okay then. We do it tonight."

Kris stared at her, jolted.

"They got her at a party, didn't they? So we get him at a party. Poetic justice, yo."

"I can't," Kris says. "I can't be there."

Jade got that. Not to mention that Kris would never get into one of those parties. She looked too much like a real person with real thoughts, instead of a blow-up doll.

"I can," Jade told her. "I can handle this just fine."

Chapter Twenty-Five

There were only two hundred or so miles between Santa Barbara and San Diego, but Roarke's only option from Santa Barbara's airport was a connecting flight through Phoenix: six-hour travel time, and airport hassle on both ends. If he started in the dead of night, he might be able to drive to San Diego in four hours. During peak traffic, which was nearly all the time now, it might take up to eight.

Which left the Pacific Surfliner, an Amtrak train that hugged the coastline. The website ad boasted, "To get a closer look, you'd have to be on a surfboard," and true to the advertising, a stunning view of the ocean opened up minutes after the train left the downtown station. Roarke leaned back in his seat, luxuriating in the view, and replayed the Janovy interview in his head.

Was Janovy a Bitch? Highly likely. Was she a leader? Quite possibly. But *the* leader? His strong suspicion was that there were dozens, hundreds of Janovys across the country. Educated. Each with their own skill set, as Janovy had said. And angry.

Roarke stared out the window, and his thoughts turned to Cara's cousin Erin McNally. The fog drifting in the coastal cypress took him back to the last night he'd seen her. Golden Gate Park had been blanketed in the mist of the December Cold Moon.

Erin was the ulterior motive that Epps had been right to be suspicious about.

Roarke still felt Erin was as good a suspect as anyone for the series of pimp and john murders at the time of Cara's incarceration and after, the Santa Muerte Murders. If Andrea Janovy was one of the maddening loose ends of the case, Erin was another.

Erin had been on the scene. She was a survivor of sexual assault. And Roarke had an uneasy feeling that the young woman might have gone as far as murder to create a kind of firewall to further protect Cara from prosecution.

His best guess was that Erin's disappearance had something to do with Bitch. That she was working with them, now.

And it had occurred to him that Janovy's surrogate, the one who had used her ID (and whom he was sure Janovy knew, quite possibly had sent), and Erin McNally were the only two people who had visited Cara in jail.

Could the two women be connected?

All of those nagging loose ends. And Santa Muerte, whoever, whatever she was, on the loose still, from that night.

So yes, he was going to San Diego to check out the Morton trial. But there was no doubt Erin was on his mind.

If the real assignment here was to track down Bitch, Erin might be a way in. He just wasn't sure he wanted to know.

Chapter Twenty-Six

Singh scribbles on the screen of the delivery man's device to accept the bouquet, a spray of coral roses. The man looks over her desk and gives her a knowing smile as he turns to leave. "Have a good one."

If Singh were in the habit of blushing, her cheeks would be the color of the roses. They are not the only floral arrangement on her usually pristine desk. Her workspace is overflowing with flowers, gift boxes. The fragrance surrounds her.

Valentine's Day. Not a holiday she has grown up with or has any real attachment to. Yet in lieu of his presence, Damien has taken it upon himself to shower her with presents.

Every hour, on the hour, a different gift has been delivered. A mirrored milagro, in the shape of a burning heart. An etching by Remedios Varo, her favorite Surrealist. A statue of the goddess Saraswati for her collection. A book of Sufi poetry. A stunning necklace. Other items . . . unsuitable for public display.

Her dark mood from the morning has dissolved into a pleasant haze, mildly erotic. The whole day has been a typically extravagant gesture from Epps, who, she suspects, is partly feeling guilty about not being with her for the day. But she also knows what all this is leading to.

She has no doubt that Damien is the partner of her heart.

In her spiritual practice, she is familiar with the concept of astral bodies. That in sexual union, in deeper relationships, the auras of both partners combine in one entity that is the couple. She has felt her own astral force comingling with Epps'. And she knows it is right, and good.

And she has been immensely grateful that he understands her fear and rage since the election. That as an African American man, he has intimate knowledge of those feelings. There are things that do not have to be voiced between them. They understand the peril the country is in.

It has never gone away—the racism, the misogyny, the relentless hold of the patriarchy.

But now it has full, unimpeded voice. It is becoming, more quickly than she could have imagined, in dozens, hundreds of small ways and large, the law of the land.

They are lucky to be living in one of the most liberal cities in the country, even in the world. And yet they have discussed quitting their jobs.

To have a man, a partner, a soulmate, who understands every heartache of the times, who feels the horror of each new announcement, who is willing to support any move she feels she has to make— that should be a given. Instead, she knows it is a luxury few women will ever know. With Damien, she is safe, loved, cherished, supported—in body, mind, and soul. It is a grace.

And still, she has felt herself pulling away from him. Hiding the depth of her anxiety. She feels constantly on the verge of explosion, that she could at any moment shatter into pieces that might never again be assembled into even a facsimile of a human being. She is over-come sometimes with the feeling of wanting to rip off her own skin.

The pressure inside her to run, run as far as she can go, is something she cannot express, not even to Epps.

Today, because of his thoughtfulness, this outpouring of affection, she has been given a reprieve. She has not been plagued by the constant dread, the sudden waves of panic at random moments, any time the remembrance of the new reality hits.

But even as she thinks it, a pop-up flashes on the screen that she has programmed to notify her when there is activity in certain threads in the men's forums with certain key words.

She glances around the office to be sure Reynolds is nowhere in sight, then pulls out her own laptop to log in.

And in the "Rape Cara Lindstrom" forum, there is a new post with the most chilling keyword of all.

> Get that **bounty** ready. We have eyes on the
> bitch. Bringing her down today. Watch this space.

Singh's heart constricts. She quickly grabs a screenshot of the post, then watches the forum intently for responses.

Other users are already responding to the post, demanding details.

But less than five minutes later, the post suddenly disappears.

Ortiz, she has no doubt. She can see he has logged in to the forum under one of his aliases.

This poster, or posters, was sloppy. Unable to resist crowing.

And you jumped on them for it, did you not? As soon as you saw it. But not soon enough.

She sits back from the computer, feeling ill.

It has begun.

Someone has taken the bait. And Ortiz intends to pay these monsters to deliver Cara Lindstrom to him.

Chapter Twenty-Seven

Wind spirals around her, blowing thick flakes of snow. The blizzard has moved in.

Everything is white. Flakes settle on her lashes, blinding her, as she watches the tent from her rock circle above it.

She knows she must find shelter soon. The rocks are some buffer against the wind, and her white parka is Arctic rated, but hardly enough to keep her alive in this weather.

But she stays, because she knows the snow will force the hunters back to the tent. It should not be long now.

And even as she thinks it, she sees a dark shape in the whiteness.

A bulky male figure, and the unmistakable silhouette of a rifle.

A rifle.

She loathes guns.

But guns make men cocky. Guns make them think they hold all the cards. She can get him if he is alone.

Where is the other?

She scans the rim, searching her snowy surroundings for any sign of camouflage. Not the smartest attire for the weather—the hunter had been easy to spot against the pure white.

There is no sign of the second hunter. And this one is so close now . . . she may never have such an opportunity again.

Her eyes search the ground, and she sees what she needs. She stoops and seizes the round rock, bigger than a baseball, hefts it in her hand. A good two pounds of lethal force. She sets her sights on the hunter . . . breathing in, breathing out, focusing. When he is angled in just the right direction, she summons the strength of her loathing, and throws the rock at his head.

It hits him with a sickening crunch, staggers him. Not a knock-out blow, but he is dazed. He regains his balance, puts his hand to his temple. His fingers come away red.

Now he turns in a clumsy circle, looking around him. And when his back is to her, she takes that moment of disorientation to dart out of the rockfall and run at him. Charging him full bore. Curling into herself and slamming into his back, knocking him flat, face first into the snow with her full body weight on top of him. She feels the sick, shuddering impact of his fall.

And she is on him, scrambling up his back to sit hard on his spine, pinning his arms beneath him with her weight, trapping his rifle underneath him. She digs her knees into his spine, wraps her hands around his neck, holding his face in the snow, finding a grip to twist his head, snap his neck—

In the whiteness in front of her she sees a blue-pink thread of light.

Then she jumps a foot in the air, flying backward . . . as she is hit in the chest by twin barbed darts packing fifty thousand volts of raw pain.

The electricity rips through her, like someone burrowing inside her body to claw her muscles apart with a fork.

Her entire body convulses in muscle spasms, and for jerky, white-hot seconds, pain is all there is.

Five agonizing seconds later, the pain is gone.

What remains is far more terrifying. Total neuromuscular incapacitation.

She knows she's been tased. She forces herself to think through the disorientation. She has to get up. She has to force herself to move before they can get to her.

Get up.

But her body will not obey the command.

She hears the crunching of heavy footsteps on ice.

Just feet away, the hunter who shot her bends to help his fallen comrade up.

Then the boots plow deliberately through the snow and stop beside her. A dark figure looms above as he gloats.

"Well, looky here. We got ourselves the prime bitch."

She feels fingers in her hair, and her head being yanked up. He backhands her, a vicious blow against her jaw.

"Easy now," the other says. "'Undamaged,' the man said."

The hunter tightens his grip on her hair, leers into her face. "Just means we have to clean up after ourselves. Let's get her to the tent."

Cara feels blinding rage, and summons all the will she has. This will not happen. Not while she has breath.

And then there is a hideous cracking, like the world splintering open . . .

And she falls.

Chapter Twenty-Eight

Roarke jolted awake with his heart pounding, his body roiling with a feeling of overwhelming sickness.

Falling . . .

He sat straight up, looking around him. He was on the gently rocking train, surrounded by passengers. A woman with a small boy glanced at him surreptitiously from a nearby seat, and he could only hope he hadn't shouted in his sleep.

He had to take deep, slow breaths to fight down the nausea.

Motion sickness? Or was it something from an uneasy dream?

He could remember nothing . . . when he closed his eyes there was only whiteness.

When the dizziness was past, he looked out the window. The train was just sliding past San Diego's harbor, home to an active naval fleet.

Almost there.

Roarke sat still, racked with an unease that he couldn't define. But then he stood to gather his overnight bag.

The new San Diego Central Courthouse on Union Street was a towering, all-modern, rectangular edifice of white concrete, framing sail-like metal panels that captured the changing sunlight.

Several dozen protesters lined the building's steps, lifting signs.

RAPISTS DESERVE PRISON

NO JUSTICE, NO PEACE

And some even more pointed:

JUDGE BLACKWELL: THE WHOLE WORLD IS WATCHING

Many of the protesters wore the now ubiquitous pink knitted pussy hats. An idea that had in theory seemed quaint and silly had turned out to be a genius move, a female banner of the new resistance. The pinkness was unmissable and unmistakably feminine. It was a rallying symbol for fifty-one percent of the US population. The no-longer-sleeping majority.

So Janovy was right about one thing: this trial was on the radar.

In the lobby, Roarke went through security, which included relinquishing his cell phone.

As it turned out, he'd managed to make it there in time for at least some of the main event—the testimony of the accused.

Upstairs, he took a seat in the courtroom and saw a middle-aged white man in a robe on the bench and a clean-cut young white man on the witness stand.

Taylor Morton could have been popped from the same mold as the young men of the KAT house. Morton's haircut, his suit, his shoes, his physique—all of these said that his parents could more than afford to buy justice. The well-heeled couple in the first row probably were the parents, right up front, supporting their baby boy.

The defense spoke smoothly. "Mr. Morton, you've testified that you'd been drinking that night."

"Yes, sir."

"Would you explain to the court the drinking habits of your teammates?"

The prosecutor was on her feet. "Objection, Your Honor. Irrelevant."

"Goes to state of mind, Your Honor," the defense attorney countered.

"I'll allow it," Blackwell said.

Morton answered dutifully. "The team set no limits on drinking. It felt like that was just being part of the family."

"Can you describe the team's typical behavior at parties?

"Your Honor—"

"Overruled."

"I witnessed countless times that the guys I looked up to would go to parties, meet girls, and take the girls they had just met back with them. There were always girls coming back to the house to keep the party going."

Roarke felt contempt. No way not to see where this was going. *"I was drunk, she was drunk, everyone was drunk, we all did it, everyone does it."*

He tried to listen to the testimony through the pounding in his head. Morton had met the plaintiff in the bar line. They danced. She was obviously into it. They kissed. It got heavier and she wanted to go "someplace private." It was all her idea, of course. He offered his room and they left together. Back in his room they started making out.

He claimed he'd asked for and gotten verbal consent. He insisted that the plaintiff was fully conscious and responsive throughout the "encounter." She was moaning, she had her arms around him. At no time did he think she was not willingly participating. He was completely shocked when the police arrived the next day to arrest him.

To listen to him, you'd think he was fresh off the farm, seduced and then accused by a worldly and predatory woman. But it didn't have to make sense. Because, after all, it was his word against hers. All he had to do was establish reasonable doubt. *Deny, deny, deny.*

And it worked. Even when the jury convicted, there was no guarantee of any reasonable sentence.

Because thirty years ago this judge had *been* this boy. Looked like him, had the same kind of parents, went to the same kind of school, belonged to the same kind of fraternity.

If Roarke was feeling anger, then what would it be like to be one of these young women?

No wonder they were taking matters into their own hands. No wonder Bitch was taking its protests to the streets. Anything to force attention on the repeated, continuing injustices that sent the same message over and over again.

That ninety-eight percent of the time, you can rape and get away with it.

Chapter Twenty-Nine

T he rest of the day was prep.

Jade had been doing recon, figuring her strategy. UCSB daywear was casual. But the parties were slutfests. That was the whole point. From the flyers she'd seen, from the Instagram and Facebook and Twitter posts she'd been cruising, this was going to be an all-out lingerie party. Valentine Bros and Hos.

Yeah. Original.

When Kris and Jade walked the Loop earlier in the day, they'd passed a party shop with some of the sluttiest getups Jade had ever seen, and that was saying a lot.

The party shop had been full of sorority girls shopping for the big night, giggling and playing with fetish equipment they had next to no clue how to use. Pink feathers on a stick. A riding crop that might work on a My Little Pony . . . or a unicorn.

Like any guy wants to be tickled with pink feathers or lightly lashed by a fake riding crop.

The little that college guys knew, they picked up from porn. The aggressive ones want to fuck you in the ass and then the mouth. The nonaggressive ones, you could just grab them by the balls and stick a finger up their ass to get the whole thing over with ASAP. Wham, bam, next customer.

She watched the Disney princess-slash-sluts move on to the lingerie, and felt a wave of contempt.

Valentine hos, someone got that right. Dressing themselves up for rapists. How stupid could you get?

The more she thought about it, the more she thought Kris had the right idea. Shaved head, gender-neutral clothes . . .

Why should anyone play that Barbie doll game? This shit is good for a costume, no doubt. But for reals? It's the biggest trap ever invented.

She was on the verge of just walking out of the shop. But then she spotted a glittering little number that would do just fine.

Oh yeah.

She could have some fun in that.

Chapter Thirty

Just as Roarke was feeling he had to get out of the courtroom before he punched someone, the judge adjourned.

"This court will be in recess until Tuesday."

As Roarke stood with the rest of the spectators, he realized it was the start of the weekend.

He walked with the crowd out of the courthouse, into the downtown twilight, seething with tension.

Hundreds of lawsuits had been fought on campuses by young women all over the country, precisely because of the dismal chance of ever getting justice from the legal system. And now the secretary of education might decide to drop them all. And a judge with Blackwell's history could be deciding cases on the highest court of the land.

Roarke still had the feeling that Janovy was playing him. But Janovy, and Singh, and for that matter, Reynolds—all of them were right. Of course Bitch was monitoring any number of hot spots in the state and in the whole country, and mobilizing for the next protest or escalation of action. The war had begun.

He stopped on the sidewalk to get his bearings, and realized he was right on the border of San Diego's famed Gaslamp Quarter, former home to saloons, gambling halls, and bordellos. It had been revamped into a cosmopolitan playground with historic Victorian buildings crowded side by side with modern skyscrapers, celebrity restaurants, craft breweries, happening nightclubs, and a hopping street-fair culture.

He'd turned his phone off when he'd left it at security in the courthouse. He reached for it now and thumbed it on, looked down at several messages, all from Singh.

He tensed instantly, and punched on the first.

Singh's recorded voice was tense, as well. "I did not know whether I should . . ." She seemed to choose her words carefully. "If I should disturb you with this. But I have been watching Detective Ortiz's online accounts, his activity in the men's rights forums. Particularly the Cara Lindstrom threads."

He was slammed by a jolt of adrenaline and worry. He didn't even play the message through before he was dialing her back. "I just got your message. What's going on?"

"I believe something is happening as we speak."

His throat was dry as dust. "Tell me."

"You are aware that Ortiz has offered a bounty for information on Lindstrom's whereabouts. There was a posting today in that forum—"

"Send it," Roarke said tightly.

"I am sending it."

Roarke clicked on the email. The short message turned his blood to ice.

> Get that bounty ready. We have eyes on the
> bitch. Bringing her down today. Watch this space.

Bringing her down today.

Had Cara been captured?

By the kind of scum that posted in those forums? The kind that would answer a bounty offer? He was cold with fear for her.

"Where did it come from?" he asked aloud, struggling to keep his voice neutral.

"Chief, I am working on it. Ortiz is posting with a certain level of encryption. So are the—people—he is communicating with. I have not yet been able to trace the origin of the message."

Roarke was silent, struggling with himself.

"Chief?" Singh's voice was laced with concern.

"I'm here."

He could feel her presence at the other end of the connection. Calm, waiting.

His thoughts were racing, out of control. He could get to Palm Desert, Ortiz's home, in two hours.

"Will you . . . keep monitoring Ortiz on the forums?" he asked her, through a dry throat.

"Of course," she said gently.

He didn't say where he was going. He was sure she knew.

He disconnected with Singh, then used his phone to search for the nearest car rental company. There was one just a few blocks away.

He turned abruptly to walk in that direction.

And saw a flash of a familiar face as someone ducked quickly into a doorway. Quickly, but not fast enough.

He was being followed.

Chapter Thirty-One

S ingh disconnects, and sits. She feels slightly nauseated, and realizes the feeling is empathy, triggered by the level of pain in Roarke's voice.

She looks over her desk at the flowers, all the gifts from Epps.

Her own happiness makes her ache for Roarke's excruciating, insoluble dilemma. To love—and she has no doubt it is love, though she will never say it aloud—someone so tragic and lethal . . . to know there is no place on earth, no place even in his own mind, that would ever allow consummation . . .

To care for someone as she knows he does for Lindstrom, against all odds, and be helpless in the face of life-threatening danger to that person . . .

It is unbearable to contemplate.

She looks at the lineup of Epps' gifts, every one of them thoughtful enough to stand on its own.

It gives her the shield she needs to wade back into the cesspit of the forums.

If there is a clue there to Lindstrom's whereabouts, she will find it.

Chapter Thirty-Two

Roarke turned on the sidewalk and continued walking, past break-dancers and vendors with buckets of red roses and heart-shaped balloons, and he looked at the shop fronts as if he were window-shopping.

The glass reflected the street and sidewalk behind him. He walked more slowly, staring into the windows, scanning the reflections for his pursuer.

One window after another, the decorations were all roses and lace hearts and lingerie. And finally the penny dropped. It was Valentine's Day. He hadn't even noticed the date.

He forced his mind away from a brief, painful memory of Rachel—

And then he spotted her, a specter in the glass.

Erin.

She was still too thin, her olive skin stretched tight over high cheekbones, her hair now chopped off into a feathered cap. But the last time he'd seen her she'd been in the midst of some kind of self-destructive breakdown, dazed, suicidal. She was much more pulled together now, edgy, focused, intent.

He paused in front of the nearest shop, staring into the window display . . .

And then he turned on his heel and strode straight across the sidewalk toward her.

She wasn't able to duck into a doorway this time. He saw a quick look of dismay on her face, immediately replaced by a forced look of pleasure. She walked toward him.

"Agent Roarke. It is you," she said, stopping in front of him.

"You were following me," he said shortly.

"Yes, I thought I saw you coming out of the courthouse. I wasn't sure."

To her credit, she had a good cover story ready. He didn't believe her. How many messages had he left since she'd disappeared? She could have called him back any time.

"Erin, I've been trying to find you for—" He'd almost said "months," but the truth was it hadn't been more than six weeks. He suddenly felt old. "I've called your house, talked to your roommate. Called your brother in Japan."

"Last month . . . was a bad time," she said obliquely. "There were some things I was working out. It's better now. That's why I was trying to catch you. I wanted to thank you for taking care of me that night—"

More lies. Maybe Janovy had let her know he was coming down, and sent her to find him, watch him. But he didn't have time for this. Not anymore.

"I need to get a message to Cara," he said over her.

That brought her up short. She answered warily. "We're not in touch. I haven't seen her since the jail—"

He ignored that. "You need to tell her she's in danger. There's a police detective named Ortiz. Out of Palm Desert."

Her face went still. "I remember Ortiz."

That surprised him. Erin had been—how old when Ortiz began his pursuit of Cara? Not even ten.

"What do you remember?"

"He came to our house, when Cara was visiting. Asking questions . . ."

"He's still coming after her."

He told her, briefly. About the "Rape Cara Lindstrom" forum. The bounty.

Erin visibly paled as he talked. "Okay," she said explosively, and he stopped speaking. "Okay, I get it."

"I don't know if they're serious," he started.

"Don't you?" she slammed back at him. "Really?"

"Then you'll want to contact her."

"I told you, we're not—"

He interrupted her again. "Cara stole my phone." His mind went unbidden to the night on the beach in Santa Cruz. To how she'd gotten the phone from him. He forced himself away from the thoughts. "I believe she still has it, not with her, but somewhere. I haven't disconnected the number. If you leave a message, she may get it."

He fished for one of his old business cards and extended it to her. Erin looked at it without taking it.

"Why don't *you* call?" she asked, pointedly.

"I have."

He had. He'd tried. There was never an answer, of course. But the line was live. It was his familiar mailbox message.

Her face was stormy, conflicted. "Why shouldn't I think this line is tapped?"

"It's not."

She was more and more nervous. "That's not something I can ever know, though, is it?"

"I guess not. But. Take it anyway. Please. Someone should warn her. Someone she can trust."

She took the card, stood holding it. She suddenly seemed very young.

He touched her arm. "I have to go. Take care of yourself, Erin."

Chapter Thirty-Three

Back at the apartment, Jade found Kris at the kitchen table, nervously smoking cigarettes, a bottle of vodka open in front of her.

"Didja get it?"

Kris opened her hand, revealed the eight-ball, a baggie of white.

Crystal courage.

"That's what I'm talking about," Jade muttered.

Kris had sprung for blow, not meth. Jade needed the clarity that coke would give her.

She cut the powder on a piece of glass and they did some lines before Jade went in to dress. It had been almost two months since she'd gotten high and the blast took the top of her head off.

It made dressing feel like one long orgasm, the teasing slide of silk on her naked skin.

It seemed like a long time since she'd dressed up to do the street. The feeling was white hot.

Then she saw the shadow in the mirror. He was standing behind her.

Danny.

Those long black dreads, leather pants tight on his hips, steampunk jacket.

He looked into the mirror, smiled, whispered, "You like that? That feel good, baby?"

She spun around, her heart racing.

Ohgodohgodohgod. It wasn't a dream. He was *there.*

He winked at her. "Thass the hot mama I like to see. Thass my girl. Where you been, baby?"

He snapped his fingers, like you would to a dog. "Come to Daddy, now." He whistled softly.

"No . . ." she mumbled.

And then he was gone.

She stumbled on too-high heels, sat down hard on the bed, her heart heaving.

Nothing. Nothing. Never there. He's dead.

She forced her breath to slow.

I'm in charge, now.

This time no one was shoving her out there. This time she was working for herself. And she was going to do some damage. The frat rat was going down.

She stood.

When she stepped out of the bedroom, the living room/kitchenette was thick with smoke from the cigs Kris had been chain-smoking.

Kris looked up . . . and her face was priceless. Completely stunned.

Jade had chosen a glittery bodysuit with a snakeskin pattern of gleaming greens, pinks, purples, silvers, and plenty of peekaboo cutouts. It was camouflage: the bodysuit perfectly concealed her tats. Anyone looking at her would see the skin and the sparkle, not the art. But it was also a kick-ass costume. She'd slicked her hair to her scalp with glitter gel and painted her face with luminous greens and purples and silvers. Sparkly fuck-me heels made her legs seem about a mile long. She looked like an exotic snake.

She did a slow, slithery slut walk in front of Kris, pivoted for the full effect. "So?"

Kris looked genuinely knocked out. "You look fantastic. Scary great."

Jade stopped to look herself over in the mirror. "It'll get the job done." She walked over to the table, looked down at the remaining coke. "Where's the other?"

Kris reached into a jeans pocket, pulled out another baggie of several pills.

Jade took the glassine bag, removed two of the pills, and started to crush them down.

"Let's get this party started."

Chapter Thirty-Four

Her head is throbbing. Her body is throbbing. There are rock walls, ice, and snow all around her. She is half buried in it.

She has never been so cold in her life. It galvanizes her because she knows in the final stages of freezing to death, you feel warmth, not cold. There is still time enough to survive.

She breathes in, and pain stabs her chest. Her ribs, she thinks. There is blood trickling down her cheek. She is quivering, aching. But she is alive. And she can move.

She tilts her head to the gray sky.

She is on a ledge, staring up a sheer rock wall. The cliff edge where she had been fighting the hunter is at least thirty feet above her.

The rock slab must have broken off and slid straight down the cliff face until it crashed on the ledge.

Which means . . .

Adrenaline shoots through her in a jolt of liquid fire and she sits upright.

No more than ten feet away, two dark shapes are sunk into the soft snow. The two hunters are with her on the ledge.

Alive? Or dead?

Her eyes widen and she scans the ground around her. In the white of snow, she spots a dark shape like a flashlight: the Taser. She stretches out a hand toward it . . . agony knifes her chest.

Too far.

But she reaches down her side to her boot with a trembling hand, grasps the handle of the knife she has concealed there.

She crawls through the snow toward the first shape, fighting the fire in her chest. She raises the knife and stabs it through the hunter's throat, feels the warm blood cascading over her trembling fingers. The warmth, the movement of the blood tells her.

Alive. Not for long now, but it means the other—

She feels a hand grab her ankle, toppling her from her knees, dragging her backward in the snow. Pain stabs through her ribs. She kicks out at the second hunter, kicks his face savagely.

He grunts a curse. His arm flails in the snow, feeling for the rifle that has landed three, four feet away.

"Bitch. You bitch. You can't . . . can't . . ."

She can. She does. Stabs her knife straight through his throat, and watches the blood gushing, black against the white of snow.

She pulls herself shakily to sitting in the snow between the bodies, panting. The adrenaline is white hot, exhilarating, canceling her pain.

But as her breath slows and she looks around her at the towering cliff walls, the truth overcomes her.

There is no way off this ledge.

Survival rises up in her, an instinctive *NO* to the dark that jolts her to her feet. She stands, swaying on shaking legs.

But then she pauses, as another thought emerges through the panic.

Freezing to death, now? After everything?

To let go of the fight. To be free of this for all time. To surrender herself to the canyon, its implacable mercy.

No more.

The thought floods her with a strange peace.

I've fought. I've fought as hard as anyone could fight.

She is so tired. So very tired.

Her legs shudder and fold underneath her. On her knees now, she gazes out over the bleak, timeless, terrible beauty of the canyon.

Yes. Here. I'm ready.

And now she lies back into the snow. No longer cold, but soft, like a blanket. Soft, pure, clean. And surrenders herself.

Her last thoughts before the dark are of Roarke.

Chapter Thirty-Five

H e drove the rental car like a maniac, burning up the roads, feeling he was racing against some invisible clock.

In this desert place, so close to where Cara had killed her first man, he thought of the child she had been.

The five-year-old slashed by a monster. The twelve-year-old condemned to youth prison for the offense of defending herself against two predators. The fourteen-year-old who faced off against a serial rapist and killer—because no adult was aware enough to see the monster under their noses.

No one had protected her. And for that reason alone, he was not going to allow *this* monster to get his hands on her.

He drove toward the rising moon.

He knew Ortiz lived in Palm Desert; he knew his address. Singh had compiled a file for him when Ortiz was a suspect in the serial rape case Roarke had been drawn into out in the desert.

What he hadn't known was that Ortiz lived on a golf course.

There were many in the area, but that didn't mean they were afford-able on a lawman's salary. It was surprising.

Roarke stopped his rental car on the dark street outside the sprawl-ing landscaped complex.

A security gate barred the entrance.

Maybe that means you should keep out.

Instead, he put the car in gear, drove up to the guard booth, and flashed his credentials wallet at the retirement-age guard. He put all the authority of the Bureau into his voice. "I'm here to talk to the grounds manager."

And when the guard reached for the phone, he said, "Don't."

The guard hesitated, but nodded, and raised the gate. "Make a right on the second cross street. Manager's house is at the end on the right."

Roarke followed the directions and turned down the short block, then circled back to find Ortiz's address, a condo in a two-story triplex. He parked at a distance, headlights off, and surveyed the front of the building. There was an SUV in the carport labeled with Ortiz's number.

Ortiz was home.

And now what?

Insane scenarios flashed through Roarke's head. Storming up to the house, demanding entry, seizing the man . . .

And what? What could he actually *do?*

Arrest him for illegally obtained and ambiguous posts on the Internet?

Beat the living shit out of him?

If Roarke bided his time, there might be a case here. Abduction and transportation across state lines for the purposes of sex. Reckless endangerment. They were all offenses that fell under FBI jurisdiction. However, the victim in question was also a fugitive. A fugitive who was not his case anymore.

He tried to calm himself, to think.

It's not like Cara was actually *in* there. Ortiz would never bring a hostage to his own home.

And the poster had said only: *"We have eyes on her."*

But that was hours ago.

Have they caught her by now?

He turned off the engine, stepped out of the car into the dry desert air. He kept to the shadows as he moved around the side of the triplex toward the course. He wasn't much of a golfer, but he knew how these golf communities were laid out. The houses backed up to the green. And people were paying for the view, which meant walls of windows and glass doors.

He stayed close to the building and edged out to see what the setup was.

The sprawling fairway was softly, dramatically lit, landscaped with huge old pepper trees. Grassy hills and sand traps were manicured to perfection.

And sure enough, all three of the condos in the unit had small patios with just waist-high walls separating them from the golf course. As he'd hoped, the condo had sliding glass doors, designed for an unimpeded view of the green.

But that view went both ways. The rooms inside Ortiz's condo were dark, but Roarke could see a hunched shadow seated at a table in the dining area between the small open kitchen and the living room.

Ortiz was bent to the keyboard, tension in his neck and back, typing furiously. Roarke caught a flash of Ortiz's face, illuminated by the light of his computer screen.

Watching him, Roarke felt some relief. He was there, he was alone. Cara was safe from him, at least for now.

"We have eyes on the bitch. Watch this space."

Was there some ambush being planned? Were they taking her down right now?

To deliver her to what?

But Roarke knew. The titles of the forums said it all.

He'd met Ortiz, had faced his irrational anger, had seen up close his obsessive rage that Cara was still free. The blasphemy of a woman killing men, killing men for cause, had deranged him. The forums proved there were any number of men like him.

The profile of online trolls was dire. Psychologists had found high levels of all four traits of the so-called "dark tetrad": narcissism, Machiavellianism, psychopathy, and sadism. And the more these men indulged their sadistic fantasies online, the more likely they were to cross that line from fantasy to practice. If the target of Ortiz's rage had been a journalist or politician, Ortiz would have harnessed those like-minded men to troll, stalk, harass, threaten her into silence. But Cara had no address, no online presence. She was immune to the ordinary mental torture of trolling. So Ortiz had plans for actual physical torture.

As Roarke watched Ortiz typing, his gut was roiling. Was he even now arranging for Cara's "delivery"?

His disgust and rage built until he was afraid he would cross a line, force entry into the house, do all kinds of criminal damage. He turned from his view of the glass doors, the aquarium of filth, and moved into the darkness of the golf course.

He stopped under the shadowy fronds of a pepper tree and caught his breath, tried to calm his racing thoughts.

Remember, Singh is watching Ortiz, too. If there's a way to intercept messages, she'll find it.

But all he could think was—

It's not enough.

So under the feathery shadows of the tree, he picked up the phone to call Cara Lindstrom, the mass murderess, the object of any number of manhunts.

He didn't identify himself. He was sure he wouldn't have to. And he didn't say her name, though it filled his mind as he listened to his own voicemail greeting on the other end.

Then he spoke.

"Wherever you are, you need to get out. There are people coming to get you . . ." He could barely swallow through the tightness in his throat. "Please let me know you're all right."

He disconnected before he could be tempted to say more.

Almost immediately the phone buzzed. He stared at it, for a moment not breathing, unable to move.

It couldn't . . . could it? It couldn't be.

He lifted the phone . . . and saw Singh's name on the screen.

He clicked through to her voice.

"I have been monitoring the forums. There has been no more online activity from the hunters since then."

Along with the insane relief, Roarke felt the weight of his own indefensible behavior. "I don't want you to—I'm not asking you to do this, Singh. I don't want you to do anything that you feel is—outside the lines."

There was a silence. Then she spoke. "This is a matter far beyond the threat to Lindstrom. Detective Ortiz is a serving law enforcement officer who is engaged in a criminal conspiracy to incite and/or commit rape, torture, and quite possibly murder. We have no idea who else he may intend to target. He is a clear and present danger to any number of people, perhaps anyone he comes into contact with. He is abusing his office in a manner that diminishes all of us." Her voice, always so serene, was shaking with the force of her anger. "To ignore this threat would be indefensible. It is imperative that he be brought to justice before he can harm—anyone."

Roarke realized she was right, and felt a fresh guilt: he had been so focused on the danger to Cara it hadn't occurred to him that with an obvious sadist like Ortiz, other women might be in danger.

"I'm in Palm Desert," he confessed.

"Of course," she replied softly.

He was about to speak when the lights snapped on in Ortiz's living room. Even from a distance, Roarke could see him grabbing his coat, heading for the hallway to the front door.

Roarke whispered to Singh, "I have eyes on Ortiz. He's on the move."

He shoved his phone in his pocket and ran for his car.

Chapter Thirty-Six

Isla Vista was in full party mode. Blowouts raged at every other house on the block. Strings of red lights festooned the yards and patios, along with clusters of heart-shaped balloons, laser strobes, mirror balls. Students and civilians lined the sidewalks, hoping to get past the yard guards into the houses.

Jade and Kris pushed their way through the chaos in the streets, weaving through the mass of young humanity toward the Tau house. The ground under their feet rumbled like a small earthquake with the combined force of dozens of sound systems, bass turned up to the max.

Jade's snakeskin costume was well hidden under a light coat. No point in drawing attention to herself until she was inside. Not that anyone was likely to take note of her in this chaos. Especially because the majority of people were already stumbling drunk.

Which made all of this so much easier.

Her eyes focused ahead on the four-frat-house complex.

Dudebros guarded each gateway, with backed-up masses of hopeful partygoers waiting in line. The sorting process was obvious even from a distance. Sorority girls in lingerie got in, after a whole lot of ogling. Guys in groups of more than two were turned away.

As they neared the house, Kris grabbed Jade's arm. She was suddenly white as a sheet, breathing shallowly. "Wait. Wait. You don't have to. Maybe we should just go back."

"I've got this," Jade muttered. "Hold up." She pulled Kris into the shadows between two buildings. In the semidark, she turned her back to the street and fished the snuff bottle on its chain from between her breasts. She dipped the spoon, snorted powder, felt the tingly rush . . .

And feels herself blasted into the absolute present. Her eyes gleam as she wipes her nose.

Are you ready for me, asshole? Tonight's your unlucky night.

She slips off her coat and hands it over to Kris. "I'll text you."

Getting into the party is no big. She's dressed like a hooker and underage, the biggest frat-boy bait there is. She can see the door guards drooling as she slinks up to the gate in her glimmering bodysuit.

One of the guards leers at her while he stamps a red heart on her hand. Kris's story flashes through her mind: *She had these—Ks—stamped on her back.*

Yeah, Jade knows something about branding.

She moves past the guards, through the wide front doorway into the hall. The party is ear-crushingly loud. The strobe lights are blinding. The pounding of the speakers is like being compressed in some factory grinder.

In this crush of humanity there is no such thing as walking. Instead, she lets herself be carried by the human current, into a dark room throbbing with techno, jam-packed with lingerie-clad college students. Sorority sluts in their Vicky's Secret sequins, dudes in their Calvins, reeking of beer and sweat. Despite her level of undress it is stiflingly hot.

Guys shout in her face and she just smiles. She can't hear a thing over the sucky electronic music.

Kegs are lined up on a long table. The floor is already wet with spilled drinks and God knows what else, so disgusting no one would dare take off their shoes. Not just the floor, *everything* is covered in some unidentifiable sticky liquid. She knows the bathroom will be grotesque—puke in the sink and piss in the shower.

She thanks her lucky stars she's high. There is no other way this would be bearable. You'd have to be wasted out of your mind to think this was any kind of good time.

She forces her mind off the squalor and makes herself inhabit her role, moving her body with the sinuousness of a snake. She sees jaws dropping around her as she glides through the crowd, taking in her surroundings in quick flashes as the body-thumping techno music blares.

A swaying crowd around the beer pong table.

Two girls making out on the dance floor while a circle of frat bros records them with iPhones.

Another group of guys pointing at a younger girl, chanting, "Fresh. Fresh. Fresh."

Of course people are texting and snapping selfies like mad. 'Cause it's irrelevant whether or not you're having a good time as long as it *looks* like you're having a good time on Snapchat and the Gram.

She glances into another room, sees three sorority girls wall-twerking—doing handstands against the wall and pumping their hips frantically. Another sorority chick is bent over, hands on the floor, grinding her ass as a frat boy dry humps her from behind.

Jade knows she's done worse—way, way worse—but the sight fills her with disgust. It occurs to her that any kind of performing for men, boys, fucktards, whatever you wanted to call them, was doing way more harm than good.

But she has no time to dwell on that. She has work to do.

She steels herself and moves into the crowd in the main room.

Being alone, she is instantly targeted. Which is the point. She can feel the ripple of electricity as she pushes her way through the crowd.

She is a glittering serpent among all the trashy Victoria's Secret Angels. Male eyes follow her and female rivals rage in her wake. She has left them all in the dust.

It is so much more than the costume.

After all—the whole party is packed with amateurs.

What Jade knows comes from volumes of hard-earned experience. She knows the ultimate secret: that most people—men and women— are subs. Men who are all dom—those are the assholes you have to look out for. She's had to deal with more than her share of those. And most men who are that kind can only pull that shit on kids, teenagers, or junkies. But men who are on the sub scale—all you have to do is take charge. And you can take charge with just a look—a look that says, *"On your knees."*

She doesn't know which Topher will be, dom or sub. But she's looking forward to finding out. Either way, she's ready to play.

She finally spots him as he steps up to a long table to play flip cup amid cheers from some of the bros and most of the girls.

The two teams of three take their places at each end of the table. At the signal, Topher and the head player of the other team lift their full cups, chug beer. Topher gets to the bottom first, places his empty cup faceup on the edge of the table, and uses one hand to flip the cup over so it lands face down. He sticks the cup on his first try, to a huge cheer, and the next player on the team takes over, chugging his cup . . .

Right.

Is there a stupider game on the planet?

But Jade watches as if old Toph is the most fascinating thing on earth. Watches him, until he feels her eyes on him and turns to look. She lets him catch her looking. That's the key, to stare right into them. Works every time.

And he sees her, all right.

She's a pro. Come on hot, then look away, pretend to falter, to be out of her depth.

She sees him start to strut, show off a little. Voice louder, gestures bigger. *God, so easy.*

She watches the whole game. When he wins, because of course he wins, the crowd jeers and cheers.

She makes a point of disappearing into the crowd as his friends are doing that pileup thing guys do, 'cause when do they ever pass up a chance to grope each other? So when he looks for her, which she knows he does, she is gone.

Let him find her, think he's the one in control.

She moves into the one dancing room that isn't playing shitty house music. Looks over the room, chooses her spot. A table solid enough to hold her weight, against a wall so she'll be even more noticeable.

Yeah, that'll do.

She sways along with a couple of dudes trying to coax her onto the floor, and then she sees him come into the room. Pretending not to be looking for her.

Right, dude. You just keep pretending that.

And at that same second, an actual good song starts.

Meant to be.

She makes eye contact with King Frat Dude so there's no doubt at all that she's doing this for him. And then she steps up on the table, all shimmering fish-scale legs and glittery fuck-me heels, and starts to work it. Dancing against the wall. Body waves, rippling, sinuous.

The whole room is watching her, guys howling and cheering, girls fuming.

Her hands are all over herself, her neck, her tits, her thighs.

Oh, he's watching now.

Her eyes graze his a time or two, letting him know who this dance is for.

All for you, douchebag.

As the song ends she throws back her head and pins herself, legs spread, against the wall.

The whole room—well, half of it—explodes in cheers.

She holds his gaze across the room—then she reaches out her hands to two guys below her and they lift her down.

Topher comes to her, silent, authoritative, the crowd on the dance floor parting for him like he's some frat boy Moses. He stops in front of Jade, looking down at her, and they start to dance without speaking.

His hands move slow circles on her hips. She stares up into his eyes, daring him.

He bends to her and they are mouth to mouth. She sucks his tongue into her mouth, lets him taste the coke on her tongue.

"Whoa . . ." he breathes, and plunges deeper. She pushes him away with one hand on his chest . . . then slides a finger into his mouth for him to suck.

He licks her finger, licks her palm, groans with pleasure.

It's not just sex, this. He's just discovered she's dipped her nail in powder.

"Oh, that's what I'm talking about," he purrs.

"Want more?" she challenges him, letting her tone convey layers of meaning. He stares back into her eyes.

"I want it all."

She runs her hand down her hip to one of the cutouts of the bodysuit. Besides the vial around her neck, she has another stashed there, a professional little tube.

She pulls it out, discreetly flashes it at him in the palm of her hand. "Know someplace quiet we can share this?"

Chapter Thirty-Seven

Roarke followed in the rental car as Ortiz drove his oversized SUV through the dark. The silhouette of the San Jacinto and Santa Rosa mountain ranges towered above them, massive and black against the deep blue of sky, outlined by the silver of the moon.

Ortiz motored down one of the seemingly endless highways parallel to the mountains, past more golf courses, strip malls under development. He turned on a side street and pulled into the parking lot of a restaurant with a blinking neon cactus sign under the word NOPAL.

Roarke idled his rental car outside the parking lot, watching Ortiz park near the front of the lot, then get out and go inside the restaurant.

Only then did Roarke turn into the parking lot and park in a space with a view of the front door and Ortiz's SUV.

He sat in the car in the dark, itching to go in.

Is he meeting someone? Is that someone already in there?

Chances were there would be a vestibule inside the front door, where Roarke would be hidden from the diners in the main room. He could look over the scene without being spotted.

He reached for the door handle—

Wait, instinct whispered.

He sat back in the seat. Slow minutes passed.

He was just reaching for the door again when another car pulled into the lot. A bulky Tahoe that got Roarke's attention.

The driver parked at the edge of the parking lot, and a man stepped out of the car. Dressed in khaki trousers and a sport coat, thick around the middle—but he came out of the vehicle with a "don't fuck with me" authority and was instantly scanning the lot in a wide sweep, taking in his surroundings. He shut the car door behind him while still keeping an eye on the whole lot. And there was the unmistakable give-away—his right elbow kept bent and slightly pressed into his body, guarding the pistol in his waistband.

Law enforcement. Present or ex, but yeah, this guy is a cop.

This is the one Ortiz is meeting.

The man walked toward the restaurant, back straight, a heavy and confident stride.

Roarke waited for him to open the front door, to disappear into the restaurant. And then he got out of his own car and followed.

At the restaurant entrance, he held his breath and opened the door, took a quick glance into the entry.

He'd been right: there was a waiting area with a few leather benches, the cashier's counter, and the hostess's stand.

He stopped at the stand and reached for a takeout menu, then moved over to a wall, pretending to study it. With his head bent over the menu, he looked to the side, scanning through an archway into the dining room. Sure enough, Ortiz was in a back booth, with the new guy seated opposite him. They were already deep in conversation, Ortiz's body language tense and agitated, the cop/ex-cop's defensive.

The hostess breezed by Roarke, leading a couple into the dining room. While she was occupied, he walked back out the front door.

In the parking lot, he pulled out his phone and crossed over to take photos of the new guy's vehicle and license plate. He checked quickly through the windows to see if there was anything revealing on the seats or in the seat wells—but the car was well kept, barren of any interesting evidence.

Roarke turned away and returned to his rental car. Inside, he phoned Singh to report.

"I need you to run a plate on a Chevy Tahoe." He gave her the number.

"One moment," she told him, and he waited in silence, watching the front door of the restaurant.

In no time, Singh was back on.

"The owner of the Tahoe is Corey Parker. DOB 4-20-62. Resident of Rancho Mirage, home address 4525 Mariposa Avenue. Parker is formerly of the Palm Desert branch of the Riverside Sheriff's Department. Retired four years ago, now does private investigation work. I am sending a file."

Roarke told her, "Ortiz is meeting with Parker right now, in a restaurant near Ortiz's house."

Hiring him to track Cara? Or is it something else? He'd put out a general call for anyone willing to go hunting for her . . . so what is he doing with a PI now?

"Chief?" Singh asked.

Roarke realized he'd been silent for some moments, lost in his own dark thoughts.

"I'm here."

"Do you intend to speak with this Parker?"

Roarke didn't see any use in pretending. "I'm thinking about it."

Instead of warning him against it, Singh continued carefully. "If perhaps Parker is communicating with these—bounty hunters—and you were able to obtain an email for them, I would be able to retrieve their IP address by sending an email to them, ostensibly from Detective

Ortiz. I could put a pixel inside the email that would give me the IP if the recipient opened that email. And that would give us an idea of the hunters' current location."

Cyber was not Roarke's field of expertise. "So, you would send an email to them from Ortiz's email address?"

"I could, if I hacked his account," Singh answered dubiously. "However, Ortiz is being quite cautious, using routers, encryption, scrambling his IP. He will certainly be monitoring for any hacking attempts. What we need is to induce him to send an email to *us*, to an account I will then have control over. As for the hunters, judging from their communications, these men are . . ." she paused, as if searching. "Rather dim bulbs. I believe I could compose an email they would open."

I bet you can, Roarke thought, with a flash of amusement.

The amusement didn't last. He fell into silence, and a mounting dread. Were the bounty hunters on the road with Cara right now? Bringing her back to Ortiz, subjecting her to inconceivable horrors along the way?

His whole drive here he had been sick with escalating anxiety. He felt danger.

Singh spoke out of nowhere. She was still on the line. "Why is it, do you think, that Lindstrom does not use firearms?"

Roarke was startled. It was a question he was drawn back to again and again.

It wasn't entirely true to say that she didn't use guns. His first real encounter with her had taken place just three months ago, at an abandoned cement plant being used by a drug and human trafficking ring. There had been a shootout, and Cara had taken an automatic rifle off one of the gang members. Her proficiency with the weapon made him think it wasn't the first time she'd held one.

But the team had never turned up another instance of her using a gun to kill. She used knives, fire, up-close accidents, and of course her default M.O.: a straight razor to the throat.

It was exactly why his fear for her was so elevated now. These mouth-breathers were hunting Cara—and not with knives. She was without question a ruthless, skilled fighter, but all the skill and smarts in the world didn't mean much against a high-powered rifle.

He turned the question back to Singh. "Why do you think she doesn't?"

There was a silence on the line.

"I do not know what occupies Cara's head. But I know I could not be a field agent. I have my service weapon. I am certified. I keep my training current. But I never pick it up without feeling . . ." She hesitated. "Diminished."

Roarke found himself nodding. It wasn't the first time he'd thought that Singh had an understanding of Cara that went far beyond what he could grasp.

He was about to respond, when the restaurant door opened and Ortiz walked out.

"Ortiz just exited the restaurant," he said, low.

His hand slipped to the holster of his Glock. It was all he could do not to leap out of the car, jump the man, shove him against the wall . . .

But he remained seated. He knew what Ortiz was: the worst kind of predator. But he also knew where to find him. And he was betting he had a better shot at answers with a private citizen like Parker.

So as Ortiz drove off, Roarke sat back in the rental car, watching.

It was a few moments later, but when Parker emerged from the door and walked out through the parking lot toward his car, Roarke was ready.

Parker beeped the Chevy open, reached for the door handle—

And froze, as Roarke stepped out of the dark, holding his credentials out.

"We're taking a walk."

Parker pulled himself up, blustered, "Like hell. Why would I—"

"So that I don't arrest you for that little meeting you just had, there."

"Arrest me, motherfucker," Parker snarled. "And get me a lawyer."

Roarke refrained from backhanding him. "Oh, I'll be happy to arrest you. Let me spell this out for you. It's Friday night of a long, long weekend. I can make sure you're in federal custody for the whole two days and three very long nights." He knew he didn't have to remind Parker how well retired law enforcement does in lock up. Even if Parker or Ortiz had local pull, it wasn't a chance any man in his right mind would want to take.

Roarke continued, "Then I'm going to charge you with abduction, sex trafficking, and criminal conspiracy."

He stopped, let it sink in. Parker had gone very still.

Roarke lifted his hands. "Or—we can talk, like reasonable people. We can come to an understanding. Entirely up to you."

Parker stood, fuming, but he knew he was busted. Roarke could tell from his reaction—he didn't even have to go into detail on what he had on the PI, which meant what Ortiz and Parker were up to was big enough to scare Parker into compliance.

"So what'll it be?" he asked.

Parker ground out through his teeth, "Let's talk."

"I hoped you'd see it that way." Roarke nodded out toward the dark desert beyond the parking lot. "After you."

Chapter Thirty-Eight

It is all going exactly as planned.

Jade and Topher walk, drunk, dizzy, down the few short blocks to Del Playa, past other drunk, dizzy people. Stopping every block to make out, dry humping. She massages him through his jeans, enough so he gets a taste of how very good she is. But she steps away every time, leaving him groaning in her wake.

Del Playa is block-to-block people, with music blasting from every other yard and balcony, but Topher grabs her hand and steers her expertly, if unsteadily, through the crowd to the KAT house.

Inside is more pulsing music, but compared to the chaos of the main house, this one is a sanctuary. This house is dark, lit only by random strings of Christmas and red chili lights. And it has nowhere near the volume of people. This is the fuck palace, the private party for the upper echelons of the fraternity.

Of course he takes her straight to the Basement. Leads her down a narrow flight of stairs, opens the door.

Jade's eyes skim her surroundings quickly.

It's a long rectangle of a room, with a wall of glass opposite, looking onto the deck and the shimmering ocean beyond. She can hear the rumble of the waves below the house.

There are candles, tiny red lights, and couples in various stages of undress. A built-in bar area: sink, cabinets, island counter crowded with bottles and cups. Couches and armchairs occupied by people making out, one pair openly humping on a sofa. And the pot smoke is thick enough to choke a horse.

Topher's the boss. When he orders, "Everybody out," they all grab for their clothes and scramble out of the way.

The ensuing disorder gives Jade all the time she needs.

When the last throbbing, disgruntled couple is gone, he locks the door and turns.

She has already cleaned a space on the bar, used a convenient plate of mirror to cut some lines.

And now his drink has something extra. She's spiked a shot of tequila with roofies. She knows it's his drink tonight because she's been tasting it when they kiss. Not that it matters. By now he'll take anything she gives him.

She presses a shot glass into his hand and they down the shooters. Then she passes him the mirror and a rolled-up bill.

He hoovers a line up greedily as she watches.

The lines are from the vial she cut with Rohypnol. And that's not his first dose of the night, either. The bumps he did on their walk down to Del Playa were from that same vial. She doesn't know exactly how much he's had, but it's slowing him down. His coordination has been deteriorating by the minute.

She pushes into him, dancing against him teasingly, stroking him off at the same time.

And smiles as he wobbles, stumbles.

She swings him around, pushes him down on the couch, straddles him. She has another spiked shot in her hand, but at this point he doesn't look like he can hold it without spilling. So she takes the tequila into her mouth—and then bends over him, kissing him, gushing the shot into his mouth so he swallows yet another dose.

On top of the rest, possibly enough to kill him already.

His head drops back against the armrest. She rides him, grinding against him, and he's breathing unevenly. "Oh yeah, baby . . . yeah . . ."

And then he's silent.

Chapter Thirty-Nine

She is slung over someone's back, being carried. Someone is climbing a rock face, seemingly straight up. The figure is slight, mere flesh and bone, but unbelievably strong. She hears muttering from whoever is carrying her.

She knows it can't be happening. But whatever is going on, she is too weak to struggle.

She gives in to whatever it is, and slips back into unconsciousness.

Chapter Forty

Roarke and Parker walked in silence, out from the lights of the parking lot, away from the blinking neon of the cactus sign, twisting past sagebrush and real cactus. Roarke caught a whiff of creosote in the wind.

The music of the restaurant bar faded behind them and there was only the soft crunch of sand beneath their feet. The night was clear and the moon nearing full. It was no hard thing to find their way between the scrub, the delicate fronds of mimosa, the occasional Joshua tree.

Finally they were far away from the sight of the last cars, with the moon and stars the only light. Roarke stopped and motioned to a large flat rock. "Have a seat."

Parker did as he was told, reluctantly. And Roarke rattled off what Singh had found out about him. "Your name is Corey Lewis Parker. You served in the Riverside County Sheriff's Department from 1984 to 2013. You worked with Detective Gilbert Ortiz in Major Crimes from 2005 to 2007. You're now a private investigator, company name

Private Solutions." He paused. "And you're doing a little work for Ortiz under the table."

"Sounds like you know it all," Parker sneered.

"I want to know what Ortiz hired you to do."

Parker was truculently silent.

"Lockup, then?" Roarke suggested.

Parker grimaced. "I'm investigating responses to—" He broke off.

"His bounty offer?" Roarke said. "Conspiracy to commit murder?"

Parker smoldered. Roarke looked out into the dark of night, and saw a Joshua tree.

For a moment he could almost see the skeleton of a girl.

Ivy.

He turned back to Parker, with barely contained fury. "A serving law enforcement official offers a bounty for rape and murder, and you're profiting from that." His voice dropped, low and deadly. "Tell me why I shouldn't just kill you now."

For the first time, Parker looked truly worried.

"Oh—you're *getting* it now, aren't you? You could really not come out of this alive."

Parker spoke fast. "I'm hired to check out people who respond to—the offer. I do background checks."

"What are you checking for, specifically?"

Another long pause. "Criminal convictions. Firearms ownership. A history of activity in—certain online forums."

Roarke didn't have to ask what online forums he was talking about. "I take it none of those are disqualifiers. That's a list of the minimum requirements."

Parker gritted his teeth, but nodded.

"So you're looking for people with records."

For blackmail purposes, and to increase the chances that respondents would actually follow through.

"Yeah," Parker answered.

"And these firearms—I'm guessing they're not legal."

"Right."

Roarke paced on the sand, a million jagged stars above him. "And if candidates pass that threshold?"

Another pause. "Then my understanding is that certain information is passed on to those individuals."

Roarke felt sick. "Information like . . . location? What?"

Parker shifted on the rock. "I don't know. That's not my part of this."

"He's recruiting hunters to bring him Cara Lindstrom."

"Yes."

"Does Ortiz have Lindstrom right now? Does somebody?"

"I don't know."

Roarke felt anger well up in him, and before he could check himself, he was dragging Parker up by his collar.

"I swear I don't," Parker choked out. "All I do is screen applicants."

"I want a list of these *applicants*."

"All right. Yes. Yes."

"I mean *now*."

Roarke pushed Parker away and the man fumbled for his phone. He tapped, scrolled, finally handed it over to Roarke.

There were eight names, with addresses in California, Nevada, Arizona.

Roarke swallowed, gathered himself. "You've checked all of these men out in person?"

"Yeah."

"And then what?"

"I do a report. Living situation, family situation, finances. How they present."

"How much has Ortiz paid out for this, so far?"

"Upwards of twenty-five grand."

Roarke didn't react, but he was shaken. It was a steep price for . . .

For what? Revenge? Rape? The opportunity for a private murder?

The chill he felt had nothing to do with the desert night.

"Send it all to me. Everything you have. Now."

Roarke gave Parker an email address. It was a Hotmail account that Roarke had as yet never used. He'd set it up when he'd taken his hiatus, just in case. *In case of what?* was an interesting question. But the account wasn't in his own name, or any variation of it.

He watched as Parker fiddled with his phone again. When Parker looked up, nodded, Roarke checked the email account, opened the file, read enough to know that Parker had sent the real thing. Then he turned back to the man.

"Why were you meeting Ortiz tonight?"

"There's another couple applicants that came in today he wants screened."

The posters from the forum?

"Are those on the list?"

"Yeah. The last two."

"You always meet Ortiz in person?" It seemed an unnecessarily risky way to do this kind of business.

Parker frowned. "We don't, usually. Not since the first time."

"So why did you meet in person tonight?"

Parker looked honestly bemused. "I'm not sure."

"Guess," Roarke said tightly.

"Ortiz has gone paranoid," Parker admitted. "Thinks he's being monitored. Wants to know who he's talking to."

It was the first truly spontaneous thing Parker had said that night. It was interesting. Roarke believed him. And now he saw an opening to get the contact Singh said they needed.

"All right. You're going to get back to your employer and clear your latest potential clients for contact. The guys ticked every box, passed with flying colors. Except—you're going to give Ortiz a new email to use to send information to 'them' from now on. *My* email. If I'm not contacted in the next twelve hours, I'm kicking down your door with a warrant for your arrest for criminal conspiracy. And you're going straight to lockup. Are we clear?"

Parker gave a sullen nod.

"I have your name. I have your address. I have your online accounts. I have your phone number. You are now under twenty-four-seven surveillance. Any news on Lindstrom, I expect to hear it from you immediately. Any move you make to contact Ortiz will be monitored. Don't fuck up or I'll make you regret it for the rest of your life. That's a promise."

Roarke walked the PI back to the parking lot, staying at a distance behind Parker. He watched as Parker got into his vehicle, drove the SUV off.

Back inside his car, he phoned Singh.

"Ortiz is using Parker to screen hunters. I've got a list of men he's met with and passed on to Ortiz, and their contact information. I think the last two are the ones who posted in the forum today."

Roarke paused. Singh answered his unspoken question simply, "Send me the list."

"Thank you, Singh."

He ended the call, and stood alone in the moonlight. And hoped he was not already too late.

Chapter Forty-One

J ade sits on top of Topher, not moving, staring down at him. His breathing becomes longer, deeper, labored.

She stands up, watching him. He doesn't move.

Now she is free to drift around the room. She takes the vial from between her breasts, the unspiked vial, and bumps.

She stumbles. And giggles.

Okay, that last blast may have been a mistake.

There is movement in the corner of her eye, in the dark beside the wall opposite the bar. A flash of bony white.

She spins . . . and sees the skeleton hovering against a black curtain.

She gasps.

The vision fades.

She breathes in, focuses.

And realizes that the black curtain is draped across the wall where no window would be.

She frowns, walks unsteadily across the room . . . reaches out and pulls the curtain aside . . .

And stares up at the Trophy Wall.

Printed-out shots on plain paper, glossy paper: the collage of female body parts. Naked breasts and thighs with Greek letters drawn on in marker. Beaver shots. Naked girls passed out, being fingered, being fucked.

Fury rises in her, rushing though her veins, blinding her.

She sees flashes in her mind, camera flashes. Danny shooting photos for the online sites, Backdoor, Redlight. Ass shots, breast shots.

Do it and smile. Do it or get beaten.

She chokes out a strangled cry of rage. She turns in the room . . . then strides to the bar, looking over it, her face burning up.

She starts yanking out drawers, scrabbling through them . . . until she finds what she's looking for.

She straightens up, holding the knife.

She walks deliberately over and looks down at Topher, hard. And the red Christmas lights gleam on the blade.

"Now it's your turn, motherfucker," she tells him softly.

Chapter Forty-Two

Cara wakes to the feathery brush of snow on her cheeks.

Then nausea overtakes her and she sits upright with the overwhelming need to vomit. Suddenly she feels a slender dry hand on her head, and someone is holding a bowl for her to be sick into.

She is sick for a long time, vomiting up all the bile from her dreams, from the hunters, from the photos, from the world.

Finally the retching stops. She is empty and shaking. But the sickness is gone.

Her face is cold, but the rest of her is warm. The pain in her ribs has faded to a dull ache.

She opens her eyes. She is on a bed of piled furs, buried in them. Around her, a curve of rock wall creates a cave. Beyond the semicircle she can see straight into the snowstorm, as if she is in the eye of it, high, high up in the sky.

A tiny, ancient woman stands on the rock floor of the cave, looking at her. She wears antelope robes and a necklace of bones around her neck.

Cara is suddenly shot through with terror, her mouth dry as dust.

This is a different fear from what she felt with the hunters. It is primordial.

The sheer power emanating from this being is terrifying. This is not human. It is goddess energy. It is not real, and it is far, far beyond real. It is mind cracking.

The old woman takes the bowl and goes to the edge of the rock and throws it out. All of the sick turns to dark ash as it floats down into what Cara now knows is the canyon, hundreds of feet below.

It is not the color and shape of the rock that tells her where she is. It is not the dizzying height, or the expanse of snowy sky.

It is that small, wizened, robed figure.

She is on the spire of Spider Rock.

She feels her mind straining to encompass it, feels her mind on the verge of breaking with the strain.

The old woman turns to Cara. Cara drops her eyes. She cannot look into this being's face. It takes her breath away. She has always lived on the border of sanity, but now it seems she has finally crossed over. Or perhaps she is dead.

She hears the ancient, bony voice in her mind, not aloud.

Breathe, child, Spider Grandmother says. *There is work to do.*

DAY FOUR

Chapter Forty-Three

Cara huddles in the bed of furs, dreaming awake. The naked bodies of the hunters are piled in a corner of the cave circle, on top of a heap of other bones.

The old woman sits on a stool, rocking slightly back and forth. Her words come relentlessly in Cara's mind.

It is not your time to die yet, granddaughter.

The words make Cara colder than the ice around her: equal blessing and curse.

You have protected the canyon. You have the thanks of the First People.

Beneath the rush of pride and gratitude, Cara understands that there is an ultimatum coming.

But you cannot stay here. Here is no longer safe for you. And it is not your land.

Cara knows this is true, and fair. But the fear of what is outside, waiting for her, is almost too much to bear.

The goddess's voice is implacable.

The white rapists are in charge now. They are raping the Mother, and all the mothers, and all the daughters. They are raping the land. They are raping the planet. All of us. All of us.

There is wetness on Cara's cheeks, on her throat.

"I can't. Grandmother, I can't—"

Listen. I will tell you what may be.

Cara swallows, silences herself. The tiny, magnificent being continues.

A woman can put a stop to the Great Pretender. A woman who wears the white man's skin. Who can walk the corridors of power.

Cara struggles to understand, struggles to answer with her mind.

But how can I? When everyone knows my name—

Do not think, Spider Grandmother orders. *Listen. You will know when you know. They have woven a web. Cut one thread and the whole will unravel.*

The old woman's eyes are bottomless, shining like obsidian.

The young are rising up. You must not fail them.

Cara gasps as the pile of corpses in the corner suddenly moves.

The hunter on top is still alive.

The old woman goes over to him and kicks him viciously, then grabs his arm. Cara can hear bones snap as the shoulder breaks from the ancient one's sheer, unthinking strength. She extends his arm to Cara.

Take his hand.

Cara flinches back.

Take it. You must read the secrets of the Glittering box. You will need what is inside.

In some part of her mind, Cara knows what she is saying. As long as the hunter is alive, she can use his thumb to unlock his phone.

She struggles to her feet. The furs fall away and she realizes that underneath them she is wearing a hunter's parka.

The pockets are heavy, and when she slides her hand into the right one, she finds a phone inside.

She approaches the pile of bodies on shaking legs, and kneels beside it.

The hunter on top is nearly blue with cold, more corpse than human, but she can see his lips move in a shallow breath.

She reaches for his arm, grasps his hand, uses his thumb on the Home button.

Then she drops the almost-dead arm and scrambles backward in the snow, away from the bones and corpses.

She looks down at the unlocked phone. And taps the Settings button to remove all security.

Chapter Forty-Four

R oarke jolted awake.

His dream slipped away from him like a wave retreating on sand. He kept his eyes shut and reached for it with his mind.

His first thought was Mother Doctor. Some warm and slightly terrifying female presence . . .

And then it was gone, replaced by awareness of cold, stiffness, a cramp in his neck. He opened his eyes. He was in the front seat of his rental SUV. Through the windshield, dawn shimmered in silver and purple over the sheer cliff wall of the San Jacinto/Santa Rosa range.

He sat up gingerly, feeling every muscle in his body complain. He'd slept in the car, down the street from Ortiz's house.

Okay, this is absolutely off the rails.

But Ortiz's SUV was still in his carport. He hadn't gone out last night. No one had come to him.

Cara was probably safe. For now.

"Get a grip," he told himself softly.

But he reached for his phone, checked the email inbox he'd given Parker.

His heart started to race as he saw there was an email from an account he didn't recognize. From Ortiz. It had to be. No one else but Parker had this email address.

He clicked on it, read the terse message.

> Tuesday delivery will work. Send update when package is in hand.

"When package is in hand."

When. The rush of relief was instant.

So the bounty hunters didn't have her yet.

And this email proved he'd scared Parker into passing off the dummy email account to Ortiz as belonging to one of the hunters.

He would see any message from Ortiz with instructions for delivery. And Singh could get to work monitoring Ortiz's communications and tracking the hunters' location.

And then what? his mind whispered.

He couldn't go after her.

He *couldn't* go after her.

If there was anything he knew about Cara, it was that she could take care of herself. And weirdly, the sense of danger that had gripped him for most of the day yesterday had dissipated. Maybe all it had taken was to see Ortiz for himself.

"Do your job," he told himself softly. And like it or not, the job was in Santa Barbara. He'd let Singh do the tracking for now.

There was also the best reason for going back to Santa Barbara. Leaving meant that he wouldn't be tempted to do something truly insane, like kill Ortiz.

It was early Saturday morning; there would be the lightest traffic he could hope for in Southern California. He could take a break somewhere along the way. There were truck stops on the 101 that had showers.

He took one more hard look at Ortiz's house . . . then turned the key in the ignition and hit the road.

Somewhere near Riverside, he stopped for coffee and a bathroom, washed his face, and stretched his legs as he waited for a breakfast burrito.

He'd only been back on the freeway twenty minutes when his phone buzzed.

He grabbed for it, expecting Singh. But it was Epps' voice on the other end.

"That frat boy president? Stephens? He went missing last night."

Chapter Forty-Five

The road to the Stephens home was up the same canyon road as the route to Andrea Janovy's. As Roarke drove past the Mission again, he found the proximity vaguely worrisome. If Topher really was missing, Roarke himself may have given Janovy and/or Bitch ammunition to go after the kid, by mentioning the KAT house to Janovy to begin with.

But that would mean Janovy had actually found something incriminating on Topher.

Following the satnav's tinny prompting, he turned up a winding road. The Stephens home was a newish Santa Barbara mansion perched on a cliff, looming over the city. Roarke rolled up in the looped driveway and parked behind Epps' rental car. An unmarked car, clearly a law enforcement fleet model, stuck out like a sore thumb beside a couple of gleaming luxury vehicles.

As Roarke got out of his own rental car, he checked the dummy email account again. Nothing more from Ortiz or the bounty hunters. Or from Singh.

He felt the relief of it. Then forced himself to put his anxiety for Cara out of his mind.

A housekeeper opened the front door, and Epps was right behind her to meet him. They stepped into a vast entry hall with marble floors and columns, a double curved staircase. More like a museum lobby than a private home.

Epps stepped close to Roarke, spoke quickly, low. "There's a detective from Santa Barbara Sheriff's CID here, too. And Sandler. He was here before I was. 'Supporting the family,' the man says. They called him first, then he called me, thinking he'd get you, no doubt."

Roarke nodded. "But there's still no ransom demand, no contact from anyone at all claiming to have abducted him?"

"Nothing. Kid didn't show up for Mom's birthday breakfast downtown, that's all, and now they can't get hold of him. Thing is, the Taus had a big blowout last night. Valentine's Day. I don't even want to think about the hangovers, right?" Epps shook his head. "You figure some of those clowns won't wake up till next week. But the Stephenses are about ready to call out the National Guard."

Roarke saw his point. It didn't make any sense.

Epps added, "I sent the Isla Vista cops over to the Tau house to make sure they didn't clean anything up."

"Good work."

"Yeah, you're welcome, but I'm standing down now. I'm sure Mom and Pop will be more comfortable talking to a—ranking agent," Epps said, managing to keep a straight face.

Roarke caught the subtext. "That bad?"

Epps nodded silently toward a framed photo on the wall, a stock political contributor photo of a man in a power suit shaking hands with the new president. Which said it all.

"But hey. They did let me in through the front door."

Topher's parents were in the luxurious living room. Mr. Stephens, he of the political photo, was standing. His wife was seated on a sofa behind him. A perfectly matched couple: tailored, polished, Botoxed. The one percent. Fraternity boys and sorority girls hooked up, got married, and grew up to be this. "Consolidating the wealth" was what Janovy had said.

Kirk Sandler stood at the window, and the powerfully built Latino perched awkwardly in a too-small chair was obviously the sheriff's detective.

All eyes turned toward the door as the agents entered.

Epps made quick introductions. "Mr. Stephens, Mrs. Stephens, Detective Huerte, this is Assistant Special Agent in Charge Roarke."

Stephens nodded at Roarke curtly. The mother was silent and seemed out of it. Roarke took a discreet look at her eyes. Her pupils were tiny. Opiates, he'd bet. Prescription pain pills. Oxy. Percocet.

"Mr. Stephens, Mrs. Stephens, I'm sorry to have to meet under these circumstances. As Agent Epps has no doubt told you, I was on the road—"

"Can we just get to it?" Stephens's voice was an aggrieved whine.

"Of course," Roarke answered. "Here's the thing. It's still morning after what I understand was a big party last night. Yet you seem very convinced that some kind of harm has come to your son."

"Isn't that fucking obvious?" Stephens snarled.

Roarke was impassive. "I'm sorry, sir, but it isn't. Your son is an adult. Technically he's not even a missing person yet."

Stephens flicked a hand at Epps without looking at him. "We've been through this with your man. Topher would never have missed his mother's breakfast."

This bit of hypocrisy was coming from a man who was obviously a product of a frat himself. He had either a short memory or a long history of denial. *How the hell do they know he isn't just passed out somewhere?*

Stephens clearly picked up on Roarke's skepticism. "He hasn't called. He hasn't responded to texts. None of his brothers—his Tau brothers—have seen him."

"And there's been a rash of hostage attempts in the Santa Barbara area over the last six months," Sandler supplied.

Roarke and Epps turned to the sheriff's CID, Detective Huerte. The detective nodded. "That's true. But as I've explained to Mr. and Mrs. Stephens, this doesn't look anything like those ransom scams. What those perps do is track their targets' whereabouts online. When the target is out of contact for whatever reason, they call the target's family and demand an immediate ransom. The callers sometimes represent themselves as members of a drug cartel or corrupt law enforcement. They can be very convincing. But there've been no phone calls here. No ransom demand."

Roarke looked at Stephens. "That doesn't sound related to me. So why are you so sure that it's a hostage situation?"

Stephens bristled. Everything seemed to make this man defensive. "I didn't say it was a hostage situation. I said foul play."

Roarke turned to include Mrs. Stephens with his next question. "Is there a specific reason you think your son would have been targeted for 'foul play'?"

Mrs. Stephens blinked, a small flinch. Mr. Stephens was instantly livid.

"What the hell are you implying?"

"I'm mystified that you're jumping to the conclusion that foul play is involved. You haven't been contacted by anyone claiming that they've hurt your son—"

"The timing says everything. That attack on the colleges and universities specifically targeted fraternity members. Two of the boys in the Tau house were already attacked. The way that mannequin was slashed up . . ." For the first time, Stephens faltered. "And now Topher . . ."

"But you all seem to be seeing that vandalism as having a direct relevance to your son. Why?"

Sandler broke in. "He's the fraternity president. That alone could make him the target of retaliation for any number of slights or grudges."

There was a vague logic to that, although something Stephens had just said bothered Roarke in a way he couldn't put his finger on.

What he was sure of, sure enough to stake his whole reputation on, was that Stephens and Sandler knew a whole lot more about the situation than they were telling.

But he nodded, pretending to go along, and spent the next ten minutes running through the standard questions as if he really believed this bullshit. Hoping that somewhere along the line, someone would slip up and give the agents a clue to what they all were so frantic about.

"Does Topher have a girlfriend? Is he fighting with anyone? Has he received any threats? When was the last time you saw him in person?"

The answers they got back were standard, too. *"No one steady for a while, now. No. No. A week ago."*

Roarke knew that the frat brothers would almost certainly have more useful details about last night and about Topher's habits than his family would know—or admit to. But he continued on to the more emotional questions.

"What was his mood? Was he worried about anything? Anxious? Depressed?"

"You're implying suicide now?" the father demanded, at the same time the mother lifted her chin to respond, "Of course not."

"I wasn't implying suicide, no. But if there is some personal issue we should know about, we've got a much better chance of finding your son before . . . something happens. So if there's anything you can tell us . . ." He allowed his eyes to connect briefly with Mrs. Stephens's gaze. "We need to know."

"We've told you what we know," Mr. Stephens said, with barely concealed rage. "Now what are you going to *do*?"

Roarke turned to Epps. "You have Topher's phone numbers, his home computer, his bank account numbers?"

Epps gave him a nod.

"The Sheriff's Department is monitoring for activity on all those accounts," Huerte added.

Roarke saw Epps grimace. The protocols about adult missing persons never seemed to apply when the missing person was the offspring of wealthy citizens.

But Roarke nodded thanks at Huerte, swiveled back to the parents. "We'll question everyone at the frat house, everyone who attended the party that we can find. We'll work the house as a crime scene."

Even as he said it, he knew how daunting the prospect was. He remembered Isla Vista parties. They were looking at potentially hundreds of attendees.

But that means someone saw something, *right?*

Stephens was looking at him balefully. "Get to it, then."

The agents left the house, but Roarke stopped beside the cars in the driveway.

"Let's wait for Huerte."

Epps nodded, and glanced back at the house wryly. "Well, they're lying their asses off."

"Except for one key thing. They absolutely believe something happened to the kid."

Epps looked at him sharply. "You think Bitch took him? Or—something?"

It was the $64,000 question.

The organization—entity—whatever you wanted to call it—had never done anything like it before. One or more of its affiliates may have committed murder—the pimp and john killings in the Bay Area and in other places around the country remained unsolved. But if Bitch had organized those killings or had anything to do with them other than using the media to call attention to them, that link had not been proven.

Roarke shook his head. "I think if Bitch did something, we'd already know. Why would they take Stephens and not publicize it? And why him? Such a small fish in the grand scheme of things. If they were going to send a statement, wouldn't they pick someone more high profile?"

He was thinking aloud. The truth was, he had no idea. He finished, "I'll tell you for damn sure, though, I'm sick of everyone knowing more than we do."

The agents turned as the front door opened and Detective Huerte came out. He moved down the steps toward the agents, and Roarke stepped forward.

"Detective Huerte, has the Sheriff's Department received any rape complaints against Topher Stephens or the Tau house?"

Huerte glanced at Epps. "I told Agent Epps. Not that I know of. Is there something you guys know?"

"Just that there's bound to be something," Roarke advised him. "If you can dig deeper, that's the place to dig."

"I'll get on it."

"We'll head over to the Tau house and check in later."

Chapter Forty-Six

She wakes up drenched with sweat, weak from the fever. But it has broken.

The light is dim. There is no cave. There is no snow. The walls around her are wood plank, familiar.

She is in the cabin at the bottom of the canyon. In her own bed.

She sits straight up, looks quickly into the corners of the cabin. There is no pile of bodies, either.

No. Those are elsewhere. High at the top of the spire.

She goes cold with the thought of it.

Madness.

She is accustomed to signs and portents, to the physical manifestation of nature, to hidden forces given concrete form. But this . . .

She thinks of the—*Dream? Encounter? Vision?* Approaching it carefully in her mind, not letting the full thing in at once.

Did any of it really happen?

But at least some of it was real. She wears the hunter's parka. And when she slips a hand into the right pocket, there is a phone. In another pocket there is a Taser. No—two of them.

It is all there. Everything but the bodies.

She rises, puts on fresh clothes, goes outside the cabin into blinding sun and white snow. The sky is icy blue, cloudless.

The ancient voice whispers in her head.

You cannot stay here. It is no longer safe for you. And it is not your land.

And there is the prophecy.

She pulls the phone from the pocket of the parka.

Just as in her dream, or whatever it had been, the phone is not locked. Inside is a wealth of information.

She goes back inside the cabin, builds a fire, and sits with the phone to read.

Chapter Forty-Seven

The morning after a rager was never a pretty sight.

Roarke and Epps stood in the middle of Camino Embarcadero and surveyed the party detritus up and down the block. The blizzard of red plastic beverage cups on the sidewalk, in the yards, stuck in bushes. Drying pools of vomit. Scattered clothing. Crushed velvet bunny ears.

"Fun times," Epps said sardonically.

Yeah, fun times. If you like binge drinking to unconsciousness, waking up in a pool of your own or someone else's puke.

Roarke said a silent thanks to the void that he'd left those days far behind him, that by whatever twist of luck or karma he'd escaped the alcoholic gene.

The agents walked through the debris on the street toward the Tau house. The Valentine theme was in the decorations: red ribbons and red lights still hung from palm trees and bushes. Deflating heart-shaped balloons flapped in the wind.

Is Valentine's Day significant, somehow? Roarke wondered.

Beyond that, the particular trouble they were going to have with this investigation was glaringly apparent: the party had been a huge, four-house event. People had been wandering freely from house to house all night long. And to other houses all through Isla Vista, no doubt.

They turned through open gates into the K-Tau patio, walking past a soft drink machine, sound equipment, dildo-shaped light sticks.

Roarke stepped closer to a bush to get a look at a crimson bit of material. It was a red velvet thong. Various other pieces of lingerie hung on another hedge nearby.

He turned, pointed it out. "Looks like someone's been collecting trophies."

Epps' face tightened. They'd seen photos of similarly adorned trees along the California border, where coyotes had hung underwear taken from female victims. The men called them "rape trees."

As the agents waited on the front porch, Roarke pulled out his phone and sneaked another look at the dummy email account. Nothing more from Ortiz or the hunters. Was this good news or bad news? He had no time to think before a sleepy pledge opened the door.

Inside the house was more party carnage. More red cups. The floor was sticky with spillage. Some angel wings were draped on a chair. Red cellophane dangled limply from the lights.

Roarke imagined someone halfway conscious had stashed away the beer bongs and any drug paraphernalia. There had been some basic attempt to clean up, but not by professionals—Epps had said he'd sent orders to stop all cleanup. It was, after all, a potential crime scene.

Downstairs in the dining room, several dozen frat brothers were seated at rows of rectangular tables. Tablecloths had been thrown over the surfaces, but the floors were still tacky.

Looking over the assembled faces, Roarke could see the telltale signs of paralyzing hangovers. Concealing sunglasses. A greenish tinge under the tans. Dry mouths and shaky hands. All the joys of the party life.

He moved to the front of the room and began. "I'm sure you've been told that I'm Agent Roarke and this is Agent Epps. First off, we need to know: Is there anyone else from the house that you can't find?"

One intrepid member stood. He looked as shaky as the rest of them, but gamely stepped up to answer questions. "We've texted and messaged anyone we haven't seen today. All accounted for."

"And what's your name?"

"Alex Foy, sir. Chapter vice president."

Chain of command, Roarke thought. "Was that your idea, Alex?"

"Kirk Sandler asked me to."

Roarke felt Epps shift beside him.

Foy continued. "We've all already talked about it. No one's seen Stephens or gotten any texts or messages from him today."

"All right. What we need to establish is a timeline. When was the last time anyone saw Stephens last night?"

The young men looked around at each other.

"Did anyone see him after midnight?"

The brothers shifted in their chairs. Finally Foy spoke. "It's hard to say what time anything was after a point."

Then a hand went up: a brother with longish, curly black hair. "I came in at maybe quarter to twelve. He was playing beer pong."

Roarke nodded at him. "That's good. Does anyone remember seeing him after that?"

More shifting, no responses.

"Did you see Stephens with any one girl in particular?"

No response.

"Anyone?"

No response.

Roarke felt ire rising, but kept his voice calm. "Listen, guys. You're not doing him any favors by holding out. The more we know about what went on, the better chance we have of figuring out what's really happened here."

Then, just as with the family, the agents went through a series of the usual questions. *"Was he beefing with anyone? Were there any fights that night? Did he insult anyone? Did anyone threaten him?"*

All answers in the negative. So Roarke got more specific.

"This was a Valentine's party. You guys have any special games lined up?"

He might have been imagining it, but it seemed to him that the room got just a little bit more still.

"Just the usual," Foy replied. "Best costumes get free drink tickets, that kind of thing."

"There's a hedge by the front door with ladies' underwear hung on it. What's that about?" Roarke looked around the room. "Whose underwear is it?"

Foy was the first to speak up, defensively. "No one's. It's just decoration, man. It was a lingerie party . . ." His tone implied *"Get it?"*

"Was there a photographer last night?"

Foy gave him a condescending look. "No one official. No need. There's always gonna be pictures."

"Then we want to see everyone's photos of the night. Anything you have. Costume photos taken at the door. Private photos and videos. Things posted to Instagram and Tumblr. No one leaves this room until we get all of it, so get to work."

The guys at the tables started pulling out phones.

Roarke added, "And one more question before you get going on that. Does anyone here think that Stephens being missing has anything to do with the vandalism of two nights ago? The dummy hanging from Storke Tower?"

There were a few surreptitious glances.

"Anyone?" Roarke repeated, his voice harder.

Still silence.

Roarke looked around at the gathered brothers. "Here's what's tiresome. You're all lying. You know it. We know it. We all know it."

He looked to Foy. The young man's face was a polite blank.

"And you need to *get* this. Your friend, president, dudebro, whatever he is to you—may well be in serious shit. And hey, one of you might be next. So somebody has to step up to the plate here—"

He was interrupted midsentence by the buzzing of his phone in his coat pocket. He fished it out, glanced at the screen. Singh.

His adrenaline spiked. He stepped aside, turning his back on the assembled brothers, and put the phone to his ear.

"Yes."

"Chief, you need to turn on the television. Now."

Chapter Forty-Eight

The smell brought him slowly back to consciousness. A musty, mold-like stench. Old wood. Dirt. Something scratchy against his face. And a faint greenish smell, too. There was something vaguely familiar about it, a throwback to childhood.

He was freezing, and hungover as fuck. And then he moved, and felt something hard and cold around his wrists.

His eyes flew open.

Dark. Thin slivers of light high above illuminated floating motes of dust.

He was in a stall. In a horse barn. Lying in a pile of moldy straw. A lump of dry horseshit right beside his face.

"What the fuck?" he raged, jerking up to sitting. The chains linked to the cuffs around his wrists snapped him back.

He was chained to the wall. And he was naked.

In his disorientation, a freaky thing happened. Half-digested memories of Jeffrey Dahmer, John Wayne Gacy, Randy Kraft sped through his brain. And for a moment, his bowels turned to water and he felt primal terror.

Because once in a while . . . just once in a while, rape happened to men, too.

Adrenaline shot through him as he realized he wasn't alone. Two tall shadows loomed above him. Too tall to be real. With white blurs of faces . . .

He scrabbled back, frantically focusing. "Fuuuuuck."

The chains snapped tight, stopping him.

Through the pounding of his heart he finally realized what he was looking at. Two figures sat on the chest-high gate of the stall, dressed in dark capes with hoods—and wearing skull masks.

Jade stared down at Topher from behind her mask.

It had been hard not to just do him right there in the Basement, while he was passed out. Take care of him once and for all. But it was names Kris wanted, so names were what they were going to get. Jade had put the knife away and texted Kris to bring the car to the end of the block and come down to the deck outside—it was easy enough to do from the park side where they'd been that afternoon.

Then she'd roused old Toph with a few blasts of coke—woke him enough to get him on his feet so she and Kris could walk him right out the sliding glass doors. That was the beauty of roofies, after all—as any rapist frat boy could tell you. Total compliance.

They didn't even have to take him out to the street: the sandy trail ran behind the park, along the whole edge of the bluffs. They took him for a little walk, with the moonlight pouring over the waves below them, and the euphoric tingle of the coke and the thrill of it. At the end of the block they veered off the trail and walked him straight to the car.

And in no time he was passed out again in the back seat. But of course they tied him then.

And now that they had him, helpless, chained, Jade felt *good*. *Get yourself a taste of how it feels, you prick.*

The skeleton creatures were very still, looking down on him.

"I think he just pissed his pants," one said to the other.

A feminine voice, for sure. And that made him mad as hell.

"You cunts," he raged. "You are in such fucking trouble you don't even know."

One of them laughed shortly. "Really, dude? Hold on—who's the one in chains here? That would be *you*."

"My dad is going to roast your sorry asses."

"You think Daddy can help you?" the figure jeered. "How's he even gonna know what happened to you?"

The other one added, "Do *you* even have any idea where you are, loser?"

His mind scrambled to remember anything, anything at all about the night before, or how he'd gotten there.

Nothing but a blank.

"Total blank, huh? Yeah, roofies, what a bitch, right?" one of them taunted.

"I wonder what else he doesn't remember?"

"Anything coulda happened. Anything at all. Isn't that right, Toph?"

"I'm gonna kill you," he snarled. But he could hear how slurred his speech was, still. Damn, his head hurt like hell.

The taller one suddenly sounded hard. "Whoa. Really? Maybe you better think before you run your mouth."

Her words turned into a buzz as a wave of nausea overcame him. He leaned over and vomited into the hay beside him.

He could hear laughter above him. "Aw, little Tophie is sick. Went whoopsie."

He finally pulled himself back up to sitting, using the chains around his wrists.

"You bitches . . ." he coughed out, weakly.

One turned to the other, in exaggerated surprise. "Did he just call me Bitch?"

"He did just call you Bitch," the other answered.

"Well, good. He knows our name." The skeleton-thing leaned forward, glared down at him. "These Bitches are the boss of you. You hold zero cards here. So you're gonna want to do exactly what we say. Or it could go real bad, real fast."

"A couple of girls? What are you gonna do, rape me?" He gave them a leer. "Bring it on."

On the stable wall, Jade felt Kris stiffen beside her, with a short, sharp inhale of breath. Jade stared down at their captive . . . and felt a blinding rage. Because that was it, wasn't it? It was what they couldn't do. It was never the same. It would never be the same at all. *Rape* him? She didn't even want to touch him. The sight of him, naked, only made her want to be sick herself.

She shuddered . . . feeling her bile rise.

And for a moment it was her down there in the straw, chained to a post . . . while DeShawn brought guys in, one after another.

She felt a scream rising from the depths of her being . . .

She bit down on her lip hard enough to taste blood, forced the memories away. She lunged forward, sneered down through the skull mask at Topher.

"Us—rape *you*? In your dreams. But there are lots of pervs who'll pay good money to get a piece of a pretty frat boy."

She stared down . . . and saw him hesitate. A fierce triumph blazed through her. *You be afraid, for once. You fucking better be afraid.*

She taunted him, relishing the power. "How fun would that be? Since gang rape is your thing, right?"

"I don't know what the fuck you're talking about," he muttered.

But she'd seen him flinch. And his eyes were wary, now.

Jade nudged Kris, who was still frozen, mute, beside her. "Hell, yeah, we could do that. We could make some serious money off your tender ass. What does the Bible say? 'An eye for an eye, an ass for an ass'? Something like that?"

She made her voice hard.

"You think about that, while we go make some calls."

They both slid off the top of the gate, dropped out of sight on the other side of the stall, leaving Topher alone in the darkness of the barn.

Chapter Forty-Nine

Roarke and Epps stood in the library of the Tau house, watching in disbelief as the president, with his usual preening bombast, announced his nomination for the Supreme Court vacancy.

Everyone had expected a nominee who would be virulently antichoice.

What Roarke hadn't been expecting was a pro-rape appointee.

Not Judge Blackwell, the judge Roarke had just seen in San Diego.

This was worse.

Judge Neville Armstrong was a grotesque example of institutional misogyny. Women's groups had long been keeping lists of his comments about rape survivors and his light sentences and outright dismissals in rape cases.

He'd been forced to resign from the Pennsylvania Supreme Court after a firestorm of criticism rained down on him in response to his remarks that "ninety-nine percent of rape reports are false."

His most infamous ruling, although far from the only outrage, was in a case against a fifty-eight-year-old man accused of raping a thirteen-year-old girl. The defendant had images of child abuse and bestiality on his computer. Thanks to Armstrong he'd walked free with a suspended sentence.

In his comments, Armstrong had declared that the thirteen-year-old victim, who had been sexually abused by a family member, was "predatory and sexually experienced," and that she was "leading the defendant on."

A thirteen-year-old.

And *this* was the guy the new administration was going to try to ram onto the Supreme Court?

Roarke felt, not for the first time, that he'd slid into some kind of alternate reality. He could only begin to imagine how that feeling would be magnified for a woman.

It was so blatantly misogynistic, it seemed like farce.

And there was no doubt that Armstrong would be confirmed. With a Republican majority in Congress, the votes were there.

This is the ticking bomb, Roarke thought. *This is what is going to set it all off.*

And even as he thought it, the news changed. On screen, the anchor looked concerned as he read the copy. "Responses to the nomination have been instantaneous and ominous."

Beside Roarke, Epps' phone pinged with a text message. Roarke looked to him.

"Singh," Epps said, and showed Roarke an embedded link.

The two agents huddled around the phone and Epps clicked through the link.

A grainy video with a black backdrop appeared on the screen.

A skull-masked figure in a black lace dress was seated at a table with piles of paper in front of it.

It looked up, and spoke in a creepy, haglike, computer-generated voice.

"This abomination of a nominee will not be tolerated.

"We are Santa Muerte. We are legion. We are done. We will bring about the death of rape culture by any means necessary. A rapist will die every day until these conditions are met."

The skeleton lifted a sheet of paper and began reading a list of demands in that nerve-jangling hiss of a voice.

"The nomination of Neville Armstrong is withdrawn and he is permanently removed from the bench.

"Every rape kit in the country is tested and all results entered into the Violent Criminal Apprehension Program Database.

"All accused rapists on our list are removed from high school, college, and university campuses.

"All judges on our list are removed from the bench.

"All convicted rapists and abusers on our list are banned from the NFL and NBA, and accused rapists and batterers are suspended."

The skeleton figure looked up from the sheet of paper.

"We have the names. We have the addresses. We will make the lists public so the world knows who they are. Even now, the guilty are being watched, stalked, monitored. Some have been captured. Some have already been killed.

"No rapist is safe. No rape apologist is safe.

"This is a call to arms. This is a war on rape culture.

"The war begins now."

The screen went black.

Epps shifted his eyes from his phone, glanced behind them.

Roarke turned to look. Frat brothers had filtered into the room behind them and were watching their own phones in the same dazed disbelief. There were murmurs.

"They can't do that, right?"

"Are they going to kill people?"

Before he could stop himself, Roarke was turning, and answering, "Yes. They're going to kill people."

And beside him, Epps muttered, "Lock your doors, boys."

Chapter Fifty

Jade had found the stables on one of her long rides in the valley. No one could see the building from any road that she'd been able to find, and she'd never once seen anyone anywhere near it.

She and Kris had set up supplies in the stable master's quarters. Sleeping bags on the bed frame, food, gallon jugs of water, Diet Coke, vodka.

And 4G worked just fine. They were isolated, but not far from civilization.

They sat on the musty sofa they'd covered with blankets, watching the Bitch video in bemusement—and awe.

"No rapist is safe. No rape apologist is safe.

"This is a call to arms. This is a war on rape culture.

"The war begins now."

It was the third time they'd played it.

Kris was wide eyed, stunned. "What the actual fuck? Do they know about . . . ?" She looked toward the wall, in the direction of Topher's stall.

Jade narrowed her eyes, shook her head. "I don't think so. They've been planning some of this for a long time."

"What do you mean?" Kris looked at Jade, and somehow she figured it out. "Wait. You know Bitch?"

"Yeah, I know them. Some of them." Jade thought of Elliott, and felt a brief twinge of—

Guilt?

Well, fuck that. This is happening. Because we're making *it happen.*

Kris was staring at her, processing it. "So was this all . . . what we did . . . a plan?"

"No. I wasn't in on all that—" Jade indicated the phone. "I came looking for whoever did that dummy on the tower, just like I said."

Kris hesitated, then looked away. "I did *a* dummy. But I didn't do the thing on the tower."

Jade raised her eyebrows, waiting.

"I did some stuff that night, but not that. I just let you think I did." Kris looked uncomfortable. "I don't know who did it. But you came to the meeting, and you were asking for people willing to step up. I figured . . ."

"It's cool," Jade reassured her. "That's the way this all works. They put out a call to action, people jump on it in their own way. The whole point of it is, we don't *have* to be hooked up with them. Everyone runs their own campaign. And it ripples. It grows. That's how you scare people. It all starts to feel like something bigger, something exponential . . ." She reached for the word. "Something mythic."

"But this video—"

Jade was on her feet now, unable to keep still. "The video only helps us. People are going to freak the fuck out about ol' Toph being gone. Everyone's going to think he's one of those that they're talking about." She pointed to the phone, and felt a wave of excitement. "And it's suddenly a lot bigger than us."

"So . . ."

"So now we send our own message."

Chapter Fifty-One

As they played the video through again, Roarke saw a lot of confused faces, a growing alarm . . . as some of the assembled frat boys started to process the implication that they might finally be held accountable for their actions.

He nodded to Epps, signaling the door. He had no intention of talking anywhere within earshot.

The boys didn't even notice them leaving.

Outside the Tau house, the agents walked in silence through the littered street, toward the loop of shops and restaurants.

When they were far enough away, Epps spoke. "Kinda starting to look like terrorism now."

Roarke's gut was churning. It was all a bit surreal. Certainly unprecedented. He was having trouble getting his mind around it.

Epps' voice was worried. "You think this is for real? They're planning on following through?"

"It's not just for real," Roarke answered slowly. "This is someone who knows about these programs—knows ViCAP, knows the rape kit backlog, knows percentages."

The video was Bitch. There was no doubt in his mind. And the lists the Santa Muerte figure had talked about—those would be coming soon, if they weren't already being circulated online.

Epps laughed shortly, without humor. "It should put the fear of God into some trolls, at least."

Roarke had to agree. Certainly turning the online threats against the threateners was a brilliant idea. And his long experience, personal and professional, was that bullies are cowards, for the most part. It might well work to make this kind of man watch what he said.

It might start making all men watch what they said.

An uneasy look crossed Epps' face. "They could end up making it worse for women, though. I mean, *all* women."

Roarke had thought the same, himself. "I think the point is that it can't be any worse."

Epps shook his head in something like admiration. "They've been pulling all this together for a long time. Must have been. You can't just come up with this overnight."

Roarke had to agree. *But did* Bitch *take Topher Stephens?* He had a sinking feeling. *Was he the first to die?*

Epps spoke his thoughts aloud. "So the parents are right? Bitch took the kid?"

It was the obvious conclusion. And yet there was that element of doubt. That was the brilliance of Bitch's video. It claimed preemptive credit for every attack on any man anywhere. A page from the terrorist playbook.

Roarke answered, "They were ready for this nomination. They've been waiting for it. Wrote out a script. Probably made most of the video beforehand. But . . . if Stephens was their first victim, it would've been part of the video. We might even be seeing a body."

Epps gave him a sharp look. "You think he's dead?"

Roarke didn't know how to answer that. But his gut feeling—now—was that the kid was in serious trouble.

Epps didn't wait for an answer. "Stephens's parents are going to be losing it. Do we go back up there?"

Roarke didn't need more than a few seconds to decide. "We're not getting anything useful out of that crew. They're so deep in denial they might actually believe all the bullshit they're shoveling."

Just as he was talking, his phone buzzed. Epps raised his eyebrows—but it wasn't Mr. Stephens, or Sandler. Roarke showed him the call on the screen. SAC Reynolds.

The agents moved off the sidewalk and stopped under a tree. Roarke lifted the phone. "I was just about to call you."

"I just got off the phone with Kirk Sandler—"

"I'm sure you did. But all due respect, sir—I'm suspending this investigation until someone decides to be straight with us."

Epps shot him a startled look. Roarke signaled for Epps to keep quiet. He put the phone on speaker so Epps could hear the SAC, and continued. "We were here investigating the disappearance of Topher Stephens even before he disappeared. It might never have happened if someone had filled us in up front."

The SAC cleared his throat. "I didn't have prior knowledge that any of this was going to happen."

Roarke fervently hoped that Reynolds hadn't known, but he wasn't going to let it go. "It's clear that any number of people here in Santa Barbara saw something like this coming. We're not capable of conducting this investigation in the dark."

There was silence on the phone, and Roarke knew he might have pushed his boss over the edge. Then Reynolds spoke.

"No one thought the Stephens kid was going to be abducted. Not that I know of. It was the director who wanted the campus attacks investigated. He was the one who suggested Santa Barbara."

Roarke realized with a jolt that Reynolds meant the director of the Bureau. Epps met his gaze.

Roarke pressed it. "The director wanted us here investigating Bitch. So what does Stephens have to do with it?"

"The director said there were two witnesses at the Tau house. He didn't mention Stephens. I have no idea what he has to do with it."

"Sir, I don't either. His disappearance—it doesn't feel like Bitch to me. But if they really have gone after him, it's undoubtedly because they think he's a sex criminal. Until someone tells us the truth about that, our hands are tied."

"I understand that." Reynolds didn't sound happy about it, but Roarke was relieved that the SAC was going to be reasonable.

"Look. We'll go back to Sandler when it's useful to us. But the gloves come off. If he keeps stonewalling, we're out of here."

"Understood."

Roarke disconnected and the agents stood looking at each other.

Epps spoke first. "The director."

Roarke was silent.

And finally Epps exploded. "I'll tell you. I am done with these white men using their offices and their roles and their privilege to do whatever favors for their white brothers and their white sons. While anyone of color . . . any kid on the street . . ." He broke off, swallowed to compose himself. "When does this shit end?"

And that was a question Roarke had no answer to. Except one.

"Fuck this," he said. "Come on."

He pointed to the nearest bar.

The agents sat out on the enclosed patio. It had a Hawaiian, Tiki theme, with surfboards on the ceiling, stuffed puffer fish, and coconut carvings on the pillars.

Outside a strong wind had come up, rustling the dry palm-frond awning. A storm was coming in.

Epps was calmer, but still seething. "This is not what I signed up for. I'm not down with carrying out that man's agenda." He didn't say the director's name. He didn't have to. He stared out at the palm trees swaying in the gusting wind. "I think every day that it can't possibly get crazier. But now I don't think we've even seen the beginning of crazy."

He looked back, meeting Roarke's eyes. "I've got to be straight with you, boss. I don't know what I want to be doing in this new world order. And I don't know what we're going to be asked to do next."

Roarke felt a sudden chill. "You can't resign. That's not allowed. I need you."

"But how long is it going to be before we're asked to do things that I can't do?" Epps' face and voice were stormy, urgent. "The Bureau starts going after protesters, I'm out of here."

"I agree. I'm with you. But we're not there, yet—"

"It's more than that." Epps paused, gathered himself. "I'm proposing to Tara."

Epps never used Singh's first name. They didn't speak of the agents' relationship; that was a personal line that had been drawn from the beginning of Roarke's knowledge of it. Roarke was so surprised, at first he could only blurt out, "When?"

"I wanted it to be yesterday. I wasn't there. But . . . she got the picture."

Valentine's Day, Roarke thought, and then—*so Singh already knew, all that time we were monitoring Ortiz.* Not that she had any obligation to tell him. Her discretion constantly amazed him.

He wanted to shake Epps' hand, embrace him like a brother. Instead he reached across the table, clasped his arm.

"That's the best news I've heard in years. I mean it."

Epps nodded thanks, a brief moment of what was almost shyness. "We've talked about it before. But I'm not going to wait. With all this shit coming down . . ." He groped for the words. "I have this feeling, like—time is running out. I want to keep her safe."

Singh was a citizen. But it was the first time Roarke had ever considered that her status might be in jeopardy. For a moment he fully felt the shield of his race, and berated himself for the oversight. *Privileged, much?*

"Are you—" Roarke stopped himself before he said "afraid." Instead he finished, "Are you concerned she'll be deported? Because the office will never let that happen. I would never let that happen."

Epps kept his voice low, but anger pulsed underneath the surface calm. "We don't know fuck all about what's going to happen. Every day is something more unthinkable. I'm not taking any chances. Not where she's concerned." He paused, struggling with himself. "Although I might not be her best defense."

Roarke swore to himself. *What's happened to our country? How could we slide so far into darkness in so little time?*

"And neither of us is so sure we're going to be able to carry out the duties of the job. Who knows what shit's going to go down?"

And that was exactly the problem. Roarke didn't know. But when he spoke, his voice was firm.

"But we have to fight this from inside. If we don't hold the line, who will?"

"I don't know," Epps said, and his voice was haunted. "I don't know."

Roarke reached across the table, but stopped his hand without touching him. "Look. Go back up to the city now. Really. Go. Be with her. I can handle things here."

For a moment Epps looked almost sick with relief, and Roarke was sure he'd take him up on it. But then the other agent straightened, shook his head. "Let's just get this done. We'll have all the photos from the party by now. I'll go through them and see what I can see. Get the boy back to speak for himself." He gave Roarke a grim smile. "He could be innocent, couldn't he? There's a chance."

Roarke shook his head. "Anything's possible."

But the outlook on that was bleak.

Chapter Fifty-Two

The skull glared down from beneath her hood, as Jade lit candles on the crude altar she and Kris had made, setting planks on two sawhorses, covering it with a horse blanket.

She'd shoplifted a whole handful of the skull masks from the party store where she got her snake bodysuit. One of them now served as the saint's face.

The girls had started the altar as a prop for their own video message. But as they gathered cigarettes, wildflowers and candy, tequila and money and dope, all the offerings Jade knew that the saint favored, and laid them all out on the altar, she felt the saint's presence intensifying. Already the figure was becoming far more than a skeleton costume, but a real, live force, with a will of her own.

Jade could see that Kris was getting into it, too. She was scouring the barn, exploring every stall for random leftovers for the altar, and the offerings she brought were becoming more and more interesting.

An iron bit. Chains.

Now she came forward with another item: a long, rusted iron pike, and extended it almost shyly. "I found it. I thought it was a poker. But it's not."

Jade frowned, examined it. It wasn't a poker. The end wasn't pointed at all. It was . . .

She jolted with the realization. And then she smiled.

"Brilliant. Freaking awesome. This is it. This is what we do."

Chapter Fifty-Three

The ocean rumbled and crashed below him as Roarke walked the sandy trail of the bluffs outside the Bacara.

The agents had taken their cars back to the hotel. But tired as he was, Roarke couldn't bear to be enclosed in the room yet. He needed the walk. He needed to think.

Epps was right. It was clear where this was headed. The FBI director had sent them here to do reconnaissance for some kind of crackdown on Bitch. And how long would it be before any and all protesters were targeted?

They would all be forced to take a stand.

Singh and Epps deserved every great thing in life. Not this shadowy, ambiguous world of threats and alternative facts.

But was there any place they could be free anymore?

The sun dipped below the sea, and soon he was walking along the sandy trail under the faint light of the rising moon. He could see only a glimpse, through the clouds. But it was uneasily close to full . . .

Hunger Moon.

He had checked the dummy email box throughout the day to see if there had been another email from Ortiz or the bounty hunters.

Nothing.

The absence was a relief. But the constant raw worry lingered.

The waves thundered below. And the sound brought inevitable, forbidden thoughts.

Epps talking about Singh, the pain and triumph of their relationship . . .

They were thinking of giving up their jobs. Going off the grid. Together.

He'd had a taste of that, out in the desert. The freedom of living outside work, outside law.

Outside law.

It made the impossible seem . . . closer, if not entirely real.

Off the grid. Answering to no one, no law. Making my own life, on my terms . . .

And what would that look like? What are you really thinking that would look like? Here, in the dark, with no one listening. Make a wish.

Below him, the surf churned. And the sound of it brought every feeling he'd ever had about Cara flooding back. It was a straight shot through his body, to that night on the beach. He felt her, tasted her, in the salt air and the sound of the sea—

Felt the terror of her presence . . .

And let's be real. Terror is what it was.

He had held her in his arms, and what he'd felt was his own death.

How many men has she killed? A hundred? Three hundred? There's no going back from that.

His wild thoughts retreated back to the steel cage he kept in his heart.

But the sense of presence remained.

Presence.

He was suddenly straight back in the present. Because there was someone with him.

He could feel someone behind him. He was being followed. Again.

And in a rush, he felt it. The familiar shameful, fearful, exhilarating feeling . . . that she might be there, right behind him in the dark, watching him. Her eyes on him, seeing him the way no one in his life had ever seen him . . .

"Cara," he said, through a dry throat. He turned in the sand, scanned the thick, concealing saltbush. "Who's there?"

A voice spoke from the dark, some distance away, barely audible. "Keep walking."

Roarke swiveled automatically. The voice said sharply, "*Don't* turn around."

It was a young, male voice.

After a beat, Roarke turned and did as the voice said. He could feel whoever it was walking behind him.

"You came to the house today," the young man said, after a time.

"The Tau house. Yes, I was there."

"We need to talk."

As sick as he was of this miasma, Roarke felt the unmistakable buzz of a new lead. He kept walking, didn't turn around. "Why don't we go back to my hotel? We can—"

"No. Not there," the voice said, with an edge of agitation. "The trail leads to a point in about a quarter mile. I'll meet you."

By the time Roarke reached the point, fog was rolling in from the water, misting the trail. He sat on the bench at the lookout, his body angled to face the path he'd come from, his elbow pressed into his side, feeling the weight of his Glock.

A shadow stepped out from the darkness and fog. Hood of his sweatshirt pulled low, shielding a young, flawless face.

Roarke might have seen him earlier that day, in the dining room of the frat house. It was hard to say. The kid was like a thousand guys he'd gone to high school and college with. California surfer. Man-boy in sweatshirt and worn khakis, with scuffed, expensive Dockers on his feet. Athletic, easy good looks. Curly black hair, a little on the long side.

"I appreciate your coming forward."

The kid nodded. He didn't look happy about it. But he was there.

"What's your name?"

The boy hesitated, but finally said, "Ethan."

Roarke tried to be easy with him. "I know it feels like a big deal, coming to me. But this stuff—it always comes out. Always. And it doesn't take a rocket scientist to figure what we heard this afternoon wasn't the whole story."

Ethan shook his head slightly in acknowledgment.

"Were you out with those guys who got attacked?"

"No, man, I was crashed out by then. I only know what they said about it."

"So what is this about?"

Ethan glanced around him. "Someone isn't kidding around. And the house is being targeted, and . . . who knows what this person is gonna do next?"

"This person."

The kid got defensive. "Or these people. I don't know."

"Why do you think the house is being targeted?"

Ethan stared at him. "The dummy being all slashed up like that. The spray paint. Nothing too vague about that, right?"

This was what had been perplexing Roarke all along. "You think the dummy hanging off Storke Tower was a warning to the Tau house? Why? I didn't hear of anything specifically naming Kappa Alpha Tau."

"It wasn't just the shit at Storke Tower."

"What do you mean?"

"Well, look. Someone did the house, too."

Roarke felt a jolt of adrenaline, but kept his reaction to himself. "How do you mean, 'did the house'?"

"Someone spray-painted the house."

"Tell me."

Ethan shifted uncomfortably. "Same night as the thing at Storke Tower. I was up early to catch some waves. When I came downstairs a couple of the guys were outside painting over the words."

"What words?"

"I mean *word*." He paused, obviously reluctant. "Someone spray-painted RAPISTS across the door."

Finally, Roarke thought. *Finally someone said it.*

"Let me get this straight," he said aloud. "Someone painted 'Rapists' over the door of the house at 815 Camino Embarcadero?"

"No, not on Embarcadero. At the DP house."

Roarke was perplexed. "DP? Del Playa?"

"Yeah."

"KAT has another house on Del Playa?"

Ethan looked confused. "Well . . . yeah."

Del Playa. The memory hit Roarke—it was the main party drag that he'd visited in his college days.

Of course. Of course they have a separate party house on prime real estate.

Roarke felt anger burning up from the pit of his stomach. *Sandler didn't even see fit to mention there's a satellite house? What the hell kind of investigation is this?*

"So a couple of guys painted over the spray-painting that morning. Which guys?"

Ethan looked pained, and Roarke decided not to press it. Yet.

"Why didn't anyone report it to the police?"

"I asked that. To—" The kid stopped himself, quickly amended, "*They* said the house already had a downgrade from the national board and they didn't want to take another for some bullshit graffiti."

"So you actually saw them painting over it."

"Yeah, there was that and . . ." He stopped, with a strange look on his face.

"And what else?" Roarke suggested softly.

"There was a dummy, too. When I came down the stairs, it was barely light yet, and I saw it in the hall, on the bench, this body with a rope around its neck. Freaked me the fuck out—I thought someone was dead. But when I stepped closer I saw it was some, you know, clothes-store dummy.

"I went outside and the guys were painting. Then when I saw the pictures online about the dummy hanging off Storke Tower, I put it together—it musta been hanging outside in the front of the house and the guys took it down."

Roarke was struggling to stay calm. He didn't want to spook the kid when he was being so cooperative. But this was what he and Epps should have been told from the very start. The KAT chapter had been specifically targeted. The fact that it had been kept from them was a strong sign that the spray-painted charge was for real.

"And this was what, six, seven a.m.?"

"Prolly six thirty."

"Did they tell you not to say anything?"

"Well, you know. The downgrades. A bunch of houses've been suspended in the last year or two."

Roarke gave him a hard look. "Just the downgrades? That's all?"

"No . . . I mean . . ." Ethan looked away, and Roarke sensed the real story was finally coming. "I think someone got raped at a party a few months ago."

"Got raped," Roarke repeated.

Ethan looked back at him blankly.

Roarke was sick of language that left out the perpetrator. "Someone at the house raped someone."

At least Ethan got the point. "Oh. Yeah. I heard . . . someone raped her."

"In fact, more than one someone, right? The spray-painting said 'Rapists.' Plural."

"Maybe more than one. I didn't see it. I just heard stuff."

"When was that?"

"It was the Halloween party."

"Do you know the girl's name?"

Ethan shook his head.

"Anything about her? Was she a student? Her age?"

More head shaking. "I was up with my girlfriend in Santa Cruz that weekend. I didn't hear about it until like the week after."

"And you never went to the cops about it."

Ethan looked suddenly stricken. "I mean, I didn't really *know* anything . . ." He fell silent. "That sounds pretty lame, right?"

Roarke felt bone tired. "Right." He looked out on the vast, black ocean. "So why are you coming forward now?"

"The dummy was real torn up. Slashed up. Face, body . . . red paint splashed at the . . ." He gestured toward his crotch, looking a bit sick. "It didn't look like a game."

"No. None of this is," Roarke said. He could hear the bitterness in his voice.

"And . . . now Stephens is gone."

"Yes, he is."

"So . . . whoever did the shit with the dummy and the spray-painting—they're not naming names. Maybe they don't know names. So anyone in the house . . ."

Roarke suddenly got it. "You mean, you could be next."

In the darkness, he could sense the gears turning in Ethan's head. The kid finally spoke. "When you put it that way, that sounds pretty shitty, too."

Roarke didn't let him off the hook. "It does, doesn't it?"

He was silent for a minute, just looking out at the ocean, letting the boy be alone with his thoughts. Then he asked it.

"Was one of these guys Topher Stephens?"

"I don't know," Ethan said. "I know Stephens was one of the guys who cleaned up the paint and the dummy that morning. But I don't know for sure about any of the—"

Roarke waited.

Ethan looked at him. "I don't know who raped her."

Back in his hotel room, Roarke looked up the photos Reynolds had sent him of the vandalism at Storke Tower. He knew what he was going to see, but he checked anyway.

The dummy that had been hung from Storke Tower had not been "slashed up." There were no violent splashes of red at the crotch. So when Sandler, and Topher's father, had talked about the damage to the dummy, they were talking about the other mannequin, the one that had been hung at the satellite house.

The men had known about that attack on the frat itself.

"Fuck it," Roarke said, and only then realized he'd spoken aloud.

They'd been lying all along. At the very least, holding back.

He paced the luxurious expanse of the room.

He was sick of the lies. It felt like every day his team had to do this bullshit work, he was losing his grasp on the task force. There were real crimes to pursue, real perpetrators to take down.

But he wasn't going back to confront Stephens or Sandler. Not tonight.

He pulled out his phone, dialed Epps, got voicemail. *Good,* he thought. *I hope you did go back to the city.* He waited for the beep, and said, "Someone's finally decided to come clean."

He left a message filling the other agent in on his encounter with Ethan, saying that he'd follow up himself in the morning.

He disconnected, checked his email and messages quickly, then sat himself down on the sofa facing the glass doors, braced himself, and clicked on the email inbox that he'd given Parker as a contact.

He was on his feet, pacing, before he'd read to the end. He felt sick, shattered by the short message:

> Bring the package across the border on I-10. Wait
> there for instructions.

He tried to think through the panic he felt.

The message was from Ortiz. There had been no other email, nothing from the hunters that would have prompted it.

Does that mean they have her? Had he missed an email?

He was dialing Singh before he could stop himself.

"I just saw the email from Ortiz. Have the hunters contacted him?"

Her voice was eternally calm. "There have been no responses to Ortiz's email, and no further posting from their accounts in the forum. But I have been able to determine their IP address from their earlier posting. The IP indicates that they were in northeast Arizona yesterday." She paused. "I used the information you obtained from Parker and took the liberty of calling these men on their private numbers and at their places of employment. Their businesses report that they are on vacation, and their cell phones go to voicemail."

Which means what? Of course they've taken time off work to go hunting.

So the last place they were heard from was northeast Arizona.

If they had Cara, it was a day's drive from there to the California border.

He was lost for a moment, as images from road trips in the Southwest flickered in his mind.

Deserts. Mountains. Canyons.

And it hit him. A way to find her.

"Singh. Can you search for unusual murders or disappearances in Arizona, that general area? Especially with Cara's—Lindstrom's—M.O. And especially near Indian reservations."

"I will, of course," Singh responded.

Maybe he'd been right about where she'd gone, all along.

Chapter Fifty-Four

He was thirsty. And he needed a shit. Bad. He'd avoided using the bucket the bitches left for him. But he couldn't for much longer.

They were feeding him drugs, he knew. In the water they left for him in a fucking dog bowl so he had to lap it up. In the crap food they left for him when he was passed out. When he did manage to wake up he was so groggy he could barely move. His head was pounding like a motherfuck.

But right now, somehow, it seemed even harder to move than before. He flexed his arms and legs . . . and it finally dawned on him. His ankles were chained, too, now. And that finally woke him up.

There was something dark and round and gleaming squatting in a corner of the stall, on sticklike legs. His heart leaped to his throat.

Then his eyes focused and he realized it was a barbecue grill.

What? What the fuck now?

The stall door creaked open and the two cunts walked in. Dressed in those lame hoods and skull masks.

One of them carried a laptop. She set it down at a distance, facing him, and hit a key so a video started to play.

He stared at it through bleary eyes.

There was another skeleton figure on the screen.

A hissing, spectral voice came from the speakers, echoing in the dark of the barn.

We are legion. We are done. We will bring about the death of rape culture by any means necessary. One rapist will die every day until these conditions are met.

The video played through. Unbelievable bullshit about releasing names of rapists. Threatening judges.

This is a call to arms. This is a war on rape culture.

The taller cunt closed the laptop.

"Y'see, it's not all about you. Right now, people all over the country have assholes like you locked up. We're just waiting on word that says you're the sacrifice of the day."

Topher felt the burn of rage. But he was also a little nervous. Just a little. "You all are fucked, you cunts. Don't you watch the news? That feminazi bullshit is *done*. Nobody's getting away with that shit anymore. Your asses are so fried. You think anyone's gonna protect you? If you were fucked before, you are *dead*, now."

One of them answered, softly. "And that's why we have nothing to lose."

He felt another twinge of nerves. Even through the drugs, that made a little too much sense.

"Let me tell you how this goes," she continued, relentlessly. "Guys that are straight up about what they did? They get let go. The ones that keep quiet? Not so much."

She paused to let that sink in, then said softly, "On Halloween night you raped Caitlin Rose with a bunch of your friends. You're going to tell us the names of all the bros who raped her."

Now nervous didn't begin to describe how he felt.

"Fuck you," he managed.

"I'd rethink that answer." She pulled something out of her robe. A cardboard tube stuffed with newspaper. In her other hand was a lighter. "That straw you're on? Highly flammable."

She lit the tube like a torch, held it up. The light danced on the skull mask.

"You won't," he said.

"You just keep telling yourself that."

But instead of lighting the straw on fire, she touched the torch to the barbecue grill. Whatever was inside it caught instantly, roaring up in flames.

The other one held up a long, thin pole. He couldn't tell what it was. It looked like some kind of medieval torture implement.

She started to heat it in the flames.

And now the panic overcame him. He blurted out, "I don't know who this bitch was, but I never touched her."

The figure at the grill turned on him. "This *bitch*. This *bitch*?"

They both moved up to him, staring down at him with skull faces.

Then one stooped, and ripped the blanket off his body.

DAY FIVE

Chapter Fifty-Five

She drives out of the canyon at dawn, in the dead hunters' truck. She passes quickly through the sleeping town of Chinle to pick up Indian Route 15.

After nearly two months, she is on the road again.

On the road.

As always, the movement, the driving, feels natural. There is a physical pain in leaving the canyon behind. Her refuge for far too short a time . . .

But the voice is in her head:

The canyon is not for you.

The winding road crosses through a huge flat valley with distinctive low hills rising out of the middle of the land. More than hills: they are freestanding mountains, towering land masses, like gods walking in the fields.

She is armed with knowledge from the Glittering box. The phone has revealed all.

And she is armed with more than knowledge. There is a small arsenal in the back of the truck.

She is vastly uneasy, even knowing it is there. She feels the death weight of it dragging the truck down, like a lead saber at her back. But she must be prepared for all eventualities.

She has seen postings in the rape forums about Ortiz's bounty.

The lengths to which he still seems willing to go are unreal, insane. But if his hatred has festered this long, there will be no end of it until she ends him. Meanwhile he spreads his virulence to virulent men. If she is meant to re-enter the world, it is as good a place to start as any.

And as always, more will be revealed.

In his email message, Ortiz did not give the hunters a place to deliver her, only the vague direction to bring her across the border to Southern California and wait for instructions from there.

But she knows where Ortiz lives. He has never left Palm Desert. Theoretically the Coachella Valley is only an eight-and-a-half-hour drive.

His hunters are dead. But she fully intends to keep that rendezvous for them.

Chapter Fifty-Six

Roarke woke in his room at the Bacara and immediately reached for his phone.

He'd set it so that anything from the dummy email box would come up on his screen. There was nothing.

So he swiped in to check the headlines.

It was a terrible habit, he knew. No matter how many times he told himself it was his job . . .

What he saw made him throw off the bedspread and stand, reaching for the remote to turn on the television.

There were mass protests. Again. People all over the country taking to the streets.

Thousands, tens of thousands, on college campuses and in city centers all over the country, in reaction to the Supreme Court nominee.

Upping the ante, news stations were reporting that Bitch had released a list of names—accused rapists, anonymously reported rapists, domestic abusers, johns, pimps. They were calling it a death list, and promising that it was only the first of many lists to come. The lists were eclectic, and in many instances, treasonous. Not just misogynistic Twitter trolls, but half of the cabinet—and the president.

WE ARE COMING FOR YOU.

YOU'RE NEXT.

Assassination threats.

Roarke highly doubted that Bitch was going to be sending assassins after government officials. But they'd just crossed a line that the Bureau and national agencies were not going to allow them to walk back from.

It's war. Just like Singh predicted.

He pulled on trousers and grabbed a shirt from the clean ones in the closet. He was having his clothes cleaned and ironed through the hotel. It cost a small fortune, but what the hell—it was all billed to Sandler.

He made coffee with the Nespresso machine, his eyes glued to the screen as reports started coming in of online trolls suddenly receiving floods of threats, including castration images, and being doxxed—their addresses, phones, emails being posted online.

Roarke found himself unable to call up any sympathy.

A knock came at the door. He crossed the floor and pulled it open.

Epps stood in the doorway, holding a newspaper in one hand and his tablet in the other.

"Yeah," Roarke said. "I've been watching—" He gestured toward the TV.

"Not that. There's a ransom demand for Stephens."

Chapter Fifty-Seven

It wasn't an ordinary ransom demand. It wasn't for money.

It was in the form of a video sent to Mr. and Mrs. Stephens's private email accounts. Roarke and Epps watched it in the Stephenses' library, along with Topher's parents and Sandler.

It was stomach churning.

Topher is in some kind of barn, chained to the wall, obviously groggy—so drugged he can barely move. There is total silence.

There is someone in the stall with him, dressed in a black cloak and hood with a skull mask beneath. The figure rips the blanket off his body. Topher is naked underneath.

The figure turns, steps to a fire blazing in front of a Santa Muerte altar.

It took Roarke a moment to focus against the firelight, to make out that the fire is contained in a barbecue grill.

Another cloaked figure turns from the fire, holding a long metal implement . . .

Roarke stared at the screen. He wasn't sure what she was holding. A poker? The shaped tip of it glowed red.

Not a poker. A branding iron.

"Oh, shit," Epps muttered beside him.

The silence is broken by screaming as the video suddenly reverts to sound.

And the camera lingers on the flesh of Topher's back as the brand burns into his shoulder.

Roarke's jaw, his whole body, clenched at the sound. Those screams weren't faked. They were spontaneous screams of agony.

He could feel Epps equally clenched beside him.

"Turn it off," Mrs. Stephens gasped. "Please, please, please."

"Wait," Roarke ordered.

The figure blocks the camera with her back when she bends over him.

Then the figure steps back, and the camera focuses on the burned, bleeding wound—in the shape of the letter *R*.

The screen went dark and silent as the video ended.

Mr. Stephens paced the living room, raging. "I will kill them. I will sue them. I'll . . ."

He was hyperventilating, his hands clenching and unclenching, grasping at nothing. His eyes were unfocused. Roarke was starting to worry the man could have a stroke right in front of them.

"Mr. Stephens, you're going to need to calm down and focus."

He turned to Mrs. Stephens, looked her over quickly to make sure she was breathing. Then he started with "I want to stress that what we're seeing could be faked." He thought it extremely unlikely, but there was a chance, nonetheless. He nodded to Epps. "We'll forward the video to our lab, and analysts will be looking at the footage from all possible angles, with all possible methods, to see what's really going on here."

Epps stepped to the side of the room with his phone. Roarke turned back to Sandler and the Stephenses, and now his voice was hard.

"But it's time for all of you to stop this charade. Bitch's targets are extremely specific. They abducted your son because they think he's a rapist."

"That's outrageous—" Sandler began.

"Enough." Roarke cut him off. "We know that there was a gang rape at the fraternity—"

"That's not true—" Stephens protested.

Roarke overrode him. "And if you're at all interested in saving your son, we need to know everything. Anything at all that would have given the abductors that impression."

"I'm not listening to this bullshit. You can go straight to hell." Stephens slurred the words slightly. Roarke was sure the man had been drinking.

Sandler stepped in, eerily smooth. "It's slander. No rape was ever reported to the Isla Vista or Santa Barbara police. We've already checked. It didn't happen."

Roarke had to fight the urge to school Stephens and Sandler on the dismal percentage of rapes ever reported to the police. He looked around at them: the Stephens family, Sandler.

"What about the vandalism at the KAT house three nights ago? The spray-painting, the hanging dummy?"

It was only the slightest moment. But for that instant, both Sandler and Stephens froze.

"Tau members cleaned up that vandalism in secret and for some reason, didn't see fit to report it to authorities. You've known about that since it happened, and you never said a word about it to us."

Stephens and Sandler were silent. Mrs. Stephens looked bewildered.

"We're done with this investigation." Roarke nodded to Epps, who straightened and stepped to his side. "You've been withholding evidence from the start. It's deliberate obstruction of justice. I'm not going to pretend we can do our job with that kind of game going on."

As the agents turned to walk from the room, Roarke paused and looked back at Mrs. Stephens. "I hope you get your son back, ma'am. I honestly do."

"All right. All right," Sandler called from behind them.

Roarke and Epps turned back to look at Sandler.

"There was damage done at the Tau satellite house," he ground out. "Spray-painting. A dummy."

"We know that," Roarke said flatly. "We need to know what you know about the gang rape that allegedly occurred there."

"There was no rape," Sandler said. "Hundreds of campuses across the country were similarly libeled that night. Anyone can make accusations. It's no proof of wrongdoing."

Roarke gathered himself and turned to Stephens.

"Do you people not get it? Your son is terrified. He's in mortal danger. If there was an accuser, we need to find this girl. And if you're holding anything back, it may end up killing your son. We need to know the truth—"

"What truth?" Stephens said loudly. "How can there be any truth here? These animals can . . ." For a moment, he faltered. "They can torture him into saying anything they want him to."

That was literally true, Roarke knew. And as much as the lying, the denial, the covert collaboration disgusted him, he could never condone torture.

"Is there anything—anything more that you're not telling us? Anything that came with this video? Any demands?"

"There was a message," Stephens said finally. "But it's not true," he said, louder. "I can tell you right now, it's a filthy lie."

"We'll have to see it," Roarke repeated. By now he had a pretty good idea of what it said.

Stephens pulled his phone out of his pocket, held it out to Roarke.

244

It was an email message, short and to the point.

One a day until he confesses.

Roarke and Epps looked at each other.

"Get it to Singh," Roarke said. "See if she can track where it came from."

Epps nodded, stepped away from him with the phone as Roarke turned back to Stephens.

"We need to take a look at this video on a larger screen. And I don't want to waste time going back to our hotel."

After a long, smoldering look, Stephens nodded.

Chapter Fifty-Eight

She drives out of the desert wilderness on Indian Route 15 and heads west again on I-40. In a hundred miles she turns south on 17 toward Phoenix, not just because it is somewhat faster, but so as not to use the same interstate she came out on.

Her route takes her through several suburbs on the outskirts of Phoenix proper. Scottsdale is a desert version of South Beach, with an airbrushed Western theme. Galleries, boutiques, bars, and nightclubs. Postcard-perfect resort hotels with lush and carefully tended desert landscaping. Around her the sidewalks are trafficked with a brisk tourist business of snowbirds and golfers.

After the pristine, isolated, haunting beauty of de Chelly, everything about this place is too bright, too harsh, too crowded. Her senses are screaming, and she wants to flee. Everything in her wants to retreat to the canyon.

And yet she can feel something happening here. She hits the button to lower the window and feels a gathering electricity in the air.

She passes a gallery with Catrinas in the window, the Mexican skeleton dolls arrayed in fiesta finery. She stares out the car window at the skull faces.

The empty eye sockets seem to follow her as she drives past, and she feels herself go on alert for whatever is to come.

As she drives farther into Phoenix, the traffic slows to a crawl, then a standstill. The streets are lined with people carrying signs and banners, in some massive demonstration.

The sheer number of them is staggering, intimidating.

Waves of people, masses of them, the majority women. They are marching in the street with protest signs, wearing T-shirts with printed slogans.

THAT JUSTICE—NO PEACE

DUMP JUSTICE ARMSTRONG

NO JUSTICE STRONGARM

KEEP YOUR LAWS OFF MY PUSSY

THIS IS NOT NORMAL

Among the knitted pink hats dotting the crowd and the rainbow signs, the marchers wearing NASTY WOMAN shirts and jerseys, she sees dozens of the demonstrators wearing skull masks with robes or lacy wedding dresses, the symbols of Santa Muerte.

As Cara watches one of the skeleton figures, it turns and stares straight at her, then deliberately looks toward a side street.

Abruptly Cara turns the wheel, maneuvers the truck slowly past groups of people to head down that side street. There is no way to move forward in the traffic, anyway, and she is certain this delay is meant.

Miraculously, there is a truck-sized parking space open several blocks down the street from the main route.

She backs the truck into the spot, turns off the engine, and surveys the street. Despite the massive numbers of people a few blocks ahead, there is no one walking on this block.

She takes a moment to fill the pockets of her parka with essential equipment. Then she exits the truck and starts walking back toward the street with the marchers. Alert. Always alert.

Almost immediately, her purpose becomes clear.

Ahead of her, three bulky middle-aged men are getting out of a tricked-out truck. It is remarkably similar to the one she has hijacked.

Another sign.

Her body stiffens, and she tastes metal in her mouth. *Danger.*

She slows, hovering at the mouth of an alley, watching them. There is arrogance in their posture, in their belligerent swagger.

She watches as a man on her side of the sidewalk reaches into the back seat of the truck and withdraws a rifle.

He passes it to the man waiting on the sidewalk beside him, then reaches into the back seat once more to withdraw another rifle. Both men sling the harnesses over their shoulders. The driver joins them from the other side of the truck, also wearing a rifle.

Open carry. Legal in Arizona. But it takes on another meaning when the men carrying are wearing T-shirts emblazoned GRAB 'EM BY THE PUSSY and MAKE AMERICA GREAT AGAIN.

The planned intimidation is clear.

And she feels herself filling with cold rage.

Not today.

Moving silently, she follows as the men walk in a triangle formation toward the main street.

Even from this distance, she can smell whiskey on them. Liquid courage.

"Gonna put the fear of God into some pussy-ass liberal bitches."

"Let's melt some snowflakes, boys."

She catches up at the corner of the next alley, glances down it. It will do.

She darts forward toward the man who brings up the rear, grabs him by the rifle harness, and before he can shout, pulls him backward into the alley and shoves the Taser into his gut, shooting him point blank, a twenty-second, 500-volt shot with twin barbed electrodes.

His body arches backward and a jagged, strangled scream rips from his throat.

She lets him drop, leaves him seizing on the ground. She has to force down sympathetic memory pains of her own recent tasing. She knows too well how incapable he is of moving. But the scream will bring his companions.

She turns, slips behind one of the recycling bins, and drops to a crouch, pressed against the steel side, listening . . . barely breathing . . .

She can hear his companions' boots pounding on the sidewalk, heading back to the alley. Their shouts: "Lionel? What the fuck—"

The bootsteps come to an abrupt halt as they catch sight of their friend on the ground, alone in the alley.

"Lionel!"

Cara peers around the Dumpster. One of the men drops to his knees beside the man on the ground.

She aims and shoots the Taser at the standing man.

He shrieks and goes into convulsions. The kneeling man struggles to get up, bug eyed—and gets hit with the third and final Taser shot. This one emits a weirdly reverberating cry.

All three down now, the last two still quivering from the electricity.

She moves out from behind the Dumpster, stands above the men's bodies, panting. Her head is spinning, her heart pounding.

She glances to the mouth of the alley. Still no pedestrians in sight.

One of the men is still rolling from side to side, barely able to speak in a snarling gasp. "Bitch. You bitch."

Quickly, before the moaning, fallen men can even think of recovering, she shoves the Taser into one pocket of her jacket.

And pulls out her razor.

Chapter Fifty-Nine

In a side study of the Stephens house, Roarke watched the video while Epps continued to search the lists released by Bitch. He had not been able to find Topher Stephens's name on the lists, and so far there was no statement by Bitch, online or elsewhere, that they were claiming responsibility for his disappearance or the video.

Roarke started the film for the seventh or eighth time. He'd gotten past the visceral reaction to the torture and had progressed to studying it.

It was in the style of Bitch's video. But it wasn't the same. It had a more improvised, copycat feel.

He was intent on studying the movement of the black-robed figure. He couldn't shake a feeling of familiarity. Of course he'd compared what he was seeing to the database of Cara images in his head, unlikely as it seemed that she would be behind the attack. But the person on the screen didn't have Cara's ruthless strength or animal awareness.

And it's not her style at all. Cara kills, quickly, efficiently. There is no lingering on her victims' pain.

Next, he pulled memories of Rachel and Erin out for comparison: Rachel's slow, deliberate, almost-languor, and Erin's focused stillness— and her disjointed edginess in stress. He could eliminate Erin right away: she'd become far too thin to be the person in the video.

None of the three women really fit what he was seeing. He would bet it was someone younger. Slim, agile, flexible, a high center of gravity, and lacking the body strength of even a slightly older woman.

But the anger made up for the lack of strength. Oh yes, the anger was there in spades—

His phone buzzed in a pocket, startling him. He picked up to Singh's voice.

"Chief, are you alone?"

Roarke could hear the urgency in her tone. He glanced toward the door to the library. He knew the Stephenses, and Sandler, weren't far away.

"Not at the moment, but I could be. Why?"

"I believe I have located Lindstrom."

He felt that familiar adrenaline rush. And was ashamed that he could be so electrified by the words. Every time he thought he was over this, he was reminded that he was not. Not in the slightest.

He moved through the French doors, out into the large side yard.

The grounds were perfectly landscaped, with a central fountain and dramatic groupings of plants, flowers, trees. A gazebo covered in rose vines overlooked the valley. He stepped inside the structure for extra privacy, and looked out over the valley view. Cloudy, with a chance of rain.

"Go ahead, Singh."

"There was a demonstration in downtown Phoenix today to protest the nomination of Judge Armstrong for the Supreme Court vacancy. A group of women protesters arriving to join the march found the bodies of three men in an alley."

Roarke felt the familiar, queasy feeling rising from the pit of his stomach. Singh continued.

"Before calling the police they took photos and video of the bodies, which they have uploaded to the Internet and which are being widely circulated. I have sent through photos."

Roarke tapped into his email on his iPad.

The photos were graphic shots of a pile of male bodies in blood-soaked clothing. Their heads hung bizarrely from the deep slashes in their necks. The bodies had obviously been staged—there was no way the men had died in the positions they were in. They looked like a human trash heap. All three were armed with rifles; the rifles were carefully positioned by slings on their shoulders to look impotent, useless.

But the most telling sign of staging: the dead man on the top of the pile wore a T-shirt emblazoned GRAB 'EM BY THE PUSSY.

Predictably, some of the photos were already being disseminated online as a meme, with the morbid caption "PUSSY GRABS BACK."

It was sickening. Three dead men. *And yet . . .*

"They brought rifles to a demonstration?" he asked.

"Open carry is the law in Arizona," Singh answered.

Roarke sat for a moment, chilled.

Laws are being passed all over the country to curtail peaceful protest— but bringing rifles to a protest to intimidate protesters is legal.

His gut was twisting, for all kinds of reasons. But underneath everything else was a thrill of exhilaration.

This is Cara. She's alive.

There had been other instances of throat slashings that he thought were copycat killings. But here—the efficiency of the killing, the sheer reckless will it would take to murder three armed men like that . . .

Other people might say that it would take a whole group to dispatch them, but Roarke's money was on Cara.

Singh broke into his thoughts. "Bitch, of course, is already claiming the murders are part of its campaign."

"No," Roarke answered automatically.

But does it really matter? This is the whole point of a viral action. It builds on itself. One murder emboldens another . . .

"As you suggested last night, I have been looking for recent instances of murder with Lindstrom's M.O. in northern Arizona. There have been none that I could find."

But Roarke felt a prickle of anticipation, sensing there was more to it.

"However, I have found several disappearances of white men in Arizona, in the Chinle area. Chinle is a town on the border of the Canyon de Chelly region of the Navajo Nation."

"Indian nations," Roarke said.

"Precisely as you thought," Singh agreed. "Specifically, these men are recreational hunters. Three men in the past six weeks have disappeared in that area after telling friends and/or family that they were embarking on hunting trips. One of the missing men has served time on domestic battery charges. Another had a sexual assault charge that was dropped."

Exactly Cara's victim type.

"These men disappeared over the last few weeks. Now three more hunters are killed in Phoenix, with Cara's exact M.O., less than six hours' drive away. It is not a provable connection, and yet . . ."

Yet there was something resonant in it. Roarke could see it, too.

She's alive. Alive and unhurt. At least, well enough to do that kind of damage to three men at once.

The next thought was unprofessional and immoral, but he let himself think it anyway:

That sounds pretty damn well to me.

Chapter Sixty

She is cold . . .
Holes in the ceiling above her . . . with snow sifting through. Men's drunken laughter comes from the poker table in the next room.

She is more than cold. She can't move.

Hands are holding her down on the sagging bed. Now someone is ripping at her clothes, grabbing her breasts, grabbing between her legs . . .

The laughter of the men fills her ears . . . and her own screaming . . .

Jade startled awake, her heart hammering with dread.

She was on the air mattress, Kris beside her.

Only dreaming.

Dreaming of that hellhole . . . the derelict farmhouse and the men . . . the men her non-step-non-father had sold her to for turns—

She sat bolt upright, biting back a scream.

"You okay?" Kris murmured sleepily.

Jade dug her fingernails into her palms until the pain made the visions fade. "Peachy," she said, her voice hard. "Ready to brand some frat boy ass."

The first time they'd branded him, they'd gotten nothing but screaming. He'd passed out before he could name any names.

And then Kris had pretty much lost it. She ran out of the stall, out of the stables.

Jade found her puking under one of the scruffy oak trees. Jade held her hair back, rubbed her shoulders as she sobbed. "That was h-horrible," she gasped, between shudders.

She'd never seen it before. Jade had.

DeShawn had branded his girls. Once Danny had made her watch. So she would know how *lucky* she was. Because Danny would never do that to *his* girls.

He said.

Jade had treated Topher's burn with hydrogen peroxide and some antibiotic salve made for horses.

And pain pills. Don't forget that.

She kept putting the stuff on all through the day, and the burn looked as good as could be expected. Better than the burns on some of DeShawn's girls. That was for damn sure.

"I just . . . I don't want to be that kind of person," Kris said later, when they were lying in bed, smoking a joint to try to get to sleep.

"You're not," Jade said flatly. She'd never seen Danny or DeShawn crying about what they did on a daily basis, much less throw up about it. They got off on inflicting pain. Kris didn't. And Jade didn't either. It had sickened her, too, the branding. And that was what was so fucking unfair. There were so many of them, men, who just did this like it was nothing.

"Believe me, you're not," she said again. "I've seen guys do that and laugh about it." And the anger welled up. "They do it *all the time*. They don't care. And they never pay."

Kris was silent, and Jade could tell she was thinking about it.

"We don't have to get off on it," Jade said. "I don't know how anyone could. But it has to stop. They have to pay."

When they went into Topher's stall with the branding iron again, he started bawling like a baby.

"Today we have the letter *A*," Jade said. "*A* for asshole."

He gave out the names of his rape buddies so fast it spoiled the fun. Squealing, "I'll tell you. I'll tell you. It's not me you want. I swear to God. But I know the guys who did it."

"We're waiting," Jade said, with no remorse at all.

He never caught on that they were just holding the same branding iron again.

Chapter Sixty-One

The video of Topher Stephens had been sent to Mr. and Mrs. Stephens's private email accounts through Topher's own email.

Singh can see that the originating location has been blocked, though. The kidnappers have at least a basic knowledge of proxy servers.

While she has been working on tracking the email, Lam and Stotlemyre have been analyzing the video itself.

Instead of phoning the lab to check up on their progress, Singh pushes back from her desk and walks up the stairs to speak to the techs in person.

She steps into the lab, and finds blown-up screenshots from the video pinned up on boards all around her. The frat boy's naked body. The brand burned into his back.

She forces her eyes away as Lam jumps up from a stool and bows, greeting her effusively. "*Elen síla lúmenn' omentielvo.*"

Behind him, Stotlemyre sighs. "Ignore him. He's decided to learn Elvish."

Unfazed, Lam switches to English. "We're making some progress. We're thinking Stephens is being held in a barn, or stables. He's lying on old straw, and it's an unfinished space."

Stotlemyre continues, "We've done all kinds of playing around with the sound, but haven't been able to latch onto anything specifically identifying. No sound of street traffic, or industrial noise. It's either a quiet space or an isolated neighborhood, or a semiwilderness area, which is our guess. We were able to isolate bird sounds outside, very faintly, some wind—but that's the extent of it."

Lam nods agreement. "Now, the hooded figure is using a branding iron. We've grabbed the clearest shot we could of the burn on Stephens's skin, and cleaned it up to provide an image of the brand."

He moves to the whiteboard with wiry natural grace, and points out blowups of the enhanced images.

"There are thousands of farms and ranches in Santa Barbara County. The Santa Ynez Valley is riddled with them. But here's where we could get lucky. We might find the brand is specific to a ranch or stables, and that could pinpoint where he's being held. We've just sent these images in to the state Bureau of Livestock Identification to see if they can identify it."

Singh is impressed. "This is very promising. I will report to ASAC Roarke."

"No need," Lam says cheerily. "I can call him. You go home. You're looking a bit peaked, if you don't mind my saying. *Cormamin niuve tenna' ta elea lle au,*" he adds, in really quite good Elvish for a beginner.

"*Lissenen ar' maska'lalaith tenna' lye omentuva,*" she answers, straight faced, and leaves the lab, gratified to hear the techs dissolve in delighted laughter behind her.

She goes back to her office and sits alone. It is empty, now. Outside the windows is a cloudy darkness.

And it is dark in the office as well. She has left the lights off, deliberately. The washed-out glare of fluorescent bulbs always annoys her to distraction. In daylight she turns off lights when she can, and relies on the natural light from the windows. When she is alone at night, like tonight, she far prefers to work by the light of her screen.

She catches a glimpse of her reflection in it as she sits down at her desk, and looks at herself for a moment.

"Peaked," Lam had said. It is not a word she is familiar with, but she guesses it is an accurate assessment of how she feels.

She sits for a moment, listening to the silence in the office, to make sure she is really alone. Then she takes out her personal laptop and boots up.

As she has suspected, the men's rights forums have continued to explode. It has been a day and a half so far. She has not been able to keep up. Starting yesterday with the announcement of Justice Armstrong as the SCOTUS nominee, the forums have been beside themselves with glee.

Now it's open season on the bitches.

Liberal cunts are shitting themselves.

MAGA!!!!!

For the most part, she has stayed away today, for the sake of her own sanity. She is having to fight her own revulsion at the implications of the nominee. The Republicans, in the majority, have eliminated the possibility of a filibuster. A simple majority vote will put this rape apologist on the highest court in the land.

But now, as she skims the forums, she finds the tables have turned, somewhat.

Now the men are having a meltdown over the murders in Phoenix. Of course.

The messages are being posted fast, in real time. She turns off the sound to mute the constant dinging.

But she cannot help herself. She checks one of the forums she knows Ortiz frequents.

And is instantly assaulted by the vile messages.

They want a war, they got a war. A rape war.

Hunt these Bitches down.

Anal for everyone.

The hair on the back of her neck has risen, and her stomach is churning.

She stands, walks around, stretches, forces herself to breathe, trying to disengage from the poison of it.

But eventually curiosity gets the better of her.

She approaches the computer again, sits in front of it. She considers carefully, then bends over the screen and types ungrammatically:

Someone told me it this was the Lindstrom bitch.
Any sitings???

She sits back, waits. It is not long before the responses come.

That bounty still up for grabs?

I sure would like a piece of that lol

And then suddenly there was a post in all caps.

I SMELL PUSSY.

Singh goes instantly on alert. The post was followed almost instantly by another, more ominous one.

I SMELL *MUSLIM* PUSSY.

THERE'S AN INTRUDER IN HERE.

Singh feels her heart start to race.

They have of course misidentified her spiritual affiliation. Men like these cannot distinguish anything beyond their limited understanding. But clearly they know her skin color and her sex. She has been noticed. Someone has hacked into *her* fake accounts, or perhaps it is a forum administrator who has determined her identity . . .

Not good.

The all-caps messages continue, coming from several different posters.

WE KNOW WHO YOU ARE, BITCH.

BLACK CUNT.

Singh quickly logs out of the computer and sits in the dark, with just the glow of the screen saver and the racing of her pulse.

She has been playing with fire. Now the fire has turned to face her.

Look not too long into the abyss . . .

She stands abruptly, grabs her coat and bag from the back of her chair, and hurries from the dark room.

Chapter Sixty-Two

Roarke sat in the gazebo. His lower back was aching and he felt light-headed. And to his surprise, it was already nearly dark.

He'd been aware on some level that the sun was going down. Of course dusk came early; it was still winter. But somehow he'd been at the Stephens home, glued to the video of Topher's branding, all day. It had been hours since he'd eaten.

He blinked as the shadows moved.

And a figure stepped out of the dark, startling him.

"Mrs. Stephens. I—didn't see you there."

She was highly agitated, he could see. Not just nervous, but swaying slightly on her feet. Drunk, or high. Both unsurprising. A husband like that. A son like that. The cognitive dissonance must be a constant psychological tension.

She extended her arm, and he saw she held something dark in her right hand. For one paralyzed moment Roarke was sure it was a gun, that she intended to shoot him . . .

Then he realized she was holding a phone.

"What is this?"

When she didn't answer, he stepped forward and took the phone from her hand. The screen was open to a video. Roarke clicked the Play icon, stared down at a wobbly film, taken in near-darkness.

There was rhythmic breathing and drunken male sniggering. Glimpses of the backs of young men on their feet, swaying as they looked down, watching something going on . . . and a feminine whimpering . . .

Roarke felt his gut twist as he understood what he was looking at.

The male voices were slurred, but he could make out some of the drunken commentary.

"Extra points for anal."

"If he can get it up."

"Stick it in her mouth, let her do some of the work."

Roarke lowered the phone, sickened. He looked at Mrs. Stephens, standing in the shadows.

"How long have you known about this?"

She was silent.

"You got it off Topher's phone?"

"His computer."

So Mrs. Stephens was spying on her grown son's computer use. Charming. But at the moment, useful. He looked her in the face. "Mrs. Stephens, what do you expect me to do with this?"

"I thought . . . I thought if you could find the girl . . ."

He had no idea how she was going to end the sentence, so he waited.

She twisted her hands together in agitation. "She must be the one. Or she told someone. So if you find her, you might . . . you might find Topher."

He felt a wave of contempt.

She looked back at the house. "Please. Don't tell my husband. He can't know I . . ."

Roarke stared at her. She dropped her eyes. "Just find him."

"Yeah. We'll do what we can to save your son, the rapist."

Chapter Sixty-Three

Just past the tiny Arizona town of Ehrenberg, Cara crosses the California border at the Colorado River.

She stops at the agricultural inspection station, where she affirms to the inspector that she is carrying no fresh produce, and is waved on. Of course she is. She is white, blond, female. No possible threat to anyone.

Across the river, she passes Riviera Marina, a fourteen-acre park along the river, in the city of Blythe.

She knows this park.

Blythe, after all, is her hometown.

Where, as a child, she first met *It*.

She is now just an hour and forty-five minutes from Palm Desert. But she does not think that Ortiz wants her, "the package," brought to his home. He has some other rendezvous in mind.

She avoids Riviera, with its rowdy RV lots and motorboats and noisy personal watercraft, and drives instead toward the smaller, off-road Waterman Park, with its primitive camping sites.

On the way she passes ramshackle houses. Fast-food joints and burrito stands. Palm trees. Always palm trees. She can practically smell the meth cooking. Her family had lived in a much nicer area.

Not that that had helped them.

She makes a brief stop at another post office drop box she keeps in Blythe, to pick up more IDs, more cash, some accessories.

There is something else in the drop box: the phone she took from Roarke that night on the beach in Santa Cruz.

She has not carried the phone with her. It has been sitting in this drop box at her point of exit from California, with the battery removed.

Roarke had wiped all data from it almost immediately after she took it. But he never disconnected the line.

Perhaps he kept it online to catch her, if she is ever foolish enough to use it. That would be the logical explanation. But not every action is governed by logic.

She slips the phone in a pocket, returns to the truck, and continues on toward Waterman Park, stopping at a convenience store to buy water and some provisions from an indifferent young clerk. As a precaution, she is now wearing glasses, a wig. But the disguise hardly matters. The young rarely notice their elders.

At the turnoff to the campsite she puts money into a lockbox for a camping permit. Off-season, the entrance fee is on the honor system. She drives into the park and around the loop, surveying the campsites. Residents are sparse. When she has found a site with no neighbors, she parks the truck.

She walks down to the river, strips down to tank top and underwear, and wades in.

The February water is cold, but the wind is mild.

She washes herself in the water and in the wind. Washing away the memory of the men in Phoenix, the taint of their blood.

The California wind is like a lover's touch on her skin. And she is glad that she did not die so far away from home.

Back at her campsite, she sets up a tent, the small spare one she has found in the plethora of equipment in the back of the truck. The truck is stocked with everything she could possibly need. Coleman lanterns. A camp stove. And there are other useful items. Handcuffs. Chains. Leg irons. Items the hunters no doubt intended to use on her.

Now they will save her a trip to the hardware store.

She is too drained from the triple kill to face Ortiz. So she will sleep here tonight.

And she will begin in the morning.

Chapter Sixty-Four

Driving is comforting, her Lexus is a haven, and Singh is somewhat calmer as she pulls the car into the below-street-level lot of her South of Market loft building. She uses the remote to open the steel gate, then descends the steep ramp into the dark underground. The gate rattles down behind her.

She parks in her assigned space and shuts off the engine, just sitting, feeling the presence of concrete and steel around her.

Even now, she must force herself to breathe, to take in oxygen, to center herself.

The men in the forum are hardly men at all. "Troll" is the exact word for them. Small, and misshapen and filled with hate and fear.

They are nothing to her.

She visualizes light, pure and constant and warm. Surrounds herself with it. Breathes it in.

Then she gathers her laptop, her coat, her briefcase, and opens the car door to the faint, accustomed whiff of oil and gas fumes. She has locked the car and started for the inner door that leads to the lift when she senses presence.

Adrenaline shoots through her like a lightning bolt.

She is not alone in the garage.

The air shifts. She hears a rasp of breath, some twenty feet to her right.

And then a low whistle.

From the left.

Her blood freezes. There is more than one of them.

All at once the voices surround her in the dark. Multiple men, whistling, chirping like birds. She sees their shadows loom on the concrete walls . . .

And then the catcalls begin.

"Muslim cunt. Black pussy."

Faster than thought, she slips between two cars, dips low, presses her back against the door of the taller vehicle.

Her breath is rapid and shallow, her eyes wide as she scans the shadows in both directions.

She knows what is in the garage with her. The monstrous thing she has managed all her life to escape. The Beast. *It.*

The calls continue, breaking her stupor.

"Here, pussy pussy pussy . . . I've got somethin' for you."

"Get ready—"

"Gonna get fucked till your ass bleeds."

Four of them. Five.

She has told Roarke she loathes the feeling of a gun. And she does. But tonight, she is armed. Her service weapon is heavy on her hip.

She draws the Glock and calls the warning: "FBI. Drop your weapons and come out with your hands above your heads."

The laughter is immediate, jeering.

"Who do you think you're talking to, bitch?"

"Gonna wish you never left Dumbfuckistan . . ."

Singh ignores the taunts. Pressed against the side of the car, she listens, every sense straining to hear, see, smell what is out there in the shadows.

When she feels the stir of movement, she does not hesitate. She fires into the dark.

There is a shriek, and a soft thud, and an explosion as someone fires back. A bullet cracks against a nearby vehicle, shattering glass.

Singh's heart is hammering, so thunderous she fears it is echoing off the concrete walls and floor. She drops lower, bracing herself with one hand on the cold floor, listening to the darkness.

There are garbled voices.

"Fuck. He's hit."

"The bitch got him."

Singh concentrates her senses. And she hears it . . . the wet rattling of a sucking chest wound.

She slides around the side of the car, makes a break for the door to the inner stairs in a stooped crouch. She slams her shoulder into the door, grabs for the door handle, twists it . . . and is gone.

Chapter Sixty-Five

The tent is too confining. Cara takes the sleeping bag and lies outside.

The desert air is cold, mid-forties, but she has made herself a shallow burrow in the sand to hold in heat, and the sleeping bag she bought at one of Arizona's ubiquitous outdoor supply shops is rated for Arctic weather. The cold on her face is stimulating. She breathes in the desert air and feels her own body warmth radiating back from the sand beneath her.

She lies under the canopy of night and looks up at the star-crusted sky. And as she has done since she was a child, she presses her back against the curve of the earth and imagines she is looking down, down . . . at an infinite field of galaxies below her.

She is mere miles from her childhood home. But she will not go near *The House*. She hasn't, not since the night she watched Roarke there. It is too easy to stake out.

Tonight, like that night, Orion is clear in the sky. Orion the Hunter and Cassiopeia, the Queen.

She never sees Orion now without thinking of Roarke.

Her hunt is almost done, she thinks. Her reprieve in the canyon was only temporary.

But Roarke will never stop, as long as he has breath. She knows that much.

He will hunt forever, constant as Orion in the sky.

She sits up, and reaches for the phone. His phone. She sits holding it for some time.

It is a risk to turn it on. She is not even sure why she has kept it, except that it is some connection to him. To kindness. To the one person who has ever seen her.

She knows, she is sure, that Roarke himself will not come after her. Not anymore.

She inserts a fresh battery, the one from the hunter's phone, and calls his voicemail.

There are messages. For her.

"Wherever you are, you need to get out. There are people coming to get you."

There is a pause that seems to go on forever. She can hear him breathing in it. *"Please let me know you're all right."*

She listens several times through, and feels herself flushed, disoriented.

So Roarke knows about Ortiz.

He knows that Ortiz is after her. And has taken the huge professional risk of warning her.

There were several other messages, not just from Roarke, but also from her cousin, Erin. It seems that Roarke had even recruited Erin to warn her about Ortiz.

And his voice.

His voice.

She is unaccustomed to having anyone look out for her, and the feeling is strange. She cannot examine it closely, not now. Not when she must focus everything in her being on eliminating Ortiz. To become distracted could prove fatal.

But she would like to do something for Roarke.

Perhaps tonight, her dreams will tell her.

Chapter Sixty-Six

Singh showers for an hour and still does not feel clean.

Then she goes to her meditation room. With hands still shaking from adrenaline, she lights candles on her altar and kneels, touching her head to the ground, supplicating herself to her goddesses and saints.

She heard the rattling. She is fairly certain that she has killed someone.

And yet when she has regained herself and goes back down to the garage, hours later, there is no one.

Apparently the men had chosen to spirit the dead or dying man away, no doubt to prevent law enforcement from looking into their motives for being in the garage.

But she does not call the police. Nor Epps. Nor anyone else.

She goes back to her loft, back into her meditation room.

She is trembling again.

And this time she turns to the dark saint in the recessed altar.

The idol stands half-naked, four-armed, with a necklace of skulls around her neck, blood dripping from her mouth. She holds a severed head in one hand, a machete in the other, and Lord Shiva lies prostrate beneath her foot.

Kali Ma. Mother of Demons. She Who Is Unthinkable. She Who Manifests Darkness. The Fierce. The Destroyer.

Singh kneels, lights incense in the bowl, and chants the Dakshina Kali Dhyan Mantra.

Om karala-badanam ghoram mukta-kEshim chatur-bhuryam
Fierce of face, she is dark, with flowing hair and four-armed
Kalikam dakshinam dibyam munda-mala bibhushitam
Dakshina Kalika divine, adorned with a garland of heads
Sadya-chinna shira kharga bama-dordha karambujam
In her lotus hands on the left, a severed head and a sword.

She spends the night in the company of the dark goddess. And when the dawn comes, she knows what she must do.

Chapter Sixty-Seven

B ack in the villa at the Bacara, Roarke and Epps had been going over Mrs. Stephens's video for hours. Freezing images. Enhancing them. Grabbing screenshots.

Whoever had filmed it had been sober enough not to film the perpetrators' faces. So the agents combed through the video, stopping and starting, doing screen captures of the young men—body shots, identifying marks like tattoos—and of distinctive features of the room—a glimpse of curtain, a sofa pillow.

It was the kind of thing that Singh was brilliant at, but her phone kept going straight to voicemail and she hadn't yet called back. Roarke figured she had her plate full, analyzing the other video of Topher. It was hard not to think of the two videos as a matched set. Action and consequence. Crime and punishment.

"How did she even find this?" Epps asked at one point, meaning Mrs. Stephens.

Roarke didn't know—it must have been well buried on Topher's computer. But he had his suspicions. "She seems like the kind of woman who might keep tabs on her husband. He seems like the kind of husband you'd want to keep tabs on. Once you're monitoring one person's online accounts, it's that much easier to start monitoring other people. Especially people you might feel some ownership of."

Epps shook his head.

Roarke had to agree. It was no way to live.

The agents focused again on the screen.

"Wait—that." Epps pointed, intent.

Roarke enlarged the shot.

It was a lamp with a naked woman as its base, doing an impossible backbend as she balanced the globe of the lamp on her foot.

Roarke captured a photo of it. If they ever found the room, this would be a strong identifier.

The video played on. Naked buttocks moving on top of a girl whose face they couldn't see, while other male figures stand watching.

What is it about guys like this, that they get off on perpetrating this in a group?

Roarke suddenly sat up, pointed to a reflection in a glass tabletop, the briefest glimpse of the profile of one of the watchers. "That one."

Epps rewound, froze the video. Roarke stared at the shadowy face on the screen. "That's Foy. The vice president."

"Good catch."

"Let's take a break."

"I hear that."

Epps stood, cracked his neck, while Roarke reached for his phone and checked the time. Unbelievably, it was almost four a.m.

"Get out of here. Get some sleep. We'll go talk to Foy in the morning."

"Twist my arm."

Epps grabbed his jacket. As he left the room, he was already dialing his phone.

Alone, Roarke moved away from the screen, flopped down on the bed, closed his eyes. But of course his thoughts were racing too fast for him to just shut them down.

The video had evaporated any remaining sympathy for the abducted young man.

The rape had gone unremarked, unpunished. There was no doubt that even if it had gone to trial, the odds were emphatically in the rapists' favor. Not just statistically. In the unlikely event that Topher Stephens were ever prosecuted, he would have the best defense money could buy. There would be many judges predisposed to sympathy. And Topher lived in a society that found it acceptable for the president of the United States to grab women by the pussy.

He may have gotten the only punishment he was ever going to get. A letter branded on his skin.

Or was Topher being branded with the second letter right now?

One a day. Six days, six letters total.

But he would live.

One a day.

The phrase kept surfacing in Roarke's mind.

There were four rapists on the tape. Four participants.

One a day.

And his stomach turned over.

What if the abductors didn't mean the letters?

He jumped to his feet to call Epps. "I was wrong," he said into the phone. "We need to get over to the Tau house. Now."

Chapter Sixty-Eight

They move on the sidewalk in the dark, faces concealed by hoodies. Slim shadow figures, one carrying something bulky—a heavy box draped with a blanket.

There is no one else on the street as they move up to the house on Del Playa. No sound but the ocean as it rumbles beyond and below the row of houses.

Beside the porch, one of the figures takes an aerosol can of paint from her pocket, quickly sprays out a word in large red letters on the front wall.

Now the figures turn to the porch.

Getting in through the front door is easy—they have keys.

Inside, they leave the door open a crack and move silently down the dark, empty corridor to slip into the dining room.

One of them throws the blanket off the object they are carrying.

A gas can.

The figure dumps the gas out over the tablecloths on several tables. The other follows, flicking a grill lighter and setting each tablecloth alight.

Then the drapes at the windows are doused and set on fire.

And they drop the gas can and run, soft footed, fleet, and deadly.

The hooded figures burst from the front door and run down the sidewalk, feet pounding, breath heaving, dodging down a side street to disappear into the dark.

For a moment the street is quiet, the satellite house is still . . .

Then a dining room window explodes.

A smoke alarm shrieks, shredding the silence.

The door of the house flies open again. Frat brothers in underwear, shorts, robes stumble out, coughing. Some are wrapped in towels, a few are naked.

Students rush out of the surrounding houses, screaming, staring . . .

As the house on Del Playa burns.

Chapter Sixty-Nine

Roarke stared out through the windshield of the rental SUV.

The predawn streets were alive with students. It was impossible to drive at the speed limit. It seemed that all of Isla Vista was out, in various stages of undress. Half-asleep, half-drunk, half-conscious.

"What the hell?" Epps muttered from the driver's seat. He slowed the car to a crawl.

Roarke lifted the phone, dialed the Isla Vista Foot Patrol, as Epps steered, peering intently out the windshield to avoid crushing coeds under the wheels.

Roarke listened to the desk sergeant's briefing, thanked him tersely, put the phone down. "Someone firebombed the Tau satellite house," he informed Epps. He felt sick. *Are we too late?*

Epps pulled into the first parking space he could find and the agents left the car and took off on foot toward Del Playa. The gawpers and weepers parted like the Red Sea, moving hastily aside as the agents shouldered their way down the street.

Fire engines and patrol cars lined the street outside the Tau house. Cherry lights bathed the onlookers in red and blue streaks. Roarke could see a broken window in the front of the house, curling smoke.

The agents moved through this denser crowd toward the front of the house, weaving their way through sorority girls clustered on the street in pajamas, lingerie, and robes, sobbing and wailing.

And staring and pointing at the word spray-painted across the front of the house:

RAPISTS

Roarke spotted Ethan in the crowd and shouldered through the onlookers up to him, grabbing his arm. "Ethan. What happened here?"

The young man looked at him, dazed. "I don't know. Something exploded downstairs. There was smoke . . . alarms were going off."

"Was anyone hurt?" Roarke demanded, tensely.

"I don't know."

Roarke turned on the street, looking at the chaos of students. "Listen up," he ordered Ethan. "Round up the guys. Don't let anyone go anywhere. Stay together. And do a roll call. Get hold of anyone who was in the house tonight."

Ethan nodded, focusing.

"You have my number—"

"Yeah."

"Go. Now."

Half a block down the street, Jade weaves through the crowd of onlookers. She's shed her black clothes and hoodie for a sexy white cami and painted-on jeans. She scans the shifting clump of lookie-loos, spots her target. He's sleep mussed, dressed only in pajama bottoms and flip-flops.

She sidles up to him in the crowd, and speaks softly next to him, "accidentally" brushing his arm. "Jesus Christ. What happened?"

The frat boy sounds shaken. "I don't know. There was an explosion. Fire . . ." He dissolves in coughing.

"God. Here. Drink some of this." Jade hands him her juice bottle. He takes a swig, starts to hand it back. She puts her hand on his, gently. "Uh-uh. Drink it all. Seriously. You need it."

He gives her a once-over, as if he's finally seeing her. And liking what he sees. He tilts up the bottle and drinks.

Right on cue, Kris appears beside her. The girls lock eyes for a moment, then Jade asks low, but loud enough for the frat boy to hear, "Didja get it?"

Kris nods, pats her pocket, speaks under her breath. "Car's just around the corner."

Jade tilts her head toward her new friend, takes Kris's arm. "This is Casey. This is . . ." She hesitates, smiles at him.

"Alex," he says, holding her eyes.

"Alex," Jade repeats, with a lingering smile. "And I'm Mia." Then she leans in to him, her cheek brushing his as she whispers into his ear. "Want to come around the corner and do a line?"

Roarke and Epps moved on from Ethan and wove through the crowd on the sidewalk. They found Detective Huerte on the postage-stamp-sized front lawn, taking statements from students.

Huerte spotted them, nodded thanks to the student he was talking to, and took the agents inside.

Both agents shielded their faces with their jackets as Huerte moved them down the inner hall through thickly drifting acrid smoke. "We've got the arson unit working. This was the only room that actually burned."

Roarke and Epps stepped through the doorway and squinted through stinging eyes around the dining room, a smaller version of the dining hall in the house on Camino Embarcadero.

The smoke was bad, but the damage seemed strangely minimal. A blown-out window and several charred tables, as well as the blackened wall closest to them.

"This was the only damage?" Roarke asked Huerte.

"Just this room."

Roarke and Epps looked at each other. Roarke was no bomb expert, but it was pretty clear that the ignition site was a room that would cause the least damage.

"Doesn't look like a bomb to me."

"It wasn't," Huerte confirmed. "The accelerant was gasoline. It was only dumped on those tables, the drapes, and that wall."

"Was anyone hurt?"

"Just freaked out."

Roarke stood with that, thinking. No one was hurt. The boys in the house would have been scared shitless, of course. But if you were going to bomb a place to cause maximum damage, this wouldn't be how you'd do it.

"It's almost like—"

Epps finished for him. "A distraction." The agents exchanged a grim look.

Roarke turned to Huerte again. "Have we got a head count of the chapter members?"

"I've got officers working on that."

"You need to get in touch with Alex Foy immediately," Roarke said. "It's very possible he's in danger."

Huerte's face tightened. He didn't pause to ask questions. He raised his phone, punched a number, and gave terse instructions.

Epps spoke low. "You think this was all to grab the other kid?"

"Him. Or one of the others," Roarke said tensely.

One a day. It's what they promised.

The detective came back to the agents. "Haven't located Foy yet."

It wasn't proof—but Roarke wasn't surprised. He told the detective, "There are two other KAT members who could be in jeopardy. We've got a video—I sent it to you a couple of hours ago." Huerte frowned, pulled out his phone to check his mail. "You need to get with all those boys and lean on them to identify everyone in that video—the girl, if they can, and the boys. Stephens and Foy are two of them—but we have to treat the other two as targets, too."

Huerte had the video open. It didn't take more than a few seconds' viewing for him to say, "Jesus Christ."

"Yeah."

"I'll get my officers on this," Huerte said. As the detective turned, Roarke said, "Wait." He gestured to the room. "This is what they call the satellite house?"

Huerte turned back. "Right. It's owned by the KAT chapter."

Roarke glanced at Epps. "We'd like to look around the rest of the house. Is there another room with a built-in bar?"

"Downstairs." Huerte pointed to a door at the end of the hall.

Downstairs was a wide room with a wall of glass opening out to a deck overlooking the ocean.

There were sagging couches and armchairs, a fully stocked wet bar, strings of Christmas lights. And of course it reeked of stale pot smoke.

Party central.

Nothing immediately identified it as the room in the video. But the agents moved around the room, scanning the furniture and room accessories, with one goal in mind.

Epps was the one who found it. "Boss."

Roarke stepped over to the sofa. Epps pointed down at a table.

It was the lamp: the naked woman balancing a light globe on her toes.

Underneath the rush of triumph, Roarke felt sick. He took out his phone and started taking photos. Epps did the same.

"All right. What else've we got here?"

The agents prowled the room. Roarke stopped in front of the black curtain draped on a wall where no window would be.

He took the edge of the material and drew it back.

Behind him, Epps said, "You've got to be shitting me."

They both stared up at the collage. Naked and half-naked girls. Close-ups of body parts branded with Greek letters.

Objects.

There was movement behind them. The agents turned to see Huerte standing in the doorway.

"Alex Foy is missing."

Chapter Seventy

There was a clattering on the stairs, and Sandler came barreling in behind Huerte. He stopped in the middle of the room, glared at the agents. "How did you know Alex Foy was in danger?"

Roarke stepped away from Epps so that Huerte and Sandler could see the collage of body parts on the wall. He gave Sandler a moment to take a good, long look.

Beside Sandler, Huerte shook his head grimly. "These fucking guys," he muttered. Roarke noted that Sandler had no visible reaction.

Roarke took a pointed look back at the wall, then spoke evenly. "There's video footage of the gang rape that took place in this room. One of those rapists somehow figured it would be fun to record it. Topher Stephens and Alex Foy were two of the rapists."

Sandler started to object, but Roarke spoke over him. "You've known that all along, haven't you? Or suspected. It's why you panicked about the spray-painting and the dummy hung in front of *this* house. Why you stepped right up and offered your services when you heard the Bureau was sending us. You probably pulled every string you had, all the way up to the director, to get ahead of the investigation."

He glanced at the wall, the female bodies on display. "This is what your Tau house is about. This is what they've hired you to protect and keep out of the courts."

Sandler opened his mouth, but Roarke rolled right over him again.

"But it's gone way beyond a lawsuit now. Because of your lying and enabling, another of your fine young men has gone missing. Alex Foy's parents have *you* to thank that their son is in all likelihood chained up in a barn somewhere, waiting to be branded with a hot poker like his rape buddy, Stephens. Because *you* thought it was okay to cover up a gang rape. This is on you."

"You don't know who you're dealing with," Sandler growled.

Roarke laughed. "Please. I know exactly who you are. I went to high school with guys like you. I went to college with you. I played football with you. I partied with you. I know who you are, and *what* you are."

Sandler rushed him, a wild explosion of rage. Roarke grabbed his arm, twisted him around, shoved him up against the wall face first, arm bent behind his back. He spoke low behind him. "Really? Just try me. I'd love the chance . . ."

Sandler choked out toward Huerte, "You're seeing this. Arrest this man."

Huerte shook his head in disgust, gave Roarke a glance. "I'm going out to take statements about Foy."

Roarke nodded, and released Sandler. Sandler backed up as both agents loomed over him.

"You don't talk to those boys without a lawyer," Sandler snarled at them, then wheeled and followed Huerte up the stairs.

As he disappeared, Roarke and Epps locked eyes. "God help us," Epps said, hollowly.

Roarke had to agree. At the moment, he'd be happy to let Bitch burn the whole system down.

Chapter Seventy-One

All night long, in the dark of the stable, he'd worked at his bonds.

The bitches had been gone for hours, which gave him time. There was nothing he could do about the chains and shackles. Even if he could figure out how to pick the lock, he'd searched every inch of the straw beneath him that he could reach, and there was no stray bit of metal that would help him pick it. The shackles were brand new, galvanized steel. He'd have to take not just a thumb, but a whole slice of his hand off to get out of just one side. Fuck that.

But wood—wood was vulnerable. And with the bitches gone, he'd had hours to work at the hinge. Pulling, twisting, straining at the chains . . . weakening the planks beneath.

It hurt the burn on his back—his mind would not let him say *brand*—like a motherfuck. A couple of times he thought he'd pass out from the pain. But finally, finally, he could feel the wood splintering, starting to give way.

"Please," he muttered. "Please please please."

He braced his feet against the wall and started in for a really solid pull . . .

Then he froze, as a door creaked open somewhere in the stables.

Foy was heavy, dead weight. Jade had his arms and Kris had his legs, but the girls had to stop every few feet to set his ass down on the dirt floor of the stable so they could rest, panting like dogs.

Despite the rough handling, Foy showed no sign of regaining consciousness.

Coke cut with roofies, bitch, Jade thought, as she gasped for breath. *I should market that shit.*

She locked eyes with Kris, and they stooped to pick him up for one last slog, hauling him into the stall farthest away from Topher's.

Inside the stall, they dumped him on top of a pile of straw.

Kris sat hard on a crate as Jade stood over him, staring down. "Bitch is out for the count," she said.

Kris sat still, watching, as Jade grabbed the shackles and chains they'd screwed to the wall, and clamped them around Foy's wrists.

She straightened, reached into the bag slung across her shoulder . . . and pulled out a knife.

She stood over him for a moment, staring down. Then she stooped to Foy—and used the blade to cut his pajama bottoms off.

Kris stiffens, staring at Foy's body, suddenly unable to breathe.

Black underwear on tanned skin.

She is naked on the bed . . .

Can't move. Can't see.

Above her, jeering, drunken laugher. Then rough hands on her breasts. Fingers probing between her legs.

Someone ordering, "Yo, get back. It's Foy's birthday—he goes first."

Her eyes flickering open.
Black underwear coming toward her, with that bulge.
Hands stripping off the underwear, a flash of penis.
"Turn her over, boys. I'm going anal."
So many hands on her . . .
Then pain stabbing through her . . .
She stands, crying out.

Jade twisted away from Foy at the sound, to see Kris stumbling out of the stall.

She bolted out after her.

In the corridor between the stables, Kris was doubled over, gasping. "I can't. I can't. Please. I can't . . ."

"Easy. Easy," Jade soothed. But Kris's breath was so labored it hurt to listen.

Jade turned and ran to the stable master's quarters. Inside the room she put the knife on the shaky table and dropped down beside their boxes of supplies, rooting through until she found a paper bag. She dumped out packages of chips and candy and ran back out of the room.

Kris was on her hands and knees, wheezing. Jade pulled her upright, sat her against the stable wall, held the bag up to her face.

"Shh. Breathe into this," she whispered. "Just breathe." She clamped the bag around Kris's nose and mouth, until Kris wrapped her hand around the bag and panted into it.

"Easy. Breathe." Jade glanced anxiously at the shut stable doors.

We don't need those assholes to hear this.

As soon as Kris's breathing stabilized, Jade pulled her up to standing, led her back to their private room, and closed the door behind them.

"It's okay," she reassured Kris as she pushed her gently down to sit on the mattress. She sat beside her, put an arm around her, holding her lightly.

Kris was mumbling, but Jade heard her, all right.

"I don't have a sister."

Jade sat for a moment without speaking. "I know."

"It was me—" Kris stopped as Jade's words sunk in. "You know . . . ?" Kris pulled back, stared at her, shaken. "Since when?"

"From the start."

Kris seemed speechless. Jade shrugged. "I get it. You had to do something. They do you like that, leave all that shit inside you . . ."

She had to stop, get hold of herself. She made her voice hard.

"You've got to get it out of you. Be something else. Be some*one* else. Anything." She shrugged. "So hey—whatever works."

Kris's voice was trembling. "This morning . . . when we took him . . . He doesn't even recognize me. I was just a piece of meat."

"Yeah. That's how they do." Jade leaned forward, touched Kris's knee. "He knows who you are now."

But now that she'd started talking, Kris couldn't seem to stop.

"I went to that Halloween party and I was drinking . . . so so much. I don't remember anything after an hour."

Of course not. You were drugged out of your mind. That's how they get us.

"I danced with him. T-Topher. He had . . . his hands all over me. That's the last thing I remember until I woke up in the Basement. There were four of them. Standing around . . ."

There are four of them, plus Darrell. Playing cards in that broken-down farmhouse, while she's off in a back bedroom, trying to sleep. But she can't sleep. Somewhere inside, she knows why Darrell offered to watch her that weekend. And Alison, that joke of a mother, just let him. She let him . . .

"They were laughing," Kris choked out.

The drunken laughter.

"And saying things . . ."

The snow sifting down from the cracks in the ceiling.

"I couldn't move. Someone was holding me down."

Hands all over her, pinching her breasts, holding her down.

"And they fucked me. They kept fucking me . . ."

One after the other, over and over again . . .

Fuck them. Fuck them to hell.

A sound fills the room, a wild keening sound, and Jade doesn't know if it's coming from her or from Kris.

But Kris is standing, swaying. She grabs for the knife that Jade left on the table, runs out into the line of stalls.

She throws open the gate of Foy's stall. The gate slams against the wall.

The sound jars Foy to consciousness. He struggles to sit up, and his face changes as he sees Kris bearing down on him, raising the knife.

"What? What the fuck—"

They are his last words, as Kris slashes at his throat with the knife. His scream dissolves into a horrible wet gargling sound.

Jade stands in the open gate, watching as Kris stabs him again and again and again. Blood sprays and he gurgles, choking on his own blood.

After a time, Jade walks over to Kris, puts her hand on her back until she twists around to face her. Blood flies. Jade reaches out fast, grasps her wrist . . . and eases the knife away from her.

Down at the other end of the stables, Topher is screaming. "What the fuck? What the fuck? What the fuck?"

Jade turns around, leaves the stall, walks down the outside dirt corridor.

She steps into Topher's stall.

He is on his knees, straining against the shackles. One has come loose from the wall.

Topher jerks around and sees her standing there. She knows how she must look: blood spattered in her hair, on her white cami . . . and the bloody knife in her hand.

But he's staring at her face. *"You,"* he chokes out.

"Where do you think you're going?" she says, flatly.

He scrambles back in the straw, yanking at his chains.

She steps slowly forward, staring at him. "You really don't get it, do you?" Her voice is toneless. "You still think you're going to survive this. Be some kind of hero for escaping your evil captors. You don't get that you're the *bad guy*. And you can't be allowed to live . . . because you don't even get that you did anything wrong."

He is on his knees, jerking and twisting the chains, raging. "You can't kill me. *You can't fucking kill me—*"

She steps forward, grabs his hair between her fingers, and slashes his throat.

Then steps back and watches while he bleeds out onto the straw.

"I just fucking did," she says softly to the dark.

DAY SIX

Chapter Seventy-Two

The skull-masked figure stares out of the frame, empty eye sockets seemingly fixed on the viewer. That hissing, spectral voice reverberates from the screen.

"And so it has begun. Day one of the new order."

The video cuts to a shot of the pile of bodies in the Phoenix alley. The camera pans over the corpses, a cold, lingering look at the violence, then focuses tight on the bloody shirt reading GRAB 'EM BY THE PUSSY.

The voice continues over the image. *"Predators beware. Your words will no longer be tolerated. Your actions will no longer be tolerated. We are everywhere. We are watching. We will not stand by. Even now we are gathering your names and addresses. One a day will die, or more.*

"We will end rapists until we end rape."

Andrea Janovy sat in her wheelchair in front of the TV, watching the latest from Bitch. The footage cut to the White House spokesman, already ranting in impotent rage.

Janovy smiled a cold smile. Then the doorbell rang.

She backed up her wheelchair to go into the hall.

But before she wheeled to the door, she reached into a side pouch of the chair—and checked her gun.

She opened the front door. On the porch was a woman in a navy pantsuit, with long, lustrous black hair. She stood with remarkable stillness, waiting.

"Ms. Janovy?" she inquired in a musical Anglo-Indian accent.

"That's right."

"I'm Special Agent Singh, FBI."

There was a beat. And then Janovy wheeled back, opening the door.

Singh sits on a sofa in the living room in Janovy's house, across from Janovy in her wheelchair, and flatly relates the facts she has been researching.

"I know that you have been using your family inheritance to finance the organization loosely known as Bitch. I know there are members of that organization now living in a ranch house in the Santa Ynez Valley that belonged to your family, and now to you, though you have gone to some trouble to hide your ownership. I know that you are in constant contact with the organization."

Janovy does not react, but Singh can feel her psychic flinch.

In reality, most of what Singh is saying is guesswork on her part. There is nothing yet that she could present to a prosecutor, no actual paper trail. But the dots are there. Sooner rather than later, they will be connected.

She continues, relentlessly. "I know about the weapons you are acquiring. I know you are also at work on an underground railroad to provide women and girls access to birth control and abortion services. I do not have bank account numbers yet, but I will."

Janovy is impassive, but Singh sees the wary flicker in her eyes. "So what—you're here to arrest me? Because if not—"

"I am here to warn you," Singh interrupts. "My superior officer does not yet know what I do. But he is on your trail. You do not have long before he, too, connects the dots."

Singh must give Janovy credit: she barely reacts. It is only an increased stillness in her face that indicates she has registered Singh's words at all.

"You're here to help. You. An FBI agent," Janovy says dryly.

Singh meets her gaze. "I will not see this country turned into a third-world dictatorship for women and girls. There is no alternative but to pick a side. I have chosen mine."

She takes a data stick from her pocket.

"This is a file on a group of men who are regular posters in rape forums on the Darknet. Names. Addresses. Bank accounts. For some, criminal records. And in some cases, DNA results conclusively linking certain perpetrators to certain acts . . ."

Janovy leans slightly forward in her chair. She is moving past her initial skepticism. "So I'm supposed to trust you? Just like that?"

Singh takes a breath, and begins the story of the men's forums, the bounty offer for Cara Lindstrom, and the attack in the garage.

When she is finished, there is utter silence in the room. Somewhere else in the house, a clock ticks. Janovy slides back and forth in her chair, an almost imperceptible movement, like rocking.

Singh speaks again. "I hope you understand. It is not the attack on me personally that is my concern. Jeopardy is an element of the job I enlisted for. But there is no doubt that if these men attacked me, they will go after others. I have seen what is coming for women. What is already here. And I will not let that happen."

She finds Janovy's eyes, holds them. "It is now a government of criminals. I wish you to know that I have no qualms whatsoever about doing what must be done."

There is a deep silence, in which Singh can see all the possibilities in Janovy's head like a blizzard of images. The same images Singh has seen herself.

"I assume that trusting me will take time. I am patient. In the meantime, no one else at the Bureau knows what I know. No one else will know. This is my action alone."

She rises from her chair, turns to go.

"Agent Singh," Janovy says behind her.

Singh senses what she will see just before she turns.

Janovy is holding a gun.

And she is standing.

Chapter Seventy-Three

The Women's Center on campus was open but the corridors were hushed, deserted, the offices still locked up and dark.

Roarke and Epps waited in the silent hall. It was early in the morning, not yet eight a.m. They'd returned to the Bacara just long enough to shower off the smoke and change clothes.

They knew they were working on a ticking clock. If Foy really had been taken, and the pattern held, then the abductors would go after another of the two remaining rapists sometime today or tonight.

And Roarke didn't think the abductors were part of Bitch.

What he really thought, what he'd told Epps and Huerte, was that the kidnappings of Stephens and Foy were *inspired* by the viral video rather than direct actions by the same people who released the video.

"This is an action very specific to right here. This rape. It's personal. Which means we have to find out who the young woman in the video is."

Epps had already been to CARE, the university's office for providing confidential support and guidance to students dealing with sexual assault and domestic abuse, while Roarke was in San Diego. The office had confirmed there had been no complaint filed against the KAT house.

But the agents had the video now, and there was a chance that someone at the center might recognize the girl or have heard something of the attack. At this point they were all looking for any lead.

If we're not already too late.

Roarke glanced at Epps, but the other agent was intent on his phone, so he drifted down the hallway.

The walls outside the locked front doors of the CARE office were decorated with posters of various actions: International Trafficking Awareness Day. International Anti–Street Harassment Week. A rally in protest of the "hypermasculine culture of Isla Vista."

He stopped in front of a glass display case and stared in. Several skulls glared back at him from an altar festooned with candles, paper flowers, candy.

A printed card inside the exhibit explained the altar was a *Día de los Muertos*–style remembrance of those who had lost their lives to interpersonal violence.

Roarke cringed, thinking inevitably of Santa Muerte. But maybe it was a sign that they were finally, finally on the right track.

He checked his phone screen again, as he had been doing all morning. No new notifications from Ortiz or the hunters.

Then he glanced down the hallway to Epps, who was still glued to his own phone.

Epps' body was rigid, and even from a distance, Roarke didn't like the look on his face. He moved back down the corridor to the other agent. "What's wrong?" he asked, uneasy.

Epps put the phone down, turned. His face was lined with worry. "That was Lam. Tara didn't show for an early meeting. I haven't been able to get hold of her since yesterday."

Now Roarke tensed. "When yesterday?"

"Early evening."

Roarke quickly checked his phone for any email or texts from Singh, while Epps waited anxiously. "Nothing," Roarke told him. *Unless my notifications suddenly aren't working . . .*

And then a terrible suspicion overcame him.

He switched over to the dummy email account, dreading what he would find.

Nothing there, either.

But his thoughts were racing. Could Singh possibly have decided to take matters into her own hands?

It was so unlike her.

And yet . . .

"I think I know where she might be," he said aloud.

Epps turned to stare at him in the dimness of the corridor.

"It's Ortiz," Roarke said.

"Ortiz? What do you mean? Who's Ortiz?" Epps demanded.

The question hit Roarke like a punch to the gut. He spoke carefully. "Detective Ortiz. Riverside County Sheriff's Department." And he knew from the look on Epps' face.

"She didn't tell you," Roarke said. He turned in a circle, mortified. "I thought you knew. I assumed . . ."

Epps was having trouble containing himself. The emotional turmoil was so manifest, that for the first time since Roarke had known him, he was truly afraid for his agent.

"Epps . . ."

The other agent held up a hand until he was composed. "Not your fault," he said, his voice taut. "It was her choice." He looked around him vaguely, sat heavily on the bench behind them. "Tell me."

Roarke took a breath, and talked him through everything he and Singh had done. Everything. The monitoring of the rape forums. The bounty on Cara. Singh's tracking of the correspondence between the bounty hunters and Ortiz.

The shock, the pain in Epps' face, in his whole body, was almost unbearable.

After Roarke was finished, the other agent sat for a long time. But finally, Roarke saw him focus, become intent on a thought.

"But why do you think she would try to confront him herself?"

Roarke understood his confusion. It wasn't at all like Singh, and he knew he could be entirely wrong.

"She's been monitoring Ortiz for a while. Sometimes it's felt like . . ." He paused, trying to get at what he was feeling. "She's changed. There's something more personal to this for her." He shook his head. "Honestly I don't know her well enough to be sure. But something's going on inside her."

Epps' face was ominous. "Does this—Ortiz—know who she is? Does he know she's been keeping tabs on him?"

Roarke knew what he meant. The real question in both their minds was: *Could Ortiz have come after* her?

He tried to be reassuring. "No. Not that I'm aware of."

"But you think this isn't just posturing. You think he's dangerous."

Roarke thought of the man, his driving rage. "He's dangerous—" He was about to continue, when Epps interrupted.

"And she thinks these guys, these bounty hunters, have Lindstrom."

"She knows they're hunting her. She—" He stopped, admitted, "We've been monitoring the email exchanges. There hasn't been any word that they've caught up to her."

Just saying it as a possibility made Roarke feel ill. And then he suddenly wondered if there *had* been another email. Further instructions that Singh had deleted before he could see them.

Could it be?

Epps was on his feet, pacing, unable to keep still. "She—talks about Lindstrom." It was clearly hard for him to say. "I don't know exactly how she feels. But I know there's some connection there."

Both agents were silent. Roarke had seen the same ambiguous, ambivalent fascination in Rachel Elliott.

They're women. They're exceptional women in an exceptional time . . .

"Where is this guy?" Epps said, his voice hard.

"He lives in Palm Desert."

"That's four hours from here."

"Three and a half . . ."

Roarke could feel Epps' raw fear. "Call him. Right now. Put him on notice. Say . . . say we're coming to interview him. Make him afraid . . ."

He didn't finish, but Roarke knew what he was saying. *Put the fear of God into him. Make him afraid to do anything to Singh.*

Roarke reached for his phone, but paused. Given the depth of Ortiz's illegal activity, the depravity of it, he was more than likely to go off the grid if they made contact.

Epps started to speak, but Roarke held up a hand. Thoughts raced through his head. They could track Ortiz's email activity, or his posting activity. If he was still posting from his own IP address, that would mean he was in Palm Desert . . .

Or they could send an email through the dummy account, requesting a meeting . . .

He could call Parker, lean on him to make him make contact with Ortiz . . .

Then it hit him. There was a much simpler way to check on him.

"Wait," he told Epps. He tapped into the contacts in his phone, dialed, put the call on speaker for Epps to hear.

A clerk answered, "Palm Desert Sheriff's Station, how may I direct your call?"

"Detective Ortiz, please," Roarke answered.

Epps watched him intently. There was a long, tense pause . . . then a voice came on, the aggressive tone Roarke remembered. "Ortiz."

Roarke nodded to Epps and punched the phone off.

"He's at work. At his desk."

Chapter Seventy-Four

She is awake before dawn begins to glimmer in the sky, a delicate shimmering coral and silver light over the river.

And in these early hours, she prepares.

Inside the tent, she takes her time, carefully cutting the inside of her arm to draw blood, then ripping her clothes, using mud and blood, makeup and some strawberry and chocolate syrups she bought at the convenience store to augment the real bruises and scrapes on her skin from her fight and fall from the canyon cliff.

Now she avails herself of the hunters' equipment. The handcuffs. Chains. Leg irons.

It takes almost two hours, fiddling with lighting, with angles of the phone. But when she is done, she has several usable photos of herself, depicting her as the captive the hunters are supposed to deliver: bruised, battered, chained.

Enticement.

She looks at the photos dispassionately. They will do.

Then she types out an email on the hunter's phone, using the same terse, coded language they have used in their own emails.

PACKAGE SECURED. BORDER CROSSED. NEED LOCATION FOR DELIVERY.

She attaches the photos of herself to the email.
And hits Send.

Chapter Seventy-Five

The agents started on the road to Palm Desert immediately. Traffic was likely to be grim.

Epps phoned in to let Huerte know they were leaving. The Isla Vista police and sheriff's deputies would have to take over the investigation into the fraternity abductions. There was no chance the agents were not going after Singh.

There was no evidence. No clue to where she would be. The lack of contact was the only indication there was even anything wrong. But if there was even the slightest possibility that she needed help . . .

And the more Roarke turned it over in his head, the more certain he was that she had decided to do something—

"Crazy" was not the word.

But something beyond the pale.

Clearly Epps felt so, too. In fact, Roarke was driving because Epps was in such a state Roarke wasn't sure how present he was. He could feel the other agent's thoughts roiling, like some physical presence in the car.

"This woman," Epps said suddenly, and stopped, staring out at the winter grass of the hills beyond the highway.

Roarke knew he didn't mean Singh, but Cara. He remembered that Epps had once been alone with her, himself, and had been profoundly disturbed by the encounter.

"What *is* she?" Epps asked, sounding almost haunted.

Roarke understood what he was asking. How could Cara have this kind of uncanny power over two people Epps thought he knew, people he loved?

Epps knew Cara as the sole survivor of the massacre of her family. He knew her psychological history, the long list of foster and group homes she'd endured, her incarceration.

But last month, Roarke had learned so much more of the story.

So finally, as they drove out beyond the suburban sprawl of Los Angeles, through the windswept hills of Corona, Roarke told Epps of his dreamlike odyssey into the desert. His encounters with figures from Cara's past: Ms. Sharonda, Mother Doctor—and Ortiz.

And about Ivy—the fourteen-year-old abandoned foster child, abducted, raped, burned alive by a monster.

How Cara, just fourteen herself, had avenged Ivy when no one else would. Had tracked down the serial rapist to an isolated cabin beside a dry creek bed, where he had tortured Ivy out in the desert.

And how Cara, that desperate, haunted teenage girl, had exacted a terrible justice—by burning the rapist alive in a sandpit. The same pit where Roarke himself was nearly killed at the hands of the rapist's still-active partner.

Epps listened in silence. His reaction to the details about Ivy was quietly visceral, a tense and helpless fury.

Roarke finished, "I know I've been unprofessional. I've crossed some lines. But my feelings—" He stopped, groped for words. "Things changed for me, out there. I know her differently now. I know her as that child. I think—she's still that child."

He met Epps' eyes briefly. "I can only think of her as that child."

It wasn't the whole truth. But it was truth.

After a long moment, Epps nodded.

And Roarke drove, headed for the desert.

Chapter Seventy-Six

Singh paces the upstairs bedroom of Janovy's house.

After taking Singh's service weapon and phone, Janovy walked her upstairs at gunpoint and locked her in the guest bedroom. All with remarkable physical dexterity. Janovy has a marked limp, but clearly she has been recovered from her accident for some time. Her disability is a very clever camouflage, Singh must admit.

Singh has forced the window open—but the room is on the second floor of the house, and the house is on a hill with a sheer drop-off. Escaping through the window is not a viable option. Not without severe injury. The door is substantial, and dead-bolted.

Other women have been arriving downstairs, other members of Bitch, she presumes. Singh can hear the cadence of their voices from her room, though nothing of their words, as they talk somewhere in the house.

Discussing her fate, no doubt.

Singh knows there is a chance she will not survive this imprisonment.

But she has seen Janovy's face. She has seen the desire there, the will to believe that Singh would choose being a woman over being an agent. Janovy is not yet convinced. But she is willing to be.

Suddenly there are footsteps on the stairs, footsteps outside in the hall, approaching the door.

Singh backs up beside the open window. She can jump. But her bet is that they will not kill her.

The dead bolt slides open . . .

Janovy comes into the room, her gun trained on Singh.

The two women lock eyes.

Then with her other hand, Janovy holds out Singh's phone, demanding, "What the hell does this mean?"

Singh steps forward warily, takes the phone. On the screen is an alert labeled *Lindstrom*.

Chapter Seventy-Seven

The agents pulled off the freeway to refuel in Banning.

Roarke got out of the car to walk, bracing himself against the dry desert wind—and checked the dummy email account yet again. But this time his pulse skyrocketed when he saw there was a message from the hunters, routed from Ortiz's email account.

He clicked on it . . .

And stared down at photos of Cara. Chained, battered, bloody. Captured by monsters.

His body went weak with sheer terror for her pain.

And then there was a fury so overwhelming he felt he would explode with the force of it.

Suddenly Epps was in front of him. The other agent got one look at his face and took the phone from him.

Epps stared down at the photos. Through his own numbness, Roarke could feel the anger radiating from the other agent as he walked several paces away, walked back.

Roarke tried to focus his thoughts through the gut-punched sense of panic.

If the hunters had followed Ortiz's instructions to wait across the I-10 border, they were now in Blythe, a natural border crossing from Arizona en route to Ortiz's house in Palm Desert.

But Blythe was also Cara's childhood home. The place where her family had been slaughtered, where Cara had survived that first encounter with human evil, which she now saw as the monster she called *It*.

Is Blythe significant?

Why would Ortiz want her taken there?

He couldn't make any sense of his thoughts.

Epps typed quickly into his own phone, held it out to Roarke. The screen showed a map of Blythe and the surrounding area.

"The border on I-10 is just under two hours from Palm Desert. But I doubt he's going to have them bring her to his home. Or anywhere too near."

Roarke made himself concentrate on his agent's words. Epps was right. There was still time . . .

Epps paced back and forth, moving as he thought it out. Behind him, the wind rippled the tall dry grass. "These emails sound like he's making these hunters follow bread crumbs. Get them to one location, give them the next location from there."

"I have to go," Roarke said, through a thickness in his throat. "I can't explain it. I have to go."

"I'm going with you," Epps said.

Roarke looked at him.

"Not for her," Epps said, his voice hard. He raised his phone, punched a number, stepped aside to talk.

Roarke gave him his space, but he could hear Epps speak. "Tara. We've seen the email—the photos." He paused. "We're going to head that way, too." And then, urgently—"If that's what you're doing, you can call us. We can do this together . . ." Roarke felt the wrench as the other agent's voice faltered. "Please. Call me."

Chapter Seventy-Eight

She packs up the tent and sweeps the campsite clean, finding calm in the ritual. In the fields around her, bright yellow desert sunflowers raise their heads from clumps of gray-green sage. Spring is coming.

She doubts she will be alive to see it.

At the exact moment she finishes her clean up, the hunter's phone pings with a response from Ortiz, one terse line:

Drive west on I-10 until next contact.

She lowers the phone, sits on a boulder in the soft, dry wind, facing the river to think.

So this is how he intends to rendezvous. Throwing bread crumbs until they are right on top of each other.

He is being very cautious. But of course, he is preparing for any number of felonies. Kidnapping. Rape. Torture. Murder.

From her present location, she is one hour and forty-five minutes away from Palm Desert on the 10.

She does not think for a moment that Ortiz wants her brought to his home. He will want to be someplace deep in the desert for what he has planned. And there are so many locations to choose from along this stretch of road. Nearly infinite wilderness.

She could surprise him at his house instead, on her own time. But wherever he is leading her, or the hunters, he has carefully chosen the destination for privacy. After all, he must be as careful as she now must be. He has already done that scouting work for her. He has chosen somewhere he can never be discovered, where her body could never be found.

And that works in her favor.

It means that when she is done with him, *his* body will never be found.

She has no intention of following his instructions as sent. That can only be a trap.

She goes to the hunters' truck and fishes out the road atlas that she has bought along the way—she is never without one. She knows this part of Southern California well, but she wants to be very clear about what alternate routes are available to her.

She opens the atlas, studies what lies west along the I-10.

And she knows immediately the route she will take. Depending on the final destination, this road may take her longer than I-10 would. When she gets the next email, she will proceed from there.

Ortiz will wait. His blood is up, and he is too close now to bail out. He wants her crushed, degraded, obliterated. He is risking everything to bring her down.

He will wait.

Chapter Seventy-Nine

Singh stares out through the windshield at desert hills as she drives on I-10 toward Palm Desert.

She is aware of the irony, that Cara Lindstrom's capture has enabled her own freedom. She has no idea what Janovy, and the other women of Bitch, would have done with her had not the email with the photos of Lindstrom arrived when it did.

As Janovy watched, holding the gun on her, Singh had logged into the dummy email account to find the grotesque email from the bounty hunters, forwarded automatically from Ortiz's account.

The photos of Lindstrom—chained, battered, bloodied—had shaken Janovy to the core. Just as they had Singh.

And Singh had made her plea so quickly that Janovy and the others had let her go. For now.

She glances out the car window to the side of the freeway. Fields of winter grass. The towns are already farther apart. Civilization is falling away.

Her plan, such as it is, is weak. The hunters' email indicated they have Lindstrom at the California border, on Interstate 10.

So Singh is driving in that direction, via Palm Desert, until more is revealed.

Of course Damien has been calling, frantic. And it is of course unforgiveable, what she is doing. Cutting him out. But the decision, this action, is hers alone. She cannot let Epps, or Roarke for that matter, know her plans. Roarke has already compromised himself beyond reason where Lindstrom is concerned. He cannot think rationally in regard to her.

And Damien . . . Damien needs the structure of rules. Beyond all evidence, he clings to his belief in justice. But the world has been rewritten. Justice has no meaning any more.

She cannot involve either of them in this.

She glances in the rearview mirror, at the road behind her.

Perhaps Bitch is following. And if so, perhaps that is a good thing. She does not know. She knows very little, in fact. She knows Ortiz's address. She knows there is a good chance he will continue contacting the hunters by email, and she will be able to check that communication through Roarke's dummy account. She has checked for any activity by Ortiz in all of the forums. There has been nothing from the accounts she is aware of. Which is ominous.

But mainly, she knows she must intervene in what Ortiz has planned for Lindstrom. She will not stand by and let this happen. She will not let him loose his trolls on the world. They cannot be allowed to succeed.

She will not allow it.

So she drives.

Chapter Eighty

As the agents' SUV burned up the desert miles, Epps became more and more agitated. His long frame was always a tight fit in vehicles. Now it seemed he would burst out of the car at any moment.

And Roarke had been thinking. He hated going into a situation without the upper hand. Hated it. And they knew nothing about where they were going. Not good.

He stared out at the palm trees as they raced past the oasis of Palm Springs. And finally the answer came to him.

"We're going to make a pit stop."

Epps twisted in his seat to face him, incredulous. "We don't have time to lose—"

"We need an edge. I know someone who may be able to give it to us."

Roarke had Parker's address, and Parker lived in Rancho Mirage, which was right on their route anyway.

The address was a small, bland house on an even blander suburban street. Roarke parked the SUV down the block. As the agents approached on foot, Roarke quickly scanned the front door and windows.

He lifted his phone and dialed Parker's number from outside. "This is Special Agent Roarke."

He was greeted with silence. Before the PI could consider his options, Roarke spelled it out for him. "My partner and I are outside your door. Open it or we come through it."

It took a moment, but the door opened. Parker stood in the doorway, still in a bathrobe, glowering out. His face was bloated and he reeked of the morning after a binge.

Both agents shoved through the door, surrounding him.

"Where's Ortiz?" Roarke demanded. "And don't even try to pretend you don't know what's on."

Epps moved forward on the PI, towering over him—intimidating even when he wasn't in a righteous rage.

"I know what," Parker blurted. "I don't know where. He wouldn't tell me. I swear."

"Start talking," Roarke ordered.

And Parker spilled.

As he spoke, Roarke felt the air in the small, dim room closing in on him. It was worse than he could have imagined. Ortiz had far bigger plans than what he was going to do to Cara himself. He was auctioning her off. Men in the rape forums were lining up, paying top dollar to get a turn with her.

"Ten grand for every fifteen minutes, to do anything you want. Except kill her. You have to pay a double deposit—you lose it all if she dies during your session. That would be killing the golden goose—"

Parker stopped, choking on the last word, because Roarke had his hand wrapped around his throat.

Roarke could feel Epps step up behind him . . . and managed not to tighten his hand that fatal inch.

"What else?" he ground out, staring down into Parker's crimson face.

"He's got it all set up to be recorded, too," the PI gasped.

"To sell the video," Epps said, revulsion in his voice.

"Pay-per-view."

Roarke took a jolted step back from Parker, reeling with the sickness of it. Epps was walking the small living room behind him, equally revolted. Then through the miasma of Roarke's thoughts, another horror occurred to him. He turned on Parker.

"There's an agent of ours headed his way. Who's in communication with Ortiz. Agent Singh. A woman . . ."

Roarke felt Epps go rigid beside him.

Parker shook his head. "I don't know anything about that. But if she shows—" Something flickered on the PI's face, and he shut up, obviously thinking better of speaking.

Now it was Epps who grabbed the PI and slammed him up against the wall. "Say it, motherfucker."

Parker choked out, "I expect he could make some money off that, too."

Roarke had to pull Epps off the guy. He held him tight, restraining him, but also comforting him.

Parker doubled over, wheezing. Roarke pulled Epps to the side.

"We're going to get these guys. Listen to me. Listen to me." Epps looked up at him, struggling to focus. And Roarke said it, slowly. "Cara won't let anyone hurt her."

Epps looked at him. A morass of confusion, anger . . . and hope.

Parker coughed, and finally choked out, "I don't know where. I don't. But my guess? It's not far from Palm Desert."

Roarke forced himself to think it through, and realized Parker was right. Palm Desert was minutes from vast stretches of desert wilderness.

More privacy than anyone could ever need. Infinite places to bury a body.

He caught Epps' eye, looked toward the door. Then he turned on Parker.

"You're a lucky man. You get a day to get yourself together before we come back with a warrant."

Outside Parker's house the agents beelined for the car. Roarke was speaking before they were off the porch. "We keep driving toward Blythe. And wait for a sign."

"A sign?" Epps asked, thrown.

"A message," Roarke corrected himself.

But as they headed for the car, he wondered if he might have been right the first time.

Chapter Eighty-One

State Route 78 from Blythe is an old Gold Rush highway running all the way to the Pacific Coast, ending in Oceanside. Outside of Blythe, it passes through the spectacular Imperial Sand Dunes, the largest mass of dunes in California, famous for their appearance in *Star Wars* and other films.

For Cara, the pristine Saharan blankness of them, the shifting sun and shadows on the golden pyramidal hills, the constant ripping of the grains—all are lulling, profoundly comforting, like having her mind dry-cleaned.

It calms her for what is in store.

After the dunes, the road turns into a forty-mile stretch past date and citrus groves, following the old Southern Pacific Sunset Route toward the Salton Sea.

At the tiny town of Niland, dusty Highway 111 veers off northward, skirting the Salton Sea toward I-10, where she can pick up that interstate and proceed as directed. But there has been nothing further from Ortiz. So it is in Niland she will wait for further instructions.

She turns at the Buckshot Deli and Diner, motoring out of the city proper toward the squatter community called Slab City, known by locals as "the last free place in America."

The encampment is made up of painted RVs, long-haul trucks, old school buses, tin shacks, and outdoor art installations, all situated on and around concrete slabs—relics from a long-dismantled World War II marine base.

Here retirees occupy land with drifters, anarchists, survivalists, and criminals all living off the grid, without basic utilities—but with no interference from the law or the government. She has spent some share of time around encampments like these.

The entrance to Slab City itself is a hallucinatoric vision: a candy-colored mound of adobe three stories high. Salvation Mountain: straw bales, car parts, reclaimed junk, and ten thousand gallons of paint. The artist is several years gone on to rejoin his maker. But his kaleidoscopic legacy remains.

Cara has stopped here many times on her journeys. She is drawn to it. A massive outpouring of one man's mind, a concrete manifestation of one message: *God is love.* She admires the single-mindedness of it. The creativity and whimsy. The perpetuating drive of it. It is a human heart and soul, made concrete. It has drawn thousands of other artists, lost souls, and tourists.

It reminds her that not all is darkness. That there are things worth fighting for.

She parks the hunters' truck in the sand lot. Hers is the only vehicle here, and the wind is so strong she must wrestle with it to get the door open.

She walks around the mountain, passing freestanding art installations. A Kabbalistic Tree of Life. A life-sized wooden shark with bloody jaws. A vintage white Falcon station wagon, spray-painted with inspirational quotes.

The mountain is hollow, a literal maze sculpted of bales of straw built up with adobe and finished with an ocean of paint. The desert wind whistles in the corridors as Cara wanders through arches made of curved tree limbs, rounded rooms painted with gigantic flowers, angels, and demons.

It is a peace some people must find in church.

She follows a set of stairs toward the top of the mountain: a yellow-painted path indicating the safe ascent with a sign: PLEASE STAY ON THE YELLOW BRICK ROAD.

The view from the top is of flat, flat desert. She gazes out over mini sandstorms, and the silver glimmer of the Sea in the distance . . .

She could disappear now. No one is forcing a confrontation. She does not have to fight.

Then her pulse spikes as the hunter's phone vibrates in her pocket.

The email message is numbers only. GPS coordinates. A location from Ortiz.

And as she suspected, she will not have to go far at all.

Chapter Eighty-Two

Epps had just taken over the wheel when Roarke's phone buzzed with an alert from the dummy email account.

Roarke logged on to find an email from Ortiz.

He stared down at a weird series of numbers.

@33.3560671,-115.7414864

It took him a moment to realize the instructions from Ortiz were GPS coordinates.

His hands were shaking as he inputted the numbers into Google Maps on his phone. The map showed a spot on the eastern shore of the Salton Sea, a town, if you could call it that, named Bombay Beach.

"What is it?" Epps demanded.

"Salton Sea," Roarke said.

The Sea was less than an hour's drive from Palm Desert. It made total sense that Ortiz would have some hideout there, or maybe he was simply commandeering an abandoned building for his purpose.

Roarke knew there were any number of them in the area to choose from.

He tapped on the location and chose "What's Here?" from the list of options to call up the street view. All he got was a completely flat, dusty road. But by maneuvering around a bit, he found rows of decrepit, abandoned buildings nearby.

"Bombay Beach," he said aloud.

Epps frowned from the driver's seat. "Never heard of it."

Roarke shook his head. "You're in for a treat." He laughed, without humor. "It's like no place else on earth."

Chapter Eighty-Three

The Salton Sea lies dead center in the California Badlands, at the second-lowest elevation in the United States. The largest body of water in California, the second-largest inland sea in the country—350 square miles of salt water in the Sonoran Desert.

From a distance, it is idyllic. Flocks of migratory birds glide along the rippling blue surface of the water, past vast shorelines of deserted white beaches, under the pristine winter sun.

All an illusion.

It is a wasteland of apocalyptic proportions.

A sea that was never supposed to be, created by an engineering disaster that sent the Colorado River rampaging into an ancient lake bed. It was two years before the breach could be repaired. And the Salton Sea was born.

The area was once a thriving resort, developed in the 1950s as the "Salton Riviera." Chic towns sprung up along the shoreline in a land investment gold rush. Socialites and celebrities flocked to boat, swim, and water-ski at the popular marinas and clubs. Then a series of ecological disasters hit one after another, like plagues from God, devastating the region.

First came the recurring floods, causing massive property damage and driving residents out of the new developments. Investors pulled out of hotels and businesses, leaving a series of ghost towns along the shores. An agricultural spill from nearby farmland contaminated the Sea, killing millions of fish and hundreds of thousands of birds. An algal bloom poisoned millions more.

Now the whole region is mostly deserted, a curiosity stop for intrepid tourists.

Up close, all illusion fades. The blue water is a murky brown. The white beaches are formed of the pulverized bones and scales of millions of birds and fishes; the shoreline is littered with skeletons and dry white husks. Global warming has relentlessly shrunk the shoreline, exposing miles and miles of polluted mud. The mud bakes in the sun and turns into dust storms in the wind and desert heat; the dust, laced with the arsenic, selenium, lead, and mercury, renders the air unbreathable.

And the smell. In the cool winter months, there is only a slight whiff of sulfur, but soon the paralyzing heat will come, and the smell of dead and dying animals will draw swarms of flies and create an unbearable stench all summer long.

There are a few outposts of inhabited houses. Between is nothing but desert. Vast alien spaces. Stark desolation.

A dire warning of the consequences of mistreating the earth.

Cara drives the cracked main road along the shore, toward the GPS coordinates Ortiz has sent.

They lead to the ghost town of Bombay Beach.

She looks through the windshield at skeletons of houses half tumbled into toxic-looking green pools. Telephone poles with no wires, stretching out to the horizon like uneven lines of giant crucifixes. Rusted hulks of cars and appliances, all white-crusted with salt.

Farther up from the pale muck of the shoreline are abandoned buildings, many still filled with belongings, even cans and boxes of food, as if residents fled overnight without packing. The eeriness is compounded by the cryptic graffiti spray-painted on wall after wall.

Beyond the ten-block-by-ten-block grid of the town are paved streets with street signs—and no houses. The phantom blocks are inhabited only by dust devils and tumbleweeds. Beyond that, cracked roads just stop in the sand.

It is toxic. It is dead. It is her nightmares come to life, a postapocalyptic vision of life after a nuclear bomb. *It*, made manifest.

In the center of town, some houses and RVs are inhabited. There is a population of just under three hundred—some owners, some squatters. Stubborn previous residents. Misfits and criminals and iconoclasts.

On the outskirts, abandoned houses stand open to the elements, sand piling up in drifts in the corners. And the wind. The constant wind.

And yet, there is a terrible, menacing beauty to the place, which draws amateur photographers and artists. Some of the houses have been turned into art installations—masterpieces of graffiti, with creepy film tributes: **THE HILLS HAVE EYES** scrawled across the outside of one house, and **IT RUBS THE LOTION ON ITS SKIN . . .** on another.

The GPS coordinates lead her to a block on the edge of town, a crossroads where there is nothing but the shells of small houses. The windows have been smashed long ago, and the houses are swept clean by wind.

In the middle of a block is a whitewashed one-room house. Cara stops the truck some distance from the house to watch.

On one wall of the house, dozens of milk cartons are nailed to the plaster in tidy lines. A crude hand-painted sign sticks out of the sandy patch of yard outside:

HOUSE OF MISSING PERSONS

The wind rolls tumbleweeds past the truck, down the dusty road. Nothing else stirs.

After long minutes of surveillance, she makes the decision. She turns off the engine, and gets out of the truck.

She has dressed in the hunters' clothes. Two pairs of khaki trousers, a sweater and both parkas, to bulk herself up and create a male silhouette. And of course, the hunting cap pulled over her hair, shielding her face.

The numerous pockets of the outer parka conveniently hold weapons. A knife. The Taser she hasn't fired. A flare gun. And a real one, a Beretta. There will be a price to pay for using a gun. There always is. But here, she has no real choice. She must be prepared for all eventualities.

The weight in all the pockets help make her body heavy, like a man's, and she lumbers with the hunter's graceless stride toward the door of the cottage. Or rather, the doorway, as the actual door had been ripped away long ago.

She hovers in front of the dark opening for a moment, listening.

There is silence . . . nothing but the swirl of wind.

She steps inside.

The small, square space is completely empty, except for a table in the center of the room and the walls, where more rows of precisely lined-up milk cartons are nailed into the plaster, each with a photo of a person, a narration, and the word MISSING.

A gallery of lost souls.

A large open book lies on top of the table.

She steps to the table and looks down.

The book is a visitor guest book. A manila envelope sticks out of the pages.

She removes the envelope and opens it . . . to find the final instructions.

Chapter Eighty-Four

Singh is just past Palm Springs, less than twenty miles from Palm Desert, when her phone chimes with Ortiz's email.

It is the briefest of instructions, ordering the hunters to drive west on the 10.

So she drives.

The second email comes when she is on the long, uninhabited stretch of freeway skirting the south edge of Joshua Tree National Park to the north, and the top of the Salton Sea to the south. This time, a set of GPS coordinates that would have her turn south and drive the eastern edge of the Sea.

She drops down from the 10 onto Highway 111, driving through a corridor of massive date palm groves, through the town of Mecca and onto the North Shore.

She passes through the Salton Sea State Recreational Area, where an old yacht club in the shape of a battleship has been refurbished into a community center. A delicate purple-and-orange sunset colors the sky, stunningly reflected in the silvery water of the enormous lake.

Pelicans glide past reflections of palm trees. A glimpse of the former glory of the place.

But the old yacht club is the only sign of new life. Beyond that, only shells of abandoned concession stores, tightly boarded up and covered in graffiti, overlook the water.

Then there is just bare desert highway and the long salt-crusted stretches of sand down to the water's edge. The wind is constant, pushing at the car. The shadows of sunset creep over fields dotted with desert wildflowers, gray-green sage bushes, craggy low hills.

She motors through a lonely intersection with just two buildings: an abandoned auto repair shop with metal sun canopy, and a liquor store/video rental store. Both wide open to the elements. A tall palm tree sways precariously in the wind.

So completely abandoned, she shivers.

And then it is dark.

Behind her, she sees headlights, approaching fast. Lights that are set up from the highway, higher than a standard car. A large vehicle.

She watches in her side mirror as the vehicle bears down on her, shoots out into the opposite lane to overtake her.

A truck, with an enclosed shell over the bed.

She looks out her side window to catch a glimpse of two men in the front seat. A man with a red hunting cap driving.

She freezes. It is all she can do to keep her eyes ahead, to keep her hands steady on the wheel.

Could these be the hunters?

She has seen no one else for miles. No cars, no people. And these men are on the direct route to the GPS coordinates. Two of them.

For a moment, she is paralyzed with indecision.

She speeds up gradually, so she can keep pace without coming too near. On the dark desert highway, they are in plain sight ahead. They have come from behind, so they will not suspect her of following them.

So she follows.

Chapter Eighty-Five

Roarke and Epps drove out of the bleak arroyos of the Anza-Borrego Badlands and hit the highway circling the Salton Sea just as the sun was going down. And Epps got his first glimpse of it.

The look on his face was pure consternation as he stared through the windshield in a stupor. "What the hell is this place?"

Roarke had been here before, ages ago, on one of the endless summer vacations his academic parents dragged him and his brother on in their youth. Memory had faded, probably because it was impossible to hold the sheer weirdness of it in your mind. It was like something out of *Mad Max*.

Epps couldn't stop staring as the agents drove past scenes from the Apocalypse.

A Volkswagen bus half-sunk in a slimy pool of white. Stark driftwood trees in a mosaic of cracked mud. Toxic chemical lakes burping bubbles of sickly green and orange. Pieces of rusted machinery, crumbling boat docks, artifacts from the boomtown days—now ghostly pale, crusted with salt. A rotting armchair stuck out of what looked like sand, but what Roarke knew to be the crushed bones of fish and birds. Beyond it, a bedframe appeared to float in the water.

Roarke's anxiety spiked as he looked out over his darkest fears for the future.

Is this what we're headed for? With an unstable narcissist at the helm of the nation, how long before the inevitable?

Epps gave him a stark, sober look, and Roarke would have bet money his agent was thinking the same thing. It was impossible not to.

Ortiz's GPS coordinates led them through the outskirts of town to a block of abandoned houses with gaping, glassless window frames, random armchairs and lawn equipment scattered in the sandy plots.

The nearest match to the coordinates was the white shell of a one-room house, with a painted sign stuck in the sand plot of yard:

HOUSE OF MISSING PERSONS

On the side wall dozens of milk cartons were nailed in tidy lines. Even from the car, the agents could see the faces on each carton.

"The fuck?" Epps said.

"Ortiz's idea of a joke," Roarke answered grimly. But also, anyone stopping at the house would look like just another desert tourist, checking out the local found art.

Roarke reached for the glove compartment, took out a Maglite, slipped it into his coat pocket.

Both agents drew their weapons and got out of the SUV. They fanned out wide, then moved in on both sides of the doorway missing its door.

They took positions on either side of the entry, and Roarke called in, "FBI. Drop your weapons and come out with your hands in the air."

There was silence . . . nothing but the drone of the wind . . .

Roarke grabbed for his Maglite and shined it inside. The small, square space was empty, except for a table with a large open book. There were no inner doors—it was the only room.

Roarke holstered his Glock, stepped to the table, while Epps remained guarding the door.

The book was a visitor guest register. A manila envelope stuck out from the pages.

Roarke seized it, shoved his hand inside . . . then turned it over, vainly shaking it.

It was empty.

He turned to Epps, spoke through a dry throat. "The hunters . . . they must have gotten here already. They took the directions with them."

They stood inside the empty house . . . surrounded by the faces of the lost.

Chapter Eighty-Six

The sky is fully dark, now, the road lit only by the brightness of the moon, and Singh is easily able to follow the truck from half a mile behind. She feels exposed on the empty highway. She can only hope that she is far enough behind the hunters that it never occurs to them to suspect a tail.

The faint red taillights slow ahead, and the truck makes a sudden right turn into a dark patch of what must be another palm grove.

Singh's heart starts to race.

By the GPS, the coordinates Ortiz gave are still over five miles away.

Has she been following a local, all this time?

Should she continue on to Bombay Beach?

She slows the Lexus as she approaches the turnoff. Through the corridors of palms, she can see the dark silhouettes of buildings.

It is an abandoned motel, situated on a sea of sand. Several low white structures in rows, every door and window boarded up. The avenues between the buildings lined with more palm trees. A husk of a boat lies in the midst of a sea of tumbleweeds taking over the landscaping.

Singh stares out toward it as she approaches the drive. And then, abruptly, she makes the turn.

She steers cautiously as she enters the drive from the side. There is no trace of the truck she has been following. The huge old-style Motel sign towers at the end of the complex, three rows of low buildings away, where the former lobby must be. She is barely creeping the car now—

A figure looms up in her headlights. She slams on the brake. The car shudders as the engine stalls out. A man stands in the middle of the dark road. Dressed in camouflage and a hunter's cap.

And aiming a rifle straight through the windshield at her.

For a split second she is frozen in his sights.

Then a shadow moves behind him in the glare of the headlights . . . and the man jumps a foot in the air, convulsing, before he crashes to the ground.

The figure behind him darts forward, stoops over him . . . Singh sees a gleam of silver blade . . . and a dark geyser opens in the pale flesh of his neck.

Singh gasps. Her heart is beating so fast that for a moment she cannot breathe.

The killer stands and looks in through the windshield at her, eyes flashing reflectively, a shine like cat's eyes in the dark.

Lindstrom.

She stoops again and stands, now holding the dead man's rifle. She slings it over her shoulder, strides to the driver's side of the Lexus, and yanks at the door handle.

Locked.

Lindstrom looks through the glass, waiting. And after a beat, Singh presses the button to unlock the door.

Lindstrom reaches beside Singh to kill the headlights.

"There are more," she says. Then she grasps Singh by the arm and jerks her out of the car, pulling her into the dark, toward the labyrinth of palm trees.

Completely by instinct, Singh moves with her.

In the shadowed corridor of the palm grove, Lindstrom stops on the sand. The intense light of the moon filters through the canopy of palm fronds.

The women face each other in the moonlight. And suddenly, against all reason, Singh is flooded with intense relief, almost euphoria. "You are safe. You escaped." She cannot believe the sheer luck of it.

And then the relief fades, as a primal fear wells up from the depths of her being.

Lindstrom's face is streaked with blood from the man she has just killed. Dark crimson drips from her hair. But it is so much more than that. There is something not entirely human about her. She is an animal. She is an avatar. Killer of hundreds of men. This is goddess energy, archetypal energy, and it is terrifying to be in its presence.

Singh feels her heart rise to her throat.

Lindstrom turns away from her, to stare out through the trees, down the dirt avenue in the dark. "He has another guard on the opposite drive."

She reaches to her neck, unzips and strips off the parka she is wearing. There is another underneath it. She extends the first coat to Singh. Singh takes it automatically.

"There are cars coming in," Lindstrom continues. Her voice has a husky quality, almost erotic, yet it is strangely affectless. "There's a signal. Blink twice, then again twice. Then the guard comes to the car, escorts them in."

"For what?" Singh manages, in confusion. "You have escaped."

"Escaped who?" Lindstrom says.

Singh glances toward the motel. "The hunters. Ortiz."

Lindstrom tilts her head, frowning. "They never had me."

"But . . ."

Lindstrom looks at her. "Ortiz is in there," she says, in that strangely toneless voice. "You know Ortiz?"

"I know he is a monster."

"Yes," Lindstrom agrees flatly. Her eyes graze Singh's face. "The men who are coming. I think he's selling turns."

At first Singh is unable to think through her revulsion. "But he cannot. How can he? They never did have you," Singh says. But there is a dark understanding growing in her mind, a feeling of dread in the pit of her stomach.

"No," Lindstrom says. "He came prepared. He has a backup. He'll do this with or without me."

Singh stares at Lindstrom as the full, horrific truth dawns.

If the hunters do not deliver, there is another woman inside that Ortiz intends to use in Lindstrom's stead.

The former lobby of the motel is merely a frame now—windows and door boarded, the check-in counter still hovering eerily in the middle of a wall that no longer exists.

Singh stands with Lindstrom in a dark concrete cubicle that once housed a small laundry room, her face pressed to the rough plywood of a boarded-up window.

A crack in the plywood gives her a view into the motel lobby. The long room has been swept fairly clean and there are klieg lights on stands in various places, and video equipment. An obese young man hunches in a chair at a table behind the equipment, smoking. A swarthy man Singh recognizes as Ortiz stands over him, pointing at a screen, giving orders as he gestures behind him . . .

Where a blond woman is on top of a platform the size of a king bed. Naked, blindfolded. Restrained in a dog collar and chains. Singh catches her breath, and backs away from the crack in the window. Her legs feel unsteady; she can barely think through the horror.

Lindstrom steps forward, looks her full in the face. "You need to focus," she says flatly.

Singh realizes she is trembling with rage, and knows Lindstrom is right. She forces herself to breathe, to steady herself.

"Yes," Singh answers, low. "I am with you. We must—"

Lindstrom goes still, holds up a warning hand.

Singh hears the crunch of slow footsteps in the sand outside the cubicle they are in.

Lindstrom meets Singh's eyes, steps against the wall beside the doorframe so she is concealed from the doorway.

Singh reaches for her sidearm, but Lindstrom shakes her head quickly and shows her the Taser.

Singh nods, breathes in, and faces the doorway.

A man's shadow looms up in the opening.

"Well, well. Whatta we got here?" he says, and steps into the room, his weapon in a loose grip.

Singh has two seconds to register that he is not Ortiz.

Then he leaps in a convulsive shudder, as Lindstrom tases him from behind.

He chokes out a garbled cry and drops to the ground, seizing in pain. Before Singh can react, Lindstrom steps to his jerking body, steps on his chest, stoops to grasp his hair in her fingers, and cuts his throat with a hunting knife.

She turns to Singh, with hands dripping blood.

Singh stares down at the dead man, her heart pounding out of control in her chest. He is young, dressed in olive khakis and a T-shirt.

Troll. Rapist.

And she feels no pity.

"The guard," Lindstrom says. "One of them."

The thought is unnerving.

How many more does Ortiz have out there, helping him? How many are we up against?

"I only saw these two," Lindstrom answers, as if Singh has spoken aloud. She crouches beside the guard, starts to strip off his hat and jacket. "This is how we go in."

"It should be me," Singh says.

Lindstrom looks up from the body.

"The skin color. His hair," Singh says. "It should be me." Her thoughts are racing, calculating. She will play the guard, bringing one of the customers in. With both guards now dead, there is only Ortiz and the obese young man behind the camera inside the lobby . . .

She peels off the parka she is wearing so she can exchange it for the guard's clothes.

Lindstrom stands, slowly. She is staring at her, peculiarly. No, not at her. At her clothes, her formal suit.

"You," she says.

She reaches out and touches Singh's lapel. A shudder goes through Singh at the touch.

"It's you," Lindstrom says, and there is something like wonder in her voice. "You're the one." Her eyes are very far away. "I have to tell you," she says.

Then she leans in, and Singh can feel her breath against her cheek as she whispers something that makes her blood run cold.

Chapter Eighty-Seven

In the dark concrete cube of the laundry room, Singh and Cara take the walkie-talkie off the dead guard. Moving in tandem, they stand at the doorway on either side, and survey the dark hotel grounds.

Sand. Wind. Tumbleweeds. And the moon.

Lindstrom speaks, barely audible. "There are two customers standing outside the lobby door. The guard told them to wait."

"Two? That is all?"

"Two. For now."

So, quickly, quietly, they form a plan. The obese young man is probably armed, but is no great threat. It is Ortiz they must neutralize. In whispers, they talk it through from the hunters' point of view.

Then the two women leave the concrete square of the laundry room. Miles and miles from any town, with any electric lighting a distant memory, the night is pitch black, the grounds lit only by moonlight. A desert wind surges and retreats, rustling the palm fronds.

The women circle the motel around the back, heading for the palm grove, where Lindstrom has stashed the hunters' truck.

They sprint together over the moon-drenched sand toward the pickup. Singh feels a primal rush of adrenaline as they run, and there is more than fear in the feeling. At the vehicle, they take positions on either side of the truck and rip open the cover of the bed. Lindstrom strips off her hunter's parka and throws it across to Singh, who pulls it on over the one she is already wearing.

Lindstrom climbs into the truck bed, sits with her back against the cab. Singh uses her own handcuffs to cuff Lindstrom to the rail, her hands above her head, and as Lindstrom closes her eyes and sags as if unconscious, Singh uses the hunter's phone to take a photo of the "hostage," angling the shot to show her hands securely cuffed.

Then Singh unlocks Lindstrom, and Lindstrom positions her hands back on the rail as if she is still cuffed.

Singh gets into the cab and starts the truck, drives it out of the palm grove, into the main strip outside the motel—but not all the way to the lobby. She parks some distance away, out of sight of the two customers waiting outside the main building. She scans the grounds around her through the windshield.

No new cars. No human figures stirring.

She turns to the back window, sees Lindstrom in place in the back.

She shuts off the engine, and quickly types an email for Ortiz on the hunter's phone.

We have the package outside.

She attaches the photo of Lindstrom to the message, and sends.
In a moment, a response comes back.

The guard will bring you in.

Singh types:

What guard?

And she waits, looking out through the back window of the truck. Lindstrom's body is a slumped shadow above her.

She breathes in, turns away, and glances down at the phone. No email has come back.

She slides across the seat, gets out of the cab on the passenger side, and stands so her body is shielded by the truck, but her silhouette in the parka and hunter's cap is visible from the lobby building.

The tableau is complete: Lindstrom in the back of the truck, blond hair shining in the moonlight, apparently chained to the rail of the truck. The hunter in parka and cap, standing beside the truck.

Singh's heart is racing as she imagines Ortiz leaving the lobby, striding out to the edge of the building, peering around the corner to take the picture in . . .

And then she hears his voice call out in the dark, harsh, commanding. "Let me see your hands."

Singh slowly raises her hands in the air for him to see.

Chapter Eighty-Eight

In the black of night, so many miles from civilization, the sky was crazy with stars.

Roarke and Epps stood in the wind beside their car at the desert crossroads outside the House of Missing Persons.

What could they do? Miles in the middle of nowhere. No idea where to go next.

Epps' voice was dry, desperate. "There's only one road around the whole Sea, isn't there? It has to be close."

But which direction?

Two ways to go.

With Singh's life at stake, and Cara's, they were supposed to flip a coin and decide?

Cara, Roarke thought, helplessly.

His phone vibrated in his pocket.

He was frozen for a moment, stunned. Then he grabbed for it, hoping against hope that it was Singh.

He stared down at the number, and his stomach turned over.

It was his own number.

His *old* number.

The phone that Cara stole from him on the beach.

"What?" Epps demanded. "What is it?"

Roarke picked up to Cara's husky, emotionless voice. "Your agent is here. Ortiz has her."

In a split second his elation turned to cold fear for Singh.

Epps was staring at him, fraught.

"Where are you?" he managed. There was the ping of a text message and he checked the screen to see GPS coordinates.

Cara spoke again. "An abandoned motel on 111. Men are driving up and blinking headlights in a code. Two blinks, a pause, then two more. A guard will come up."

"I understand—"

"Hurry."

"We will," he said, and then quickly—"Cara. Thank you."

Chapter Eighty-Nine

Roarke drove like the wind.

The coordinates were ten minutes' drive from Bombay Beach. An abandoned motel complex in a grove of scruffy palms, doors and windows boarded up, connecting roads turned to sand and tumbleweeds.

The grounds were so dark the agents didn't see the complex until they were right on top of it.

Epps was raw with tension as Roarke turned into the drive. The agents stared out at an old-time MOTEL sign to the left, above the roof of a long, low building. The lobby.

Roarke slowed the car to a stop on the unpaved road, and reached for the headlights to give the signal.

"Two blinks, a pause, then two more."

The agents waited in the dark car, engine rumbling, their breathing jagged with anxiety. Around and above them, palm fronds rippled in the wind.

There was no movement in the dark ahead of them. No one coming forward to meet them.

The men exchanged a glance, drew their weapons, got out of the SUV, and stepped into the wind. Roarke had left the headlights on.

"Roarke," Epps said hoarsely, staring ahead to the edge of the light. Roarke swiveled, raising his Glock—

A body was sprawled on the sandy road, a male body, with a hunting cap. His throat cut, blackly gaping.

"Cara," Roarke said.

The agents turned as one and ran through the wind toward the lobby, feet pounding in the sand.

Near the corner of the building, Roarke stopped, held up a hand. Epps halted behind him.

There were voices on the other side of the wall.

The agents brandished their weapons, went low and high, rounded the corner of the building.

Two male shadows stood against the concrete wall, smoking.

Roarke and Epps stopped in full stance, holding them in sights. The men straightened, dumbfounded. "What the fuck—" one started.

"Federal agents. Get your hands in the air," Roarke ordered.

The one farthest from them wheeled around to run. Epps leaped after him, tackled him, while Roarke seized the other one, twisting him around, shoving him face first against the wall to cuff him.

"How many inside?" he said against the man's neck.

"I don't know," the man sputtered. Roarke kneed him in the back of the knees to topple him to the ground, shoved his head down in the sand.

"How *many?*"

"I haven't been in," the man whined. "The guy said to wait outside."

Roarke twisted to look up and around. The lobby door was under a concrete overhang. There was no light from inside.

Fifteen feet away, Epps had the other man down in the sand and cuffed.

Roarke touched the muzzle of his Glock to the cheek of the man under him. "Not a word. Not a sound."

Roarke and Epps burst through the front door into the motel lobby, weapons aimed in front of them, covering each other as they swiveled and frantically surveyed the setup.

Roarke took it in in flashes.

The video equipment. An overweight young man slumped and still in the chair behind the monitors, a dark pool at his feet.

And the platform in the center of the klieg lights. The surface red, drenched in blood.

A naked body was spread-eagled on the top of the platform, bloodied beyond recognition.

Roarke got one horrific glimpse of bronze skin, black hair . . . Epps cried out beside him . . .

Singh. Oh my God, no.

But then both men focused, and moved forward as one to stare down at the corpse on the platform: a man, gutted, sliced from neck to pelvis, skin open to mangled organs.

"It's Ortiz," Roarke said, and felt the flood of relief, even as his stomach twisted at the carnage.

But where . . . what the hell . . .

He spun to look around him at the concrete space.

A shaky voice called from behind the counter. "Damien."

Epps wheeled around, and ran. Roarke was right behind him. They barreled through the open wall frame.

A body writhed on the floor, struggling up to sitting. A slim figure in a dark and formal suit. Bound. Hooded.

Alive.

Roarke staggered, his legs buckling in relief.

Epps dropped to his knees in front of her, reached for her, pulling off the hood. Singh's dark hair spilled out . . . and Epps wrapped her in his arms, held her.

"I'm here. I'm here."

Roarke turned away with stinging eyes, leaving them.

In the main room, he paced the perimeter of the lobby, checking every corner. The young man behind the video monitors was dead, his throat cut. Roarke was even more unnerved to find the cameras were on, live, still broadcasting footage of the platform and Ortiz's gutted body.

It would come as a shock to the men who had paid to see Cara raped, live.

Maybe a lesson.

But as Roarke walked the room, slowing his frantic breath, a nagging feeling overcame him. Cara had called him. Had summoned them to Singh's rescue.

She wouldn't have left Singh like this. Not bound. Not in these circumstances.

He wheeled around on the cement floor and strode out the door, into the dark.

He jogged out past the MOTEL sign, stopped on the sand between palm trees, looking around him.

The tumbleweeds shivered in the wind. The stars shimmered in the sky. The moon was so bright it was like heat on the sand.

And he spoke to the darkness.

"Cara. I know you're here."

He turned, under the swaying shadows of palm trees and the full moon and the hundred million stars.

"I can feel you."

And he could. He could feel her in the trees, in the wind, in the earth, in the moonlight. In his blood. In his heart.

He waited, listened, heard only the keening of the wind.

He paused . . . and then said it. "I always feel you."

The wind swirled around him, and took his words out to the night.

TWO DAYS LATER

Chapter Ninety

It wasn't until the agents were back in San Francisco that they learned the fates of Topher Stephens and Alex Foy.

Lam and Stotlemyre's investigation of the branding iron registration had led to a stable in the Santa Ynez Valley, unused for years.

Inside, Huerte and the Isla Vista police found the bodies. The two young fraternity brothers, naked, throats slashed, and Foy's body stabbed repeatedly, piled in a heap in front of the altar of Santa Muerte from the video. Written large across each body in red lipstick was the single word, RAPIST.

There were photos posted online—of course there were photos. From all angles. Eerie, deadly. As blunt a warning as it could be.

Bitch claimed credit.

"One a day."

"We will end rapists until rape ends."

Roarke had no time to wonder who the killers were. He had a much, much more pressing problem.

Singh debriefed in the office, as centered and serene as always as she told her story.

Strange didn't begin to describe it.

She had been approached the evening before in the garage of her loft building by a woman claiming to be a former member of Bitch. Not Andrea Janovy, or anyone Singh had ever been in contact with before.

Singh had drawn her weapon, had taken all precautions . . . but as the woman spoke, Singh became convinced that she was telling the truth.

Just from a few minutes' conversation, Singh could see that the woman was knowledgeable about doxxing campaigns and cyber systems. The woman said that she had left the group after they began discussing murder. When she began to outline in detail how Bitch had set up the campus attacks, Singh suggested they go elsewhere to talk, and the woman agreed.

Then a male figure had appeared in the shadows across the garage. Shots were exchanged. A windshield shattered. Singh heard a sucking chest wound, was sure she'd hit someone.

Then she was struck from behind.

She had regained consciousness to find herself hooded and bound in the trunk of her own vehicle, a harrowing journey that ended at the abandoned motel outside Bombay Beach.

Ortiz and another man had taken her into the motel, still bound and hooded. They hadn't beaten her. They hadn't touched her. Ortiz had forced some pills on her that put her to sleep.

She woke several hours later in the room Roarke and Epps had found her in, behind the lobby counter. She could hear the sounds of an altercation outside, someone entering the lobby. From the subsequent scuffle she deduced someone had killed Ortiz and some other man in the room. The killer may have been Lindstrom, but she couldn't say. She hadn't seen. It had been very quick.

Then she heard something being dragged around, what she now understood was the staging of Ortiz's body on the platform.

And then there was the sound of the door as the killer left, and silence . . . until Roarke and Epps burst in some fifteen to twenty minutes later.

All perfectly, reasonably told. When questioned, she never wavered on the details.

Roarke didn't believe it.

It was true that she had been drugged. She had been roughed up. He and Epps had found her bound and hooded. And there had been some kind of gunfight in the garage of her building. Her service weapon had been fired. Lam and Stotlemyre had processed the scene, had found the windshield of a car had been shattered by a bullet, and there were traces of blood on the concrete floor some distance away.

But every other thing she said, Roarke doubted.

She sat in the conference room, serene and still, and he was certain she was lying.

Chapter Ninety-One

Roarke's feeling, just a feeling, was that Singh and Cara did it together. Singh had gotten the same message that he had, the photos of Cara bloodied, bound. And she had gone on her own to the coordinates. She had gotten to the House of Missing Persons before Roarke and Epps. She had followed the directions, had taken them with her, had gone to rescue Cara.

Except that Cara hadn't needed rescuing.

There had been no hunters at the motel. The two dead guards that Roarke and Epps had come across had no IDs on them, but the agents had identified them through fingerprints. They were not the men who had been communicating with Ortiz from northern Arizona. Those hunters and their truck were still missing.

It was Roarke's guess that the hunters had never captured Cara at all. He'd asked Lam and Stotlemyre to analyze the photos of Cara from his phone, and the techs agreed that while Cara showed real signs of severe bruising, the "blood" was not the color of real blood. Roarke believed that the hunters were long dead, and she had staged the photos herself. The truck—well, that would be found eventually. Or not.

The two live men Roarke and Epps had taken down had been customers, waiting in line. Federal prosecutors intended to offer them reduced charges on conspiracy to commit rape and conspiracy to distribute pornography, in exchange for a detailed timeline of all of Ortiz's plans and access to all of the forums where the conspiracy had been concocted.

Besides the two dead guards, there had been only Ortiz and his young camera operator inside the lobby.

It wasn't a stretch to think that Singh and Cara had arrived at the derelict motel at approximately the same time.

That Cara had already dispatched the guards in her signature manner.

That left the two customers, Ortiz, and the camera operator.

Cara had taken more men down before, on her own. And the customers had been unarmed, probably disarmed by the guards. Throughout extensive questioning, the customers swore they hadn't seen either of the women.

The young man behind the equipment would have been entirely useless in a fight. Ortiz was the only real problem.

And Cara and Singh had decided to take him down together—why?

Because Singh had reached that point of no return . . . had seen enough from Ortiz in the rape forums, in the setup of his grotesque plan, that she was willing to help Cara take him down, if not kill him herself?

Possibly.

But maybe there was something more at stake. More precisely, someone.

There was evidence of another woman's presence on the scene: blond hair that did not match Cara's found on the platform in the lobby, mixed with Ortiz's blood and viscera. Of course, Ortiz could have brought that hair in on his own body.

But given that there was potentially a lot of money involved with his little venture into rape porn, maybe he'd brought a stand-in. Just in case. And maybe that had given some extra urgency to the need to shut Ortiz and his operation down. Roarke could see Singh making that decision on the spur of the moment.

So why this elaborate story? Why not just say that there had been a hostage, and that joining forces with Lindstrom was the most likely way to effect a rescue?

Because in the real world, Cara was a mass murderess, a wanted fugitive. Singh's mandate as an agent would be to arrest her. Trusting her would be insane. Teaming up with her was not only impossible to explain, it was out of the question.

But then—what? Cara had tied Singh up and left her, and Singh had lied about it—to save herself? To protect Cara?

Or to avoid having to testify against Cara at a later date?

Maybe.

But Roarke's thoughts were increasingly worrisome.

What if there was something more to this? Another step that Singh had planned?

He didn't know what Epps believed, and he didn't know why Singh was lying.

But they had no time to find out, because once Reynolds had heard the details of Singh's conversation with the woman from Bitch, the SAC was instantly on the phone to the director, who insisted on seeing Singh personally.

Her ordeal had given her a window into Bitch, and as far as the Bureau was concerned, that was the only priority.

She was already on a plane to Washington for the meeting.

Chapter Ninety-Two

She waits on a hard sofa in the gleaming hall of FBI headquarters, outside the office of the director. She wears her sleek and formal business suit. Her back is straight. Her service weapon is heavy on her hip.

Her eyes are open, but her focus is inside, on her breath. The slow, rhythmic inhale and exhale. Grounding her. Preparing her.

The director's assistant has just informed her that the chief strategist will be sitting in on the meeting.

In her mind are the words that Lindstrom whispered to her outside the derelict motel.

"A woman can put a stop to the Great Pretender.

"A woman who wears the white man's skin.

"Who can walk the corridors of power . . .

"They have woven a web. Cut one thread and the whole will unravel."

She adjusts her coat over her arm, over the Glock on her hip.

Then she jumps . . . as someone sits down on the bench beside her.

Roarke.

"Singh," he says softly, and she has to look at him. The steady, masculine, honest presence—so familiar, so trusted . . .

"Don't do it," he says. Not a demand. Rather, a plea.

"Do what?" she asks, through the irrational pounding of her heart.

"Don't do this. We have to believe there's hope."

"Is there?" she answers, barely audible.

"We'll fight. We'll all fight." He meets her eyes with his dark ones. "I beg you. Give it one month. If things . . . if it's gotten worse, I swear I'll be there with you."

He waits. She swallows through a dry mouth. In her head she hears the pulsing of her own blood.

"Not today. Not like this," he says softly.

He looks into her face. And she feels the weight of the world balanced between them.

The young, clean-cut agent who is the director's assistant steps out of the double doors at the end of the corridor and briskly approaches the visitors' bench.

"Special Agent Singh, the director will see you now—"

He stops as Roarke rises from the bench, extends his credentials.

"Agent Singh was called away. I'm ASAC Matthew Roarke. I can brief the director instead."

The assistant frowns, hesitates . . . then nods. "I'll inform the director, Agent Roarke." He turns, walks back down the corridor.

Roarke sits back down on the bench, shaky with relief.

He rests his head on the back of the bench. And hopes with all his being that he was right.

I have to make it right.

We all *have to make it right.*

Acknowledgments

A million thanks always to:

My awesome editors, Megha Parekh, Liz Pearsons, and Charlotte Herscher, and the rest of the team at Thomas & Mercer who have continued to support and enrich this series: Grace Doyle, Sarah Shaw, Jacque Ben-Zekry, Anh Schluep.

My agents, Scott Miller, Frank Wuliger, and Lee Keele.

My priceless early readers: Diane Coates Peoples, Joan Tregarthen Huston, Eric Huston, and Wendy Metz.

My producer team: Tucker Tooley, Jason Barhydt, Al Munteanu, Claudia Schorr, Ingrid Pittana, David Scharfenberg, Hannah Grossmann, Christian Parent, and Gregoire Gensollen.

Lee Lofland and his Writers Police Academy trainers/instructors—Dave Pauly, Katherine Ramsland, Corporal Dee Jackson, Andy Russell, Marco Conelli, Lieutenant Randy Shepard, and Robert Skiff—for forensics, investigative, and tactical help.

R. C. Bray for his terrific narrative interpretations of the books.

Timoney Korbar, Amanda Wilson, Adam Cruz, and the WriterSpace team for brilliant publicity support.

Robert Gregory Browne, for the series cover concept.

The initial inspiration for the Huntress from Val McDermid, Denise Mina, and Lee Child, at the San Francisco Bouchercon.

My writing group, the Weymouth Seven: Margaret Maron, Mary Kay Andrews, Diane Chamberlain, Sarah Shaber, Brenda Witchger, and Katy Munger.

Webmistresses Madeira James and Jen Forbus at Xuni.com.

Tracy Fenton, Helen Boyce, Teresa Nikolic, and the administrators and readers of THE Book Club, who've been so supportive on the other side of the pond.

Craig Robertson, for a million things—including making it through *another* double book deadline without killing each other.

I love to hear from readers! Visit my website at http://alexandra-sokoloff.com to contact me, join my mailing list, find me on social media, and win cool stuff.

Afterword

D on't write about politics" is a warning every novelist hears at writing conferences.

I couldn't disagree more. In fact, I'm not interested in reading or writing books that aren't about politics.

I wrote *Hunger Moon* at a pivotal point in US and world history. Not only that, for anyone following the timeline of the Huntress series, the events of *Hunger Moon* fall *precisely* at a pivotal point in US history.

So as an author, I had two choices. I could either invent a world in which the election of 2016 never happened, and never had volcanic repercussions in the FBI and on American democracy—or I could write about the real world.

My series has always existed in a fictional world that is a reflection of this one. And I've never shied away from politics in my real life. I wasn't about to in the middle of a national and international crisis.

In Book 4, *Bitter Moon*, Roarke and Cara both go off the grid in January, meaning they miss the inauguration of 2017. They both come back into the world in February to find American democracy has been upended. *Hunger Moon* takes place at an exceedingly dark time in American history. The characters in the book all react to those times and circumstances. They deal with the situation as it is/was then. I have hope for the future, but I can't predict what will happen, and the book doesn't attempt to.

But we need to remember this time as it was, so that nothing like it ever happens here again.

My plea from previous books remains the same. I have not in any way exaggerated the horrific and unacceptable national rape kit backlog, the bureaucratic failure of the Violent Criminal Apprehension Program, the criminal mishandling of rape complaints on college (and high school) campuses, and the inadequacy of resources to prosecute traffickers of children and teens. Now more than ever we must all make it our responsibility to educate ourselves about what's really going on in our own communities and on the federal level, and find ways to help and to hold authorities accountable, from spreading the word through social media to volunteering with, advocating for, and donating to organizations that pick up the slack.

I donate every month to Children of the Night, MISSSEY, Thorn, and the Covenant House, which rescue and work with homeless, trafficked, and sexually exploited teens; to EROC, End Rape on Campus, which supports college rape survivors who have been failed by the insufficient and often deliberately obstructionist investigations of local police departments and the students' own campus administrations; and to Planned Parenthood, which works tirelessly to ensure that every child is planned, wanted, and cared for. If you'd like to learn more about these organizations and others in your country, state, and community, I have links to places you can start on my website, http://alexandrasokoloff.com.

About the Author

Thriller Award–winner Alexandra Sokoloff has been called a "daughter of Mary Shelley" by the *New York Times Book Review*, which also praised her books as "some of the most original and freshly unnerving work in the genre." She was nominated for the Bram Stoker, Anthony, and Black Quill Awards for her supernatural thrillers *The Harrowing*, *The Price*, *The Unseen*, and *Book of Shadows*. Her Huntress/FBI thrillers series (*Huntress Moon*, *Blood Moon*, *Cold Moon*, *Bitter Moon*, and *Hunger Moon*) earned a second Thriller Award nomination and is in development as a TV series.

Alex writes original screenplays and novel adaptations for numerous Hollywood studios, and she is the author of three writing workbooks—*Stealing Hollywood*, *Screenwriting Tricks for Authors*, and *Writing Love*—and the acclaimed blog ScreenwritingTricks.com. She has also penned erotic paranormal fiction for *The Keepers* trilogy and *The Keepers L.A.* quartet. She lives in Los Angeles and Scotland with crime author Craig Robertson.

Printed in Great Britain
by Amazon